An Innocent Man—on the Run!

"You rotten, ridge-runnin' son of a bitch," Hadley screamed, jumping up. As he did, he cleared leather with a long-barreled Colt and fired, taking Duff in the chest. Ears roaring with the explosion, Slade was on his feet too, bumping the table, sending chips slithering into disorganized heaps. . . .

Hadley cocked the gun a second time and held it on Slade.

"You better get on your horse and ride, Slade," he said. "You're the outlander and it'll be my word against yours."

"I'm not carrying a gun!"

"You knocked me in the head and took mine."

Slade was suddenly aware that if he stayed in *this* game, Hadley had him bluffed, hands down.

Racing out of the Water Hole, Slade sprinted for the livery stable and his horse. . . .

R.C. House has crafted a vintage Western novel in *TRACKDOWN AT IMMIGRANT LAKE.* . . . This is a superb entertainment, fast-moving, studded with characters plucked from our bloody past and kept alive on the printed page. One of the best traditional Westerns I've read lately."
—Jory Sherman, Spur Award-winning author of
The Medicine Horn

"*TRACKDOWN AT IMMIGRANT LAKE* crackles with excitement. Cole Ryerson is a manhunter no one wants on his trail. . . . R.C. House creates memorable characters and you'll be sorry to see them go when the last page is turned."
—Fred Bean, author of *The Last Warrior*

Also by R. C. House

Drumm's War
The Sudden Gun
Vengeance Mountain
So the Loud Torrent

TRACKDOWN AT IMMIGRANT LAKE

R.C. HOUSE

POCKET BOOKS

New York   London   Toronto   Sydney   Tokyo   Singapore

This book is a work of fiction. Names, characters, places, and incidents are either products of the author's imagination or are used fictitiously. Any resemblance to actual events or locales or persons, living or dead, is entirely coincidental.

An *Original* Publication of POCKET BOOKS

POCKET BOOKS, a division of Simon & Schuster Inc.
1230 Avenue of the Americas, New York, NY 10020

Copyright © 1993 by R. C. House

ISBN: 0-671-76042-4

First Pocket Books printing April 1993

10 9 8 7 6 5 4 3 2 1

POCKET and colophon are registered trademarks of Simon & Schuster Inc.

Cover art by Bill Maughan

Printed in the U.S.A.

Dedicated to Harold A. Geer,
pard of forty years:
"We haven't made our last camp."

Prologue

The chubby prospector scrambled over stream boulders large and small to the waterfall pool for his morning coffee water. Two Missouri mules were hobbled and grazing patiently near the prospectors' shaded campsite. Downstream, the chunky man's partner, as lean and lanky as the first man was short and squat, wrestled to adjust their wooden sluice box in the mountain stream in preparation for their day's work of digging, sluicing, and panning.

Dipping out a proper measure of water in a blackened and battered coffeepot, the portly prospector was oblivious to the fortune in gold—a gnarled globe the size and shape of a large man's fist—that lay cloaked under black-sand ooze and rocks at the bottom of the pool.

CHAPTER

1

THE THIN, LIFTING CHANT OF A MOONSTRUCK COYOTE TREM-
bled along the granite ridge where Wayne Slade camped,
knifing into the soft stillness of dark. Slade was aware of
someone coming long before he heard the hoofbeats, an
ingrown trait that had become second nature through his
difficult days in the West after the war.

Slade continued to crouch by his tiny fire, waiting, tense,
but calmly sipping his after-supper coffee. The sound of
hoofs struggling over rocks and gravel as they quartered up
the steep trail warned him of the approach of two riders.
As a precaution, he peeled back his trail coat to clear the
well-worn grips of his holstered six-gun.

The two men rounded a sharp turn in the trail to ride into the
light of Slade's fire, its glow highlighting their sinister features. He didn't know them, and hadn't expected to. It had
been a long trail from Texas up to the Immigrant Lake country.

They looked enough alike to be brothers—tall, dark, and
dirty, grown lean during a life on the dodge and scant ra-
tions. They both had black hair and flinty black eyes.

"Howdy, mister," the one in the lead said.

3

"Evenin'," Slade responded, eyeing them with suspicion.

"Hell of a road up here in the night. Seen your fire from over on the bench yonder. Figured we'd ride by for a social call. Can a man get down?"

"It's a free country," Slade said.

So far they hadn't introduced themselves, a fact that didn't particularly ease Slade's growing fears. They had a way about them that put him on his guard; his suspicions mounted that they hadn't ridden all the way up here for nothing.

"Any of that coffee left?" the other man asked eagerly, as both dismounted and moved closer to the firelight.

"If you've got a cup."

The first man went for his six-gun and held it menacingly, and on cue the second unlimbered his artillery. Slade prudently kept his hand well away from his own pistol grip; they had him where the sun didn't often shine, and he was forced to contain a fury that surged within him like wildfire.

"We didn't come up here, stranger, to sit around and sip coffee and pass the time of day. First off, we got a lame horse we're fixin' to trade with you. Might be you got some other things we could use."

"I got nothing you need, and my horse ain't for trading."

The first man cackled. "Well, ain't you the high-and-mighty one, now. Lane, keep your gun on him while I have a look-see around."

"Got 'im, Dolan," Lane said, moving menacingly closer to Slade and the fire.

"Wait a minute," Slade said, not wanting Dolan to rummage in his gear. "Maybe we can make a deal. Take the horse. Leave my gear alone. I ain't much farther ahead in this world than you are." All the while he was cursing himself for not having been more careful with his goods.

If Dolan got into his saddlebags, Slade would be minus a fat roll of cash—most of the two hundred and fifty dollars he'd brought up from Texas to get a new start, invest in a cattle spread, in the Immigrant Lake country.

"You come to a deal awful fast, mister," Dolan said.

"That tells me there's something around here you think we oughtn't to see."

Cowed by the muzzle of Lane's .44, which under the circumstances resembled the yawning mouth of a mountain howitzer, Slade wisely kept his place. His eyes squinted in fury as Dolan went unerringly for Slade's saddlebags like a dog to a buried bone.

"Hi-yee!" Dolan exulted, his fist coming out of the saddlebag clutching Slade's roll. "Our prayers been answered, Lane!" He strode back to the fire, shoving Slade's money into his pocket.

"Well, we ain't relieving you of much after all, mister. You still got all your gear and Lane's horse will be trail-ready again in a day or so. So let's part friends, sayin' we made a fair exchange. Lane, get his hogleg and punch out them ca'tridges. 'Fore he can reload, we'll be outta range."

"Hand 'er over, mister," Lane said, and Slade carefully but grudgingly complied. Lane ejected the bullets and flung them away into the night. He tossed Slade's six-gun into the gravel some distance from him. "That there pulls his claws, Dolan," Lane said.

"G'night, mister," Dolan called heading for his horse and grabbing for the reins of Slade's nearby animal to lead him away. "Thanks for all the sociability."

Slade thought fast. In Dolan's enthusiasm, he'd failed to fully check out Slade's gear. In the pocket of his trail coat was the little four-barreled derringer he'd taken off a tin-horn gambler he'd faced down in Abilene.

Walking away from the firelight they'd be momentarily blinded, giving Slade all the edge he needed. As they started to mount, he groped for the little belly-gun. He'd never back-shot a man, but there was a first time for everything; sometimes events compelled a man to betray his sense of honor. This was one of them.

The gun couldn't hit a barn wall if a man was standing next to it. Still, he swung it up at the retreating Dolan. At the second he sprung the trigger, Lane veered as he moved to mount up, blocking Slade's shot. The little gun bucked against his hand with a timid bark compared to the accustomed blast of a Colt .44. Still, the echo of the little gun's report caromed through the empty night as Dolan hit the saddle and disappeared into the dark.

"Come on, Lane!" he yelled shrilly, either still momentarily blinded or not looking back. Lane never heard the shot that bored a hole behind his right ear and, puny as the little lead pill was, embedded itself somewhere in his skull. He hit the ground and lay silent, clutching the reins of Slade's horse, keeping the animal stationary and spooked.

Slade retrieved his gray steel six-gun from the gravel and holstered it; the gun would need to be cleaned of grit in the morning. The war had conditioned him to sleeping close to the dead, so Lane's burial would also wait until daylight. He at least owed another human being that much.

Taught also through his postwar hard times to be intensely practical, he went through Lane's pockets, coming up with twelve dollars, some chicken-feed change, and the man's cigarette makin's. Lane's six-shooter was a long-barreled beauty of nearly unblemished blue steel with ivory grips aged to a rich cream color. The cartridge belt and holster were also in prime condition, expensive latigo leather. The custom-made holster had been carefully molded to the handgun's contours. A saddle tramp like Lane couldn't afford such luxury, Slade was certain. Probably relieved someone like himself of it along the trail at night.

Slade chuckled sardonically into the night. "Two hundred bucks," he murmured, "bought me a lame horse and a fancy shootin' iron. So much for high hopes." Slade chunked up the fire against a growing night chill and laid out his bedroll close to it. Dolan had missed fifty dollars in Slade's pocket.

Immigrant Lake lay like a blue mirror in the distance. A mischievous breeze frisked in his horse's mane, whisking away the melancholy of the lone rider approaching from the mountains ringing the Immigrant Lake valley to the south. The sprawl of basin presented a pleasant rolling terrain, its low hills laced with arroyos and wash beds. The town of Immigrant Lake lay like a tiny cluster of sloppy boxes sprouting deep in its center on the lake's south shore.

Slade's travel was leisurely, forced to a slow pace by Lane's horse. Lane's beautiful six-gun rig was stowed in his saddlebags.

From the distance of Wayne Slade's higher vantage point as he rode in, the buildings looked like children's toys. Gray frame and melting adobe, the structures had fanned out from the center as the town of Immigrant Lake grew. In an unpretentious town, the buildings appeared less pretentious the farther they sprouted from the center.

Riding down the land toward the lake, Slade looked over the scrub-studded valley, as broad as it was wide—twenty miles to the mountains any way you rode from town. Probably three miles across in any direction, the lake lay virtually waveless, a great disklike reflection of the sky. The lake was surrounded by miles more of prairie, the flat, grass-lush valley encircled by mountain ranges, not high and not particularly scenic. Immigrant Lake sat equidistant from four mountain passes, the southernmost of which Slade had lately crossed over. All of them were low cuts through the jagged ranges and neatly placed at the four compass points.

Intersecting the main street as though traced by a pencil and ruler was the single track of the Mountain and Central Railroad, coming down from Jackson Saddle to the east and climbing on a straight line out of the valley through Weaver's Notch to the west.

A worn map in Slade's saddlebags had given him much of this information. Because there was no one to discuss things with, a great many of his thoughts were spent in practical reverie.

His years in the West had kept Wayne Slade lean. The tall crown of his battered, sweat-stained Stetson reached well over six feet from the ground. He was long-legged, and from his waist, he tapered upward to shoulders and arms that were no strangers to hard and sustained work. Like his torso, Slade's face was triangular with a firm but friendly mouth and a thin-bridged nose of almost noble proportions.

His eyes were dark, the first thing people noticed about him. More than dark, they appeared black, deep-set, and almost hooded under luxuriant black brows. He wondered at times why his coarse Indian-like black hair hadn't turned gray. Or white. The war years could have done it, and the tough times in the West afterward almost surely should have.

The son of southern aristocratic wealth, Slade had seen his birthright rendered into a mess of scorched pottage by war's end. A pariah named William Tecumseh Sherman had seen to that. The Daniel Slade plantation had been on a direct line between Atlanta and Savannah, the route of the North's triumphant and devastating March to the Sea.

Wayne himself had been long gone, a captain under Lee. Wounded in Pickett's debacle at Gettysburg, Slade was captured and suffered a long and painful recuperation in a northern prison pen.

At war's end, he had hurried home to fulfill the dream that had sustained him throughout his imprisonment—returning to the security of home and reunion with a loving family. Instead he found his father, Daniel, dead of shock at the wanton, mindless destruction of the plantation, and his mother, Elizabeth, living with relatives in Atlanta, turned into a scatterbrain of premature senility by the horror of war she had endured. His brother, Albert, had died at Petersburg, and his sister, Rebecca, had become a worthless slut whose last-known destination two months before was New Orleans.

Crushed by this destruction of his heritage and his family, Slade had turned West where they said a promising future lay, only to find that the work was hard and that a dollar was tough to come by and bought little.

In '79, with another man and his boy, Slade went into partnership and rounded up a small maverick herd in Texas, branded them, and drove them north. He wound up with $250—much of it taken from him by Lane and Dolan and night before. Another dream gone up in smoke, he thought grimly.

Immigrant Lake was the first town he'd seen in ten days. Figuring he'd still explore its potential despite the robbery, Slade put up his horse at the livery stable, had a dinner of steak, fried potatoes, and sourdough bread at the town's only beanery, the Wagon Wheel. He emerged onto the boardwalk of Lake Street as the sun dropped its light through Weaver's Notch. The coming of night suggested finding a place to have a drink or two—and possibly a poker match to increase his holdings.

Slade had a tolerance for alcohol; his southern aristocratic background dictated that. A man who couldn't hold his liquor was beneath his contempt. His heritage had taught him as well a competence in the gentlemanly games of cards. He also knew that the cutthroat poker and shady deals along the frontier bore little resemblance to the finesse of gambling at cards that was traditional in the Old South.

Lacking a toothpick, Slade stood under the overhang in front of the Wagon Wheel, studied the darkening town, and worked with his tongue to loosen stringy bits of beef from between his teeth. His dinner had been good; even the shreds he pried loose had a memorable taste.

A short and portly man hurried along the board sidewalk, bent on an errand—the only sign of life Slade saw on the street in this early evening hour.

"Say, mister," Slade called as the man passed him.

The other rolled to a stop. "What can I do for you?" The voice was thin and reedy but friendly.

"Any action around?"

"Depends on what you mean by action. New here, I take it. Ain't been around long myself. The name's Acie Casey. Initials are A.C., that's why."

He stuck out his hand. "Glad to know you, Mr. Casey. Slade's my name. Wayne Slade. You live around here?"

"Sort of. Me and my partner got a place out south. We done pretty good fore part of the season."

"Cattle?"

"No . . ." Casey seemed unwilling to say more, and eyed the dusty, worn clothing of the saddle bum who called himself Slade. "No, we're what you might call private investors. You say you was looking for action. What kind?"

Slade smiled again, realizing he might have pried too deep into Acie Casey's business. The jolly-seeming, rotund little man could be involved in all manner of nefarious activities, Slade was aware. Out here, he knew from painful experience, everyone played his cards close to his vest, and often against a stacked deck.

"Wondered if there might be a place a man could invest five dollars and make a fast ten."

"This being Saturday night, there'll sure be one over to the Water Hole yonder, this town's one and only saloon. But mind your p's and q's. It's a fast and tough game and the stakes are high."

"Just what I'm looking for."

"Something in your voice. Are you southern?"

"Georgia. A long time back," Slade acknowledged.

"The war, I'm betting, put you in the West. Lost it all back there, huh?"

"The whole kit and kaboodle. Riches to rags, I guess. You're a Yankee, I take it."

"There ain't no more Yankees nor Secesh, Wayne. It's over and done. We're all plain Americans again, trying to do the best we can to keep the wolf off the doorsill, and maybe even get ahead."

"I favor that."

"I've also a hunch you're a straightforward man, Wayne. A bit down on your luck since the war, but good upbringing will bring you through. To tell the truth, me and my partner, Barney Wisner, we're gold prospectors."

"I didn't know this country was noted for its gold. Heard cattle was the money crop hereabouts."

"I'll grant that's true, but Barney and me have studied these hills. There's riches around here, but it'll take hard work. We figure we ain't got a lot to fear from the competition. We're just as glad nobody thinks there's any gold around." Casey paused. "We live south of town. I hope you'll stop by and say howdy."

"Yours the place you see from the road, the old adobe about five miles out, with the chicken yard?"

"The very one. You come on by . . . and good luck in the poker game."

Casey waddled off into the deepening night. Slade shoved a hand into his trousers pocket. All that remained of his nest egg after Lane and Dolan got through with him—fifty dollars—was thick but wadded flat. His silver was in a small leather pouch to save wear on his pocket.

Down Lake Street, where it curved slightly to allow for the lake bank's contour, Slade could make out the faded sign of the Water Hole Saloon. Lamplight in rectangular patches framed by windows played in the rutted street and streamed around tall batwing doors.

He shoved himself away from the post and ambled that way.

CHAPTER
2

A COAL-OIL LAMP WITH A TIN SHADE, THE UNDERSIDE OF IT painted white, dangled from three lightweight chains over the poker table in the Water Hole Saloon. The table had been fitted with a green felt covering that now was worn and dingy with wear marks where players sat, and freckled at the edges with cigarette burns.

An irregular circle of gray in the center showed where countless coins from dirty pockets had been tossed in to increase poker pots. Aside from the lamp's glow illuminating the table, the room around the three players stayed totally dark. When business had come to a standstill long after midnight, Walt, the bartender, had blown out the other lights. He'd headed for home, leaving the door unlocked. He'd also invited the remaining players to help themselves from behind the bar, but to observe the honor system in leaving money for drinks or bottles.

Hours had passed since then, and still the three played. The game that had started early on Saturday evening had had, at most, five players. When one was cleaned out, another cowboy or businessman or hanger-on had sat in and

12

left when he was picked clean—or had taken his meager winnings and left with some weak excuse.

Most of the money that had been brought to the game, however, was still on the table. Three die-hards were left—one of them Wayne Slade—each of them trying to outlast or outluck the other two.

Slade, fatigued with the nonstop tension, his many hours since sleep, a drugged-like exhaustion from the robbery, and the rigors of his Saturday ride, forced himself to stay alert. His winnings and his original twenty dollars, in scarred painted disks, amounted to about a hundred and eighty dollars. He was on his way to winning back the amount Lane and Dolan had taken from him.

Tension was visible in the other two in the game as well. Slade knew them now. They were locals who had played together before; he'd learned that early. Duff McDonnell appeared to be about Slade's age and condition. He was married, Slade had learned, and had a small spread south of Immigrant Lake. There was a wife and a pair of young-uns at the ranch, not far, he gathered, from where Acie Casey and his partner were holed up. McDonnell, also like Slade, had had a good year in the cattle market, had wiped out a few of his debts, but still had more and was looking for another good season to put him ahead of the game.

He was, however, behind the game at the poker table. Duff had come to town for a few quiet drinks and some mild poker, been drawn into the game, won enough to pique his interest, and stayed in it. Luck for Duff was a sometimes thing. He'd get ahead to the point where he'd think of dropping out and taking away his winnings, only to lose a fat pot by not playing them close enough to his vest. Then he'd stay for another round to see if he could recoup.

McDonnell owned an average build, but with thick arms and shoulders that said he knew how to turn in a good day's work. He wore a dingy gray curl-brim Stetson on the back of his head, showing a thick crop of brown hair, tightly curled and glossy. While Slade judged McDonnell was about his own age, Duff's face belied it. McDonnell had the features of a twenty-year-old, tanned but unlined. Only when he smiled did the creases show. His nose was small, a baby-button kind of snoot that reinforced his look of immaturity. His eyes were a faded blue, but hardly the baked-out blue that often came to fair-complexioned men who spent most of their lives in the merciless, cloudless sunlight of this part of the country.

Slade had also learned that McDonnell was an erratic poker player, a born loser. So far luck and not good card-playing had kept him in the game. When McDonnell won a pot, it was usually on a fluke, winning with only middling cards. Luck would give him three of a kind when the only other power turned out to be two pair. Once during the evening McDonnell thought he was building a flush, but had stupidly misread a spade for a club.

McDonnell, Slade thought, had been blessed with blind luck. He crowed once that he had successfully filled an inside straight on the draw and took the pot. Slade would have folded before thinking added ante and additional cards would complete such a nearly impossible hand. Still, McDonnell won enough to keep him in and excited. When others folded, McDonnell stayed in, still hoping to get the lion's share of the loot stacked in front of Slade's place at the table, or a similar pile in front of the third player, Quinn Hadley.

Dawn was beginning to tint the Water Hole's windows with gray as Slade studied Hadley nervously shuffling the cards. Hadley was the kind of man Slade liked to play cards with but would never in his wildest day have chosen as a friend. Hadley was tall and intense with alert dark eyes that quickly took in everything around him. He offered the kind of challenge at poker that Slade savored.

Hadley, Slade learned, was a local businessman, a cattle broker. Hadley didn't own Immigrant Lake, but seemed to have a strong enough corner on the local power. Slade had seen the name, Hadley Enterprises, in a curve of black letters against gold background accents on a large plate-glass window after his chat with Acie Casey and his stroll up to the Water Hole the evening before.

Hadley had turned out to be a vicious card player who was hard to go up against. If Hadley stayed in a game past the draw, or past a concentrated study of his hole cards in stud, Slade quickly learned that the odds were strong in Hadley's favor. It took all of Slade's cunning in the finesse of poker to stay ahead—or even abreast—of Quinn Hadley.

If Hadley stayed and could see from the progress of the betting and raising that he was beaten in cards, he could perform about as good a steel-nerved bluff as Slade had ever seen. However, Slade came to see the chinks in Hadley's seemingly impenetrable armor; he lost his temper as well when he lost what he considered a sure pot. There was little humor, little of the usual good-natured bantering, in the waning hours of this long-term game.

In spite of his own decisiveness at cards, Slade found himself pitying young McDonnell and seeking vengeance against Hadley. Slade was clever enough to shield it, but he began to find delight in holding a strong, sure-win hand and seeing McDonnell drop out with bum cards or be edged out by Hadley's bluff. Then Slade could attack Hadley's position like a prizefighter. Slade began to develop an intuition when Hadley was bluffing. When he knew he himself had a strong fistful, he savored the feeling of playing Hadley to his limit like fighting a game fish on a slender pole.

Surprisingly, Hadley appeared to enjoy being caught in a bluff and held nothing against Slade. However, when McDonnell tried it—apparently remembering only after hours of playing that Hadley was a good and a consistent bluffer—Hadley turned on the young rancher with the viciousness of a cornered wolf. Slade sensed in Hadley what appeared to be respect for Slade's shrewd poker and obvious resentment when McDonnell tried to catch Hadley in a bluff and failed.

They were still playing when Walt, the bartender, returned at broad daylight, opening the large double doors, leaving only the batwings to keep out the strong sun of the brightening morning. The realization that he had been playing cards all night bathed Slade in fatigue. Walt, a lanky man with large eyeballs and drooping upper and lower lids, resembled an old, tired hound. He owned a large and long nose, and the flesh of his lower face clung in loose wattles, reinforcing the sad-hound expression.

No one else had come in. Walt busied himself tidying up around the bar as the game went on. He came over and stood between Slade and McDonnell and solemnly regarded the progress of the game.

"Cliff go home?" Walt possessed a deep bass voice that sounded like the soft strum of a bullfrog.

"You know we cleaned him out before midnight. You was still here," McDonnell enthused, getting what appeared to be a second wind for the game. "There ain't a buck in town that ain't on this table!"

" 'Pears so," Walt said. "You fellers want me to get you some breakfast over to the Wagon Wheel? I got thirty minutes before church."

Hadley looked up at Walt and for the first time in hours, his expression turned pleasant. "Yeah," he said, as though talking for the group. "Get Jenkins to fry up about a dozen eggs and a bunch of spuds. Have him warm over a mess of ham to go with it. And bring back a pot of coffee."

Slade didn't comment, but went on shuffling the bent, dog-eared, and otherwise abused deck of cards.

"Yeah," McDonnell said. "I about had enough of your rotgut for this day, Walt."

Hadley flashed a look at McDonnell that as much as said, Who asked you? Slade stayed silent. The breakfast sounded like a good idea, and he approved of the menu.

"Winner of this pot buys breakfast. Fair enough?" Hadley asked.

"Agreed," Slade said. "Seven-card stud, gents."

McDonnell, having felt the intent of Hadley's earlier stare, only shrugged.

16

"You fellers been putting it in the till for them drinks?" Walt asked.

"Damn you, Walt," Hadley said, "do we look like a bunch of deadbeats to you? Of course we paid for our drinks. Check your lousy cash drawer! That ought to prove it."

"Just askin'," Walt apologized.

"Seven-card stud, huh?" Hadley asked, ignoring the gaunt bartender. "What, no wild cards like Little Miss Muffet here plays?"

Slade quickly glanced at McDonnell to see his eyes burning at the two small insults from Hadley in a matter of minutes. Slade tried to quench the sparks starting to dart between the two haggard players.

"All right, gentlemen," he said cheerily, "first two cards down and dirty. High up card bets." Deftly he slid the two down cards at them, dropping two at his place in turn. The round of up cards went out at the same speed.

"I'll go get your breakfast," Walt strummed, sounding as though he felt superfluous.

None of them seemed to hear.

By the time the church bell tolled, ham grease was congealing on Slade's now-empty breakfast plate on the floor beside him, and he sensed Hadley moving into a bluff. It turned out Slade was wrong. It was evident that Hadley was very tired, as he frequently pinched at the bridge of his nose with thumb and forefinger. Now he leaned back in his chair, blinked hard a couple of times to refresh his eyes, and studied his hand intently.

"I'll see that bet, Duff, and raise," Hadley said.

At his turn, Slade made the pot right. It was up to McDonnell.

"And I'll raise again," McDonnell said, almost proudly. Slade thought Duff was seeing a ruse on Hadley's part as well, and was calling Hadley's bluff.

"I'll see that raise, Duff, and raise you back," Hadley said, shoving two piles of battered wood chips into the center of the green felt.

It was Slade's turn. He looked at the two of them. "I'm a piker if I stay and don't raise," Slade said. He checked his cards. He had three of a kind, having added the third eight in the draw. He looked at the intense scowls of McDonnell and Hadley as they, too, studied their cards and mentally calculated the odds.

Three of a kind, Slade thought. Beats two pair, but that's all. One of them, he was convinced, had good cards and the other was sure to be bluffing.

"I'll drop," he said.

"Slade's no cardsharp. Okay, Hadley," McDonnell said. "You and me. I'll see your raise, and I'll raise it again." Duff McDonnell was left with only a meager pile of chips. If he did not hold the winning hand, this one would put him out of the game.

"Damn, boy," Hadley said, studying his chips. He was still amply supplied. He also surveyed the now-gigantic pot waiting in the center of the table. "You sure are playing cutthroat poker this morning. What if I raise again?"

"I'll think of something."

Slade stayed out of it. He might have offered McDonnell a loan, but he had greater respect for Hadley's hair-trigger disposition; such an offer would not set well, to say the least.

"Well, even at that, a man'd be a fool to raise again. But I believe I've got you beat. Here's your money, and you're called." Hadley counted the stack of chips in front of him and slid the proper amount to the center. Slade looked at the pile in the dirty, worn circle in the center of the green felt. It was the largest pot in the game, which had gone on about fourteen hours.

"I got a full house," McDonnell said, almost crowing. "The best you can get. Three aces and a pair of kings."

Hadley only glowered as he watched McDonnell triumphantly arc his arms and hug the heap of chips toward him.

Slade knew he shouldn't ask, but he did. "What'd you have, Hadley?"

Hadley swung his glare on Slade. "It's none of your

damned business . . . but it was a flush, a damned heart flush. Damn you, Duff, you never held an ace-high full house in your life. How the hell you come off picking up cards that way?"

McDonnell leered at Hadley, and Slade knew it was the wrong thing to do. The leer was one of victory, of a gloating superiority; it could only rankle Hadley more. "Why, Quinn," he said in a patronizing tone, "I plain drawed it, same as you did that flush. Remember, I drew only one card, so I reckon you can figure I was dealt two pair. You yourself handed me my third ace."

Hadley's voice was like the slow cut of a knife. "Why don't you roll up them sleeves, son?" It was more a statement than a suggestion.

"You suggesting you didn't deal me that ace fair and square, Hadley?" McDonnell's question was definite and emphatic.

"I ain't suggesting nothing," Hadley grumbled. "I just don't figure how this town's lousiest poker player comes up with a full house with a tall pot like that riding on it."

"Well, then, Mr. Sir Hadley, you check that deck. If I had anything up my sleeve, then I got to be hiding the one I took out someplace, don't I? That'll mean only fifty-one cards on the table there."

"You could've slipped it back when I wasn't looking."

"Slade had his eye on me too. No, Hadley, count those cards. The town's lousiest poker player sure isn't going to be slick enough to slide a missing card back into the deck with Slade there holding them. Pass the deck for Hadley to check, Slade."

Slade held his ground. He was in the middle of a battle of wits and wanted no part of it. He was the outsider and hoped to continue that way. If he'd had his druthers, he'd have gotten up and checked out. Somehow the situation compelled him to stay.

"Hand them to him, Slade!"

Slade could no longer stay neutral. "Want 'em, Hadley?"

"Naw, just deal. But you remember, Duff, I'm keeping an eye on you."

"Dammit, here," Duff growled, snatching the deck from Slade. "One-two-three-four-five; one-two-three-four-five . . ." McDonnell counted out fifty cards in ten books of five and displayed the remaining two, saying nothing. Slade and Hadley only watched. McDonnell scooped up the cards, aligned them, and dropped the deck back in front of Slade.

"Now . . . what's your game, Slade?"

Hadley's eyes still flashed on McDonnell. Dimly from a distance, Slade could hear the church congregation singing "The Old Rugged Cross." He dealt.

Proving himself honest was the turn of luck McDonnell seemed to need. He picked up the pot on Slade's deal. An instinct seemed to come over him. He'd drop and let Slade and Hadley worry over piddling pots. When the raises began coming hot and fast and McDonnell stayed in, he seemed always to have the strength in his mitt to sweep the chips into his corner. Slade watched Hadley's pile of chips dwindle—along with Slade's. He also saw the color rising in Hadley's face; he was quiet and sinister about his cards now. The tension of the hours and the game showed in the lines of his face, in the sag of his body as he slid back to study his cards. He pinched the fatigue out of his eyes more often now.

Slade was still money ahead, but Hadley's pile slid to near nonexistence. It was Hadley who began to play an erratic game while McDonnell grew steadier and more assured with each hand and each pot won. His pile of chips got in the way of his playing, and he slid them aside. Slade had dropped out, and Hadley lost again. Slade looked out the window; the sun must be pushing eleven, he thought. From the church, faintly he could distinguish the congregation singing the Doxology. He hoped Hadley would get wiped out soon and they could call this game over. He needed to find a place for some shut-eye.

"I'll ask you again, Duff," Hadley said, speaking for

the first time in about four hands. "Will you roll up those sleeves?"

McDonnell flashed Hadley a smug grin. "Uh-uh."

"Up to you," Hadley said. The words held an ominous ring.

McDonnell dealt a five-card stud game and declared deuces wild. Slade shuddered. It was not good thinking on McDonnell's part, since Hadley despised wild-card games. Duff dealt one card down and then one up. Hadley had a king showing. Slade showed an eight, and McDonnell turned over a deuce on his down card. The grin was one of unmistakable superiority, and he beamed it straight at Hadley.

"Bet twenty-five dollars," Duff said, shoving in a tall stack of his chips.

"I ain't got twenty-five dollars," Hadley said.

"But you could have a deuce or a king in the hole," Duff said. "Well, how about it?"

Hadley paused, studying Duff through tightened, tired eyes. Slade knew that a man this exhausted didn't think clearly, and his temper could be that of a maddened bear.

"I own thirty acres of unimproved land butting right up to your place," Hadley said. "It's worth, well, a good deal more. But under the circumstances, give me a hundred in chips and I'll put it up as collateral."

Slade studied his down card. It was a four of hearts to go with his eight of clubs. "Believe I'll fold," he said.

"You got the deed?" McDonnell asked.

"In the safe in my office."

"I'll have to see it."

"Slade here can be my witness."

McDonnell studied Slade. "Okay with you?"

Again Slade found himself in the middle of a local squabble. "I guess."

"Okay, Quinn," Duff said, sliding Hadley a stack of chips. "Here's a hundred, and the deed is mine if you lose it."

"Agreed," Hadley mumbled into his chest. Hadley was a

poor loser who was losing, and it showed in the slump of his body. He was a man who didn't take kindly to humiliation.

"Slade's out. Leaves you and me, Quinn."

"And thirty acres of good grazing land."

McDonnell slipped Hadley another up card and gasped; Hadley now had a pair of natural kings showing. Hadley straightened in his chair, his energy miraculously renewed. McDonnell helped himself to another card, a deuce. Hadley slumped again. "Damn Little Miss Muffet and her wild-card stud!"

McDonnell felt secure enough to let it pass. "Bet fifty dollars!"

Hadley studied his dwindling chips, obviously seeing his thirty acres being deeded to McDonnell. He slid in fifty dollars in chips, leaving himself with barely fifty to go on.

"The man's probably got three natural kings," Duff said, sounding like a jest. "We'll see what he comes up with now." He flipped a card over on Hadley's hand—a queen. McDonnell's own up card was an ace. "Three aces beats a pair of kings showing," he crowed. "Fifty dollars!"

"There comes that damned ace again. Roll up those sleeves."

"With pleasure," Duff said, setting down the deck and turning back his shirt cuffs, a wide grin at Hadley's predicament spread across his face like butter. He picked up the deck again. "It'll cost you fifty to see the last down card, Hadley."

Hadley mumbled something Slade didn't catch and shoved the last of his indebted chips into the center.

"Down," Duff said, "and dirty."

Hadley looked at his last down card, and Slade was certain he heard a sudden sharp intake of breath.

McDonnell dealt himself his last down card, set the deck aside, and looked at the last card secretly. Slade studied Duff's expression. It was tense and serious as he lifted the edge of the card. Slade saw a definite softening in Duff's features.

"What's your pleasure, Hadley?"

"It's not my option. You've got the power showing. Three aces bets."

"Call it charity. You may have it. Raise or call."

"Everything I have is in the pot."

"Half share of your business and you keep the thirty acres."

"You're crazy. Against what?"

"The rest of my chips."

"That's nothing. A couple hundred at best."

"Come on, Hadley, there's better than two-fifty. What do you say?"

"Quarter interest."

"Nothing doing. Half!"

"All right! The pot and a half interest against your stack. And we forget the land."

"It's a deal. What have you got?"

"Four natural kings." Hadley turned over his cards in triumph. Two kings lay in the hole. "I guess that cleans your damned wild-card clock!"

"Not quite," Duff said, a gloating tone dripping in his voice. "Deuces wild, remember? I've got four aces!"

"You rotten, ridge-runnin' son of a bitch," Hadley screamed, jumping up. As he did, he cleared leather with a long-barreled Colt and fired, taking Duff in the chest. Ears roaring with the explosion, Slade was on his feet, too, bumping the table, sending chips slithering into disorganized heaps.

McDonnell's chair tipped backward as the bullet slammed into his body. His gun came out as he went back, and he fired in quick succession with Hadley's one shot. McDonnell's bullet nicked the wood edge of the poker table and buried itself harmlessly in the wall.

Rigid with a spike of shock that rammed into him, Slade stared at Duff's body lying in the overturned chair, his knees still bent over the wood seat. Gray gunsmoke filtered over the table. A circle of wet crimson the size of a saucer stood in stark contrast to Duff's sun-bleached shirt.

Stunned, Slade turned and his gaze shifted slowly back to Hadley, who had cocked the gun a second time and held it on Slade, his stance and his head and neck tense, his eyes, now alert, in narrow slits.

"You better get on your horse and ride, Slade," he said, his voice low and hoarse. "If you think I'll swing for this in this town, you're badly mistaken. You're the outlander, and it'll be my word against yours."

"I'm not carrying a gun!"

"You knocked me in the head and took mine, remember?"

Slade was suddenly aware that if he stayed in this game, Hadley had him bluffed, hands down.

Racing out of the Water Hole, Slade nearly knocked over an early customer coming through the batwing doors. Recognition lanced through the chaotic jumble of terror filling his head.

Dolan!

Slade shoved past him and sprinted for the livery stable and his horse.

CHAPTER
3

THE HAMMER OF THE NAVY COLT SLID BACK WITH A BARELY
audible click.

As if in obedience, the cylinder cycled one turn on its
pin with the precision of the balance wheel of a fine watch,
the firing nipple aligning under the cocked hammer with an
almost sinister competence.

Apprenticed to a Saint Louis gunsmith in his youth, the
marshal of Immigrant Lake, Cole Ryerson, did his own
weapon repairs and cleaning. That way, he figured if there
ever was a problem he'd have nobody to blame but himself.
And he'd cuff anyone who tried to touch one of his Navys.

His favored gun company, Colt, had come out some
years before with what Ryerson sneeringly called "ca'-
tridge" guns; he still stuck with his cap-and-ball Navy mod-
els. When a man was out of "ca'tridges" in that single-
action Army, Ryerson said loudly to anyone who'd listen,
he might as well heave the damned thing at his opponent.
From the earliest days of fixed ammunition, he'd been suspicious of the stuff.

A big man pushing sixty, Ryerson heaved himself off his

cot and lumbered across the dirt floor of his one-room shanty to find his cleaning stick. Damned gun, he thought, ain't been fired in six weeks, but just carrying it around, it sure does pick up grit. He remembered going up against that kid, little Wesley Ash—well, hell, Ryerson remembered, Wesley was almost twenty—down in Waco just after the war.

Wesley, knowing Ryerson was said to be good with a gun, and overimpressed as he was with his own newly acquired abilities, had goaded Ryerson into a fight. Used his big mouth to back Cole into a corner that he couldn't get out of without a little gunplay. Ryerson, figuring to let the kid have the edge, purposely took his time going for his Navy.

Good thing, too, for young Wesley whipped some kind of nondescript old hogleg out of his belt and attempted to pry back the hammer with his thumb. The hammer made it somewhere past half cock and jammed right there; wouldn't go back more and wouldn't fall forward toward the percussion cap when he tried to pull the trigger. Ryerson always figured that the workings of young Wesley's gun were socked full of caked black-powder fouling to which negligence had added a heaping portion of trail dust.

Cole, his Navy half out of its holster, watched in undisguised amusement as the kid worked with feverish anxiety and a gray face to force the hammer back against the crap deep inside, jamming up his pistol. Ryerson stepped closer to the now-terrified boy.

"Next time you go up against a man in a gunfight, son," he said loudly for all in the room to hear, "make sure you can depend on your tools."

With that, Cole gently rapped the barrel of the Navy alongside Wesley's head just above the ear—gentle enough, that is, not to take the boy's head off. The brash would-be gunfighter landed in a heap like sacked wheat, with a welt on his head and a headache for four days and ringing ears for five. Ryerson rode out of Waco that night having added another hash mark to his growing legend as a lawman and gunfighter.

If Ryerson was insanely particular about the cleanliness

of the Colt Navy, he was considerably less so about his own hygiene and the housekeeping of the shanty with the dirt floor he called home.

"Now, where do you suppose I left that cleaning stick?" he grumbled, rummaging through a precarious stack of back-east newspapers, poorly refolded, but saved to read when he got around to it. Jasper Jones, the baggageman on the Mountain and Central train that passed through Immigrant Lake once a week, regularly saved up a bundle and dumped them off for Ryerson from the open door of his moving baggage car.

Jones had once admonished Ryerson to keep up better on current events, and took it upon himself to arrange the education of Cole Ryerson by seeing to it that Cole got the old newspapers.

"One a these days," Cole assured himself, scratching a scalp itch, "one a these days, I'm gonna make old Jap Jones happy and read some a them papers."

He found his cleaning stick and went back to lower himself heavily down on the edge of his creaking cot. He tore off a small corner of dingy ticking that held a padding of straw for his bed and worked it into the slot of his cleaning stick. He pulled the Colt's barrel wedge and removed the cylinder and went at imagined grit in the bore.

A working gunman, Cole owned two Navy Colts, but only to always be sure of having one he could depend on. Parts were hard to come by out here, and it was a long way back to the Colt's factory in Hartford, Connecticut. It was also one hell of a ride to any town large enough to have a gunsmith who could build or supply parts. Cole had come to depend on the factory.

If a sear or any other of those delicate guts parts broke, he had to be sure of a replacement, and his life might depend on a functional gun before those lazy louts back at the factory got off their idle rear ends and shipped him his replacement parts.

The gun he left at the shanty was often minus its cylinder. And Cole owned two more cylinders besides—a total of four. Whenever he left town, particularly to go on a chase after somebody who'd broken the law, he had the three spare cylinders wrapped in good quality wool in his saddlebags.

Kept them loaded, too, with powder, ball, and the nipples tightly capped. Cole remembered the time his horse lost his footing in deep water and pitched him out of the saddle for his first bath in six weeks, dunking everything in his saddlebags and bedroll. His grub, what wasn't in cans, was ruined, his bedroll was too soggy to sleep in that night, and the color all ran in his extra shirt. But his three spare cylinders for the Navy were watertight and ready to go in an emergency, particularly since he'd squeezed a chunk of tallow about half the size of a peanut inside each chamber against the ball.

He'd known what he was talking about when he told Wesley Ash that a gunfighter had to be able to depend on his tools.

He'd known the time, too, chasing a man on horseback, when he'd emptied the Navy's cylinder at the fugitive. Allowed as to how he never was much of a shot off horseback. Didn't know a man who was. On a galloping horse it would have been impossible to measure out powder and fish out lead balls and percussion caps and fumble through the loading sequence.

But he could reach into a saddlebag for a loaded cylinder, slide out the wedge and barrel, slip the capped cylinder onto the pin while riding full tilt, and be back in business quicker than scat. And he figured if he couldn't do some serious business with eighteen more rounds, then by George, he just ought to turn around and go home.

He'd learned a bit in thirty-five years as a soldier and lawman, by damn, Ryerson thought. He was young and brash himself when he slipped away from the gunsmith shop in Saint Louis, where he was apprenticed, to follow his wanderlust to the great and sprawling state of Texas.

There he'd signed on as a deputy under Mose Laramore in Abilene. After Greaser Jack back-shot Laramore in 1855, Ryerson became marshal and kept the town tame until other business called him away in 1861. Ryerson didn't fully comprehend the Secessionist cause, but adventure beckoned in names like Generals Kirby Smith, Sterling Price, and Jo Shelby. He packed his gear and headed into Arkansas and Missouri to join Smith's Confederate Army of Trans-Mississippi, signing on as a cavalryman under Jo Shelby. During four years of raids with Shelby into Missouri and Kansas and skirmishing in Arkansas, his bedroll spent more nights tied behind his saddle than it did on the ground. Valor, coupled with battlefield attrition in the officer ranks, brought about Ryerson's rise to the rank of major.

After Appomattox and Kirby Smith's and General Buckner's subsequent capitulation, Shelby, hopping mad over what he considered the Confederacy's cowardice, seceded a second time and took his Texas-based brigade across the Rio Grande to join a war brewing in Mexico. Ryerson petitioned for his discharge and went back into law-keeping, ultimately gaining an appointment as a federal marshal under Judge Isaac Winfield at Fort Walker.

Setting the disassembled Navy beside him on the bed, Ryerson reached for his coffeepot, still warm on his little cookstove. He poured a measure into his blue-flecked gray enameled cup and took a sip. It was lukewarm and strong enough to stand without the aid of crutches.

"Good Lord," Ryerson mumbled, "ought to be something old coffee should be good for besides drinking. Got to put my mind to that. Find something to do with it that's useful and maybe get rich and have me a stake put by for my old age."

Ryerson took another sip and set the cup on the stove to keep the contents warm. He cleaned the cylinder's six chambers and set it aside. He put a loaded cylinder on the pin, reassembled the pistol, and worked the hammer to check the cylinder timing for any sloppiness. He gave the gun a light film of oil. He got up to shove the Navy into its holster hanging from a belt that was looped over a peg by the shanty door. He looked out the dirty panes of the shanty's single window. Immigrant Lake dozed in the late Sunday morning sun.

"Quiet," he mused. "Quiet. And that's just as well. Maybe I can get me some time to read some a them papers this afternoon." He picked up his coffee cup from the stove. The contents were still lukewarm, but the enameled metal had heated to the point he burned his fingers and his lips.

"Judas!" he said, trotting the cup to the table that served for dining as well as for a desk. He put down the skin-blistering cup with great relief.

Ryerson topped out at just under six feet, with broad and unusually powerful shoulders. His arms were as thick as good tree limbs, and he had massive hands to match. The backs of his hands looked like old rope with wrinkles and veins brought on by continued exposure to weather and work. His fingers were stubby, the knuckles creased and swollen.

They were hardly the deft surgeonlike hands of a polished gunfighter. Still, despite his knotlike paws, Cole Ryerson could draw and fire with the best of them and so far had not met his match. He had a practiced coolness with a gun in his hands that more than compensated for mitts that were built like they belonged to a grizzly.

He always figured that because he rode on the right side of the law, he generally had the upper hand. There were damned few good gunfighters wearing the outlaw brand. Those outside the law who tried for speed and accuracy for the most part were a little strange in the head, trying for reputation and something to brag on because they didn't have anything else to recommend them.

Those kind, Ryerson knew, were usually too erratic or overanxious in their gunplay—easy mark for a man who knew he was in the right and who was skilled in the same kind of game. They were the ones to watch for, but Ryerson had come to be able to spot one a mile off—by his dress, his swaggering walk, his mouth; something would give him away. Cole thus was warned before the man ever knew Cole Ryerson was in town. This always gave the big lawman the chance to study a possible adversary and his habits and any nervous little movements that might betray a weakness. Cole avoided open confrontations wherever possible. But if it came to a showdown, Ryerson was ready and usually found he had the edge.

A fugitive was something else. A man on the dodge from the law usually was armed and, if cornered, might fight with the viciousness of a drowning rat. But if he'd run afoul of the law, it was usually over money, meaning the man probably didn't have much to begin with, either in the pocket or in the head. That meant, too, he wouldn't be carrying an especially effective weapon.

A fugitive was routine work for a lawman like Ryerson. If it had to come to a shoot-out, Cole could be sure the man's gun would probably be in about the same condition as that of young Wesley Ash. He'd seen one old seven-pound Dragoon Colt positively disintegrate in the mitt of a hard case he'd cornered out in the desert and who got the drop on Ryerson. The old pistol appeared to have been loaded and capped and then unattended for thirty years and become rusty and weak. When the hammer snapped down on the cap, it exploded with dire consequences. The two chambers on either side of the one lined with the barrel went off from concussion, and sharp shreds of metal flew in all directions—most of them into the hand of the owlhoot.

Cole tied up the man's maimed hand with an old shirt and wound a tourniquet around his upper arm and took him in. A week later the outlaw was bundled off to Yuma Prison with the stub of his right wrist swathed in white-bright bandages. The doctor in Tombstone could see no salvation for the ground-up hand and so he lopped it off and cauterized the stump, and thus the criminal set out for seven years at hard labor.

An out-of-bounds drunk was the easiest for Ryerson to deal with. Simply a matter of judgment. Cole learned early to become a keen judge of distance and how a bullet from the Navy fired from the hip would travel—where it could be expected to land at five feet, fifteen feet, or fifty feet, depending on the deflection, up or down, of the barrel. To hell with accuracy in hip-shooting; all a shot had to do was put a man out of commission.

Normally he could bulldoze a drunk; a rap alongside the head with the barrel of the Navy often was enough to put a drunk into a sound sleep. But if the man was vicious and went for his gun, Cole knew he had plenty of time to judge his shot and flesh-wound the man only to gentle him some.

A drunk's shots would go wild anyway, so why spoil everything with poor judgment and kill a man just because he had a skinful? In most cases, a drunk had a wife and kids bad off somewhere because of his carrying-on, but they'd be a whale of a lot worse off if Cole had to arrange to have the old man hauled out to the graveyard on a door.

Not that Ryerson hadn't been hit a few times himself. Always on the left side, it seemed. He figured because all the ones who'd got a slug into him fired from the right and overcompensated somehow to Cole's left. He still carried a few slugs the sawbones hadn't been able to pry out, and because of a bad hip wound in the war, he limped slightly and leaned a bit toward the left. This gave rise to remarks—and sometimes bum jokes by very good friends—about the amount of lead and other metal he toted inside him.

Bouncing around in the saddle most of his life and an affinity—but not a weakness—for booze had given Ryerson the makings of a pot gut. It was more a thickening above the belt; below the belt he was as slim-hipped and as lean as ever.

Now Ryerson fingered the cup handle, found it cool, and

brought the rim to his lips. The rim was warm and the coffee inside cold.

"Judas!" he said. "Someday I'll find a practical use for old cold coffee. Wonder if it'd be good to clean a gun?"

He riffled among the newspapers stacked precariously on the floor. The top one was the newest. Maybe he'd start with that, he thought. The quiet day was shattered by the muffled reports of two gunshots in rapid succession some distance away in town.

Ryerson put the paper down easily and stood quietly, listening for more. Somewhere a dog barked, vocally announcing his displeasure at having his early afternoon siesta disturbed.

"Christopher Columbus," he said, putting the paper back on the stack and heading for the Navy slung in its belt and holster from a peg by the door. "Something tells me there's been a shootin'. Just my luck when I wanted to get to reading them papers."

Behind him the stack of papers teetered and slewed over to spill in a mess on the dirt floor. Angrily he kicked at them as he grabbed his hat and vest and headed out the door.

CHAPTER
4

CROWDS THAT INVARIABLY SWARMED IN AFTER A SHOOTING or a brawl annoyed Marshal Cole Ryerson. These were the familiar men of Immigrant Lake, but their expressions and gestures were the same ones he'd seen in dozens of towns whether it was Texas or Arizona or Colorado. They'd fill a room as they did the Water Hole this noontime, keeping an irregular circle around the dead or beaten man, or whatever the misery was. They contributed nothing but their presence and offered no more help than to get in the way. They stood with arms folded or hands shoved into pockets, or they leaned against something, just looking and idly curious.

With them came the ever-present murmur, the low drone of questions, and the answers and the hearsay and the self-proclaimed eyewitnesses and moralists. "I knew he would come to no good. Why, I was telling Amanda just yesterday . . ."

Every now and then somebody would wisecrack, usually in extremely poor taste, about the dead man or the marshal conducting the investigation. Church was out, and this nuisance crowd had only begun to assemble when Ryerson loped up raggedly to the Water Hole and charged through the tall batwing doors.

The room was already filling with men studying the body sprawled in the overturned chair on the floor, cocking their heads like so many curious, haughty birds to get a better view of the dead man's features, or craning their necks to see over the heads and shoulders of taller men blocking the view. No one wanted to get too close to the dead man.

Walt, the bartender, maintained his position and his aplomb behind the bar. For the moment no one was buying drinks. As Ryerson entered, Walt read the questions in the marshal's eyes and strummed a response. "It's young McDonnell, Cole. He's dead."

Ryerson shouldered his way through the crowd. The gawkers' circle ringed an area around the Water Hole's single poker table. Chips were spewed haphazardly over the green felt and on the floor. A revolver of some sort lay in the center of the table amid the chips. Off to one side, Quinn Hadley slumped in a chair, his face buried behind his hands, but he was not weeping. He seemed dazed.

In a glance, Ryerson saw that it was sure enough young Duff McDonnell, good and dead. A smear of chest blood nearly covered the front of his shirt and was already drying into a scab-colored clot. Duff's revolver lay near his dead right hand, his stained gray work hat a few inches from his head on the floor. Duff still lay in the overturned chair, his knees bent over the seat.

Ryerson addressed his loud question to no one in particular. "Well, for Lord's sake, didn't any of you think to get him away from that chair and straighten him out?"

Hadley glanced up at Ryerson, said nothing, and returned his bowed head to his fingertips. There were murmurs from the crowd.

"Leave him like that for rigor mortis to set in and he'll make a hell of a looking corpse to try to lay out for buryin'," Ryerson added angrily.

Impatiently he crouched behind Duff and raised the dead man's shoulders and pulled him out of the chair by the armpits.

He could still feel Duff's body heat against his palms and wrists. As he dragged Duff away from the chair, the body straightened easily. Ryerson knelt again, gently folded McDonnell's hands over his bloodstained chest, and picked up the hat and covered Duff's face with it.

"Here you go, Duff," he said softly to the corpse. He had liked the young rancher, who had returned the friendship. Ryerson didn't have many close friends in Immigrant Lake. Some residents were openly antagonistic toward his authority.

"Did anybody send for Thompson?" he asked, looking around at the expressionless faces circling him. A few shook their heads, further annoying him. "Well, then, in the name of all that is good and evil, will somebody go get that damned undertaker!" No one moved. Ryerson stood up, feeling rage at their shocked inability to do anything at all.

"Walt!" he shouted. "Get somebody to go tell Thompson we're bringing young McDonnell over to him. It ain't Christian to leave a man lay here like this! You, you, and you, and a couple more of you fellas, come on here and get this man and take him careful over to Thompson's parlors. And treat him gentle. Could just as leave be you or one of your kin. And somebody ride on out and tell his wife. She'll probably want to come in and give him a bath and bring his Sunday duds."

A half-dozen men, energized by Ryerson's anger and authority, sheepishly stepped out of the circle and crouched over the body, mumbling commands to each other. They knelt, got their arms under McDonnell, and lifted him gently and gingerly, plainly uncomfortable with their grisly assignment. They raised him and started for the door. Like the Red Sea parting, the crowd cleared an avenue to the door only wide enough for the hasty pallbearers to move through. Those along this thoroughfare stood with craning necks, fixed eyes, and mouths agape as the dead man was carried out.

Ryerson picked up McDonnell's gun. A short smear of red showed on the floor where Ryerson had dragged the body out of the chair. The bleeding from the wound at

McDonnell's back had stopped by the time he was lifted up. A splotch or two showed where he had been carried.

With the body gone, the crowd began to clear, the murmuring still going on. Some went to the bar for a drink. Others went to the windows or the door to watch the procession to the funeral parlor down the street. Others had tagged along down to Thompson's. Some stood as they had been, watching with absorbed fascination as Ryerson checked the two guns and found that both had been fired once. He laid them on the table.

"I'll have to book these as evidence," he said, more to himself. He pulled up the chair Duff had died in and scraped it over to where Hadley sat, his head up now, his features sagging but stoic.

Ryerson had known Hadley as long as he had been in Immigrant Lake, but didn't like him; the man, in Ryerson's opinion, had an oily, slimy way about him somehow. Too damned glib for a man of Ryerson's directness. There were rumors that Hadley had friends in high, powerful places in the territorial capital and had engineered some cushy beef contracts for himself. And them.

"Well, Hadley, seeing as how you're sitting here, I suppose you know something about all this."

"It all happened so fast."

"Gunfights usually do. Want to tell me about it?"

"His name was Slade. A drifter. Others in town saw him. So did Walt. You can check. Playing poker all night. Three of us. Me, Duff, and this Slade. They was two of a kind, Cole, getting suspicious of each other all night. Both lousy poker players and kept blaming each other for their rotten string of luck."

"Nobody else saw the shooting?"

"Nope. Walt was in church."

"Hold on a minute," Ryerson said. He dug in his shirt pocket and produced a stub pencil with a barely discernible nub of lead and a wad of wrinkled gray paper, which he smoothed. He wet the pencil stub with his tongue. "Want to get this straight for later on, Quinn."

"It's okay. I understand. I want to help."

Ryerson wrote some and then said, "Go ahead."

"I was only in it because I could see that if I stayed in the game long enough, I could clean both of them out. No crime in that."

"No, sir."

"A couple of times they come close to taking a poke at one another. Along about eleven this morning, maybe it was later, this Slade fellow got up between hands and said he was going out to take some relief. When he got back, he come right up behind me, rapped me one with his fist alongside the head. As I was falling over, he yanked out my gun, and quicker'n scat he drilled McDonnell. He throwed my gun on the table there, scooped up the bills and silver that was showing, and hightailed it out of here."

Ryerson was thoughtful for a long moment. "Now, Quinn, I ain't suggesting nothing, but how much money you got on you?"

"A couple hundred in bills and silver. I was the banker, but there was some loose money on the table. He got that. Like I told you, we been playing all night. They wasn't neither of them great shakes at poker, and we was getting close to winding things up. I had just about all of their money. They just sat there blaming each other because I kept winning. That was probably why that young devil cuffed me. Lucky he didn't shoot me, too. Cole, I want to give most of this money to the widow."

"Well, that's a mighty fine Christian gesture, Hadley. You say this Slade was young. How old was he?"

"Oh, about Duff's age. I never been too good a judge of age aside from cattle and horses."

"Well, that helps some anyway," Ryerson said, making more notes. "Why didn't this Slade take your money? Was you still on the floor when he run out of here?"

"Just getting up. McDonnell, he got off one shot at him while he was going down, but he was dead already and it didn't hurt no one. Bored into the wall yonder. I believe when this Slade see what he done, he just figured to grab what was showing on the table and vamoose. And that's what he done."

"Okay, Quinn. Why don't you go home and get some shut-eye? From the looks of you, you could sleep for a week. Stick close to town. I may want to talk with you some more."

"You just going to let it go? Like that?" The inflection in Hadley's question made it more like a statement.

Ryerson looked up from his note-taking. "No, I have no intention of letting it go just like that! I'm going after the man as soon as I get my gear together and get my report telegraphed up to the territorial capital. Probably head out first thing in the morning."

"You think that's wise, Cole? He's already killed once."

Ryerson was incredulous. "Since when has my welfare become a concern of yours?"

Hadley seemed to retreat. "Well, I . . . I just wondered what you was planning, Cole."

"To bring a man in. A crime has been committed in my jurisdiction, and I'm not about to see it go unpunished. I aim to see a neck stretched in Immigrant Lake for this. Duff McDonnell was a fine lad."

Ryerson turned to the handful of men still standing awkwardly around the poker table witnessing the conversation. "Not that any of you would remember, but did anybody see which way that man rode out?"

"South," one of them said. "Albert Jenkins over to the Wagon Wheel seen him ride out south. Acie Casey talked with him last evening."

"Who in thunder's Acie Casey?"

"One of them two that has just moved into the old Stout place out south, Marshal," the man, Seth Carter, said. "Other fellow's a Wisner, I think he said. They been to town a few times. Little short fat fellow, this Casey. T'other one, Wisner, he growed the other way."

"Thanks," Ryerson said. "If I've got the time, I'll stop

off and see this Casey when I head out. You go on home, Quinn, and get some rest. You don't look much better than old McDonnell when they carted him out of here."

A lean-jawed, trashy-looking character stepped out of the crowd. "Marshal, I might be able to help you. I seen the whole thing."

Hadley instantly came alert, eyes fixed on the newcomer.

"Now we're getting someplace," Ryerson said.

"I was just comin' in, heard the scuffle, and saw what happened from the front door."

Hadley gripped the chair arms, intently watching the newcomer.

"And?" Ryerson said.

The man's eyes locked on Hadley's. "It was just like that gent, Mr. Hadley there, said. I believe you'd best take you a posse after that fella and drill 'im on sight. Cold-blooded killer if ever I see one."

"And who might you be, sir?"

"Name's Dolan. Emory Dolan."

Ryerson didn't like being told his business. Neither did he like the looks of the jasper, and his voice showed it. "Stick around town till I get back, Dolan, and I'll be the one to decide if I need a posse or not."

"I . . . I was just passin' through. Wasn't fixing to stay."

"Well, you fix now to stay, or I'll be after you for obstructin' justice!" Ryerson turned angrily and lurched out of the saloon.

CHAPTER
5

THE OLD STOUT PLACE, RYERSON KNEW, WAS ONE OF THE oldest houses in Immigrant Lake. He also knew that was hardly a recommendation. It had indeed been built stoutly, but that wasn't the reason for the name. Recent occupants had been a family named Stout. They had occupied the place about long enough for the locals to come to recognize it by that name before they moved on. The Stouts had disappeared for parts unknown about two years before, but the decaying adobe house was still acknowledged as the old Stout place.

The four adobe walls of the main building could have been laid up by Indians, possibly centuries before. Ryerson had no way of knowing. The place would thrive for a few years, lived in by industrious people who repaired or replaced the roof rafters, covering them with whatever native materials they could find or what roofing they could afford.

Then, in a matter of time, they would move on and the place would stand idle for months or years while the land turned fallow and quickly became overrun with tumbleweeds and desert scrub. Then the roof, dried out by the bitter summer sun and battered by winter winds and neglect, would disappear, only to be rebuilt when new tenants took over.

The six-inch-thick walls, however, continued to withstand the ravages of time, the elements, and indifferent residents. If the walls had once been laid up as adobe bricks, that fact was almost no longer evident. The washing of countless rains and the sandblast of wind off the desert had given the house the textured, pebbly, terra-cotta-colored surface of any baked-mud canyon in this part of the country.

The old Stout place stood a hundred yards back from South Range Pass Road, at an off-angle to the road, and on a knoll that looked down over a carpet of chaparral to the road. The lane leading up to the place, where Ryerson had been told Acie Casey and Barney Wisner lived, was a wagon track. It was hardly the shortest distance between two points and, out of convenience, followed the path of least resistance, bypassing washes and desert knobs to the house.

As he and his horse, Jo Shelby, neared the place, Ryerson noted that the roof had been recently refitted and patched and a new slab door mounted in the whitened off-center jambs that appeared to have come with the place. He marveled that the men living here must have known a bit more than most about carpentry to have made a door that would fit true in the off-kilter opening. An oblique early morning sunbeam shot a glint off a polished pane— the cabin's single window, recently replaced. The glass appeared well scrubbed and burnished.

Ryerson knew instinctively that he would like these two. They'd be a direct contrast to Quinn Hadley, who'd been much on Ryerson's mind in recent hours.

Riding Jo Shelby within hailing distance of the house, Ryerson also noted that the rubbish had been carefully picked up and the yard had been swept. Weeds had been pulled, and the sagebrush close to the house had been hacked back and pruned to look like civilized shrubs.

Ryerson knew who he was looking for. He shook his head remembering Seth Carter's quick description of Casey and Wisner—the one short and fat and the other who had "growed the other way." He surmised that Wisner had done the roof work, fixed the door, and set in the new window sash. A short, fat man would be concerned with a well-polished window and getting the weeds out and trimming back the brush.

He could also see and hear clucking and scratching in a well-fenced chicken yard, complete to a new small but sturdy roost. From the looks of their industry, Ryerson figured he would never have to chase one of these two for some crime, as he was now tracking this man Slade. He also knew neither of them would appear among the drunks he would have to bulldoze on a Saturday night.

Giving the place the once-over, Ryerson also noted that a new slanted wood shade had been fitted at one side, and there two Missouri mules stood, looking well fed and cared for, swishing their tails and twitching their hides to discourage the flies.

"Mr. Casey!" Ryerson shouted as he neared a fresh-looking hitch rail planted a few steps from the door. A tall, rawboned man appeared from behind the house, coming around the mules' rear ends. He slapped his palms together to rid them of whatever dust they had recently accumulated and beat them against his pant legs for the same reason.

The door opened and the short, fat man he knew would be Casey, wiping his hands on his canvas apron, filled the doorway.

"Can we do something for ya?" Casey asked. His tone was friendly.

"The name's Ryerson. Marshal in Immigrant Lake."

"Hain't had the pleasure yet," Wisner said, moving toward Ryerson's horse and stretching out his hand. At the same time, he stretched a grin that nearly straightened his drooping bristle of mustache. "Barney Wisner's the name. Yonder is my pard, Acie Casey."

"I've heard of ya."

"And we've heard of you, Marshal Ryerson," Casey

said, waddling over. "Glad you could come by." He, too, shoved a hand at Ryerson, still mounted. "Get down and come on in."

"Yeah," Wisner added, "come on in and have a cup of coffee. Acie keeps the best darned coffeepot in the territory. Only reason I've put up with him all these years. Got little else to recommend him."

"Sounds good." Ryerson slid out of the saddle, dropped Jo Shelby's reins, and lurched through the door. The inside of the house was dark and cool and smelled of good tobacco, good cooking, and good living. It smelled clean—a man's kind of clean—something strange to Ryerson's nose after most of the hovels he'd been in around Immigrant Lake, including his own. He mentally vowed to straighten up his place as soon as he got this current mess over and done with.

"Sit down and let me get you a cup, Marshal," Casey said. He busied himself around the kitchen corner of the big room, digging out a cup and pouring it full from the pot keeping warm on a small cast-iron stove. "I'll get you one, too, Barney."

"Obliged," Wisner said.

Ryerson took off his hat and his big trail coat and hung them from the slat-back chair he edged up to the table. He dug in his shirt pocket for his pipe and a lucifer from his battered but waterproof kidney pills can. He raised up on one flank of his rump and fired the match with one long scratch across the seat of his pants. "You fellas got you a right snug place here," he said, propping his elbows on the table and sucking fire into his pipe.

"Yeah," Wisner said. "We come by looking for somewheres to roost about a month back. Found this, did some checking in town, and found it's an open range and nobody had no particular claim to it. We got us some lumber and a few other things and come on out here and set us up to housekeepin'."

"We been prospecting hereabouts this past spring, Marshal," Casey said. "Found a bit, so we wound up the season early to spend a few months civilized in town."

44

"And chicken ever' Sunday," Wisner said. "You likely seen our yard out there. Plenty of fresh aigs, too."

"I seen it, and a couple cock-of-the-walk roosters struttin' their stuff out there. Beggin' your pardon, fellas, but there ain't never been any gold around Immigrant Lake."

"It's there all right, Mr. Ryerson," Acie said, an eager enthusiasm ringing in his voice. Wisner looked at him disapprovingly. Still he went on. "They's a coulee we worked that showed lots of promise."

Wisner horned in. "Leave it right there, Acie. The marshal's got other things on his mind." Wisner's concern telegraphed itself to Ryerson.

"Pshaw! Don't worry, Mr. Wisner. All the gold you find out there you can keep, far as I'm concerned. I want no part of pick-and-shovel prospectin'. Ain't no gold in these parts, anyhow."

About to say something more, Casey glanced at Wisner, who returned the look reproachfully. Casey's lips started to form words, but he stopped.

Ryerson worked his lips over the tipped rim of the cup of steaming coffee and carefully slurped in a thimbleful. It was hot and strong. He vowed to himself to get rid of his cussed enameled cup and get one of these porcelain mugs.

" 'Y gonies," he said, "that is good coffee! Had a trail cook down in Texas before the war that could make coffee like that. If you always keep a pot of that stuff on hand, Mr. Casey, I'll drop by often."

"Call me Acie. Yeah, I allers could make right smart coffee. Now I fetch us a hen's egg every day to put in the pot. Makes it a sight better."

"What brings you down to these parts, Marshal? I don't reckon you rode out here all the way from town just to be neighborly."

"Drop the marshal stuff, Barney. Naw, we ain't as neighborly as we used to be, nor ought to be. But to start, call me Cole."

"Proud to know you, Cole," Wisner said, sticking out his hand again and grinning.

"Yeah," Acie said. "You're welcome anytime, Cole. Come by for Sunday dinner when you can. But it is a long ride just for a cup of coffee."

"Yeah, it's more than that. I'm on official business."

"You don't want us for something, do you?" Barney asked. "We checked things out right and proper before we took over this place. The man in the land office told us there'd be no problem."

"Got nothing to do with this place. I'm after a man. That's why I can't stay long. There was a shooting in town. Yesterday noon. Got reason to believe the man I'm after may have come by here."

"What man?"

"The fellow I want to ask some questions about the shooting. A drifter by the name of Slade. I heard you two met, Acie."

"Wayne Slade. I told you about him, Barney. Yeah, I talked with him. Nice feller. Said he'd been having a string of bad luck, but he sure didn't strike me as no killer."

Ryerson chuckled. "Would you know a killer if you saw one, Acie?"

Acie shook his head. "No, I reckon not. But I seen and knowed a fair bunch of people in my time, Cole, and I believe I have come to be a fair judge. Me and Wayne Slade passed not much more than a dozen words. I tell you I don't believe him capable of such a thing. Who was it got killed?"

"Maybe you fellers know him. Lives out this way. Duff McDonnell. I mean he lived out this way."

"Can't say as I do," Acie said.

Wisner shook his head. "Uh-uh. Ain't been here that long. And we been busy."

"Had him a spread due east of here not more than five miles. You can't miss his place. Ran a few cattle and raised some groceries, that's about all. Brown-haired fellow, wore his hat on the back of his head. Had a face on him looked like he just jumped out of the cradle.''

"Oh, that one," Acie said. "Yeah, I passed him on the road Saturday evening. He was headed for town. We just howdied. I was coming home with the groceries and such. Just after I talked with Wayne Slade.''

"Got a wife and a brood of young ones over there.''

"Oh," Acie said, "that's a shame.''

"If I had the time, I'd ride over to see her. I told them in town yesterday to send somebody down to tell her, but I don't imagine anybody did.''

"Would you like me to ride over this afternoon, Cole?''

"Would you?''

"Well, nothing gives me the fantods more than having to be the bearer of bad tidings, but sure. Sure I'll do it.''

"That'd ease me some if you did, Acie. Thompson—you know, the undertaker—he's got a cool place out back in the ground, but a man'll keep just so long, and then you've got to get him buried. But that ain't the real reason I'm here. What can you tell me about this Slade?''

"Like what?''

"Things I'll need to track him down. Old Hadley was playing poker with them when Slade shot McDonnell. But that dumb bastard Hadley couldn't tell me a thing.''

"They was playing poker? Yeah, that's right. Slade asked me where he could find a game.''

"He found one. And lost the big pot.''

"He's a southern boy, Cole. Tall, maybe not as high as Barney here. Clean-shaven. Good-looking man. Got black hair. Talks well, like he's had good bringing up. He was in the war, he told me, so that'd have to make him, what? Thirty-two, thirty-three, maybe. No kid, and the war and what come after, you could see, had been rough on him. But his goodness still showed.''

"A southerner?''

"What he said. Wounded in the war, captured and went North to prison. Went home and found his family, and everything had been eaten alive. The old story. So he came west to start a new life and has been having a generally rough time of it since. Least that's the way I got it."

"Huh," Ryerson grunted. "Good southern upbringing, you think?"

"I would. How come he killed this man McDonnell?"

"Argument over cards, to hear Hadley tell it. They'd been playing all night. You know what that can do to a man, even a good one. Hadley said, though, that Slade was a rotten poker player and lost heavily."

"A rotten poker player, huh? I doubt that, even though I only talked with him a few minutes."

"How so?"

"The Old South, Cole. A boy, especially in the gentry, grew to a man knowing how to handle his liquor, his horses, and his women—and his cards. You ought to know that, Cole."

Ryerson mulled on that one a moment or two and jumped up.

"Huh," he grunted. "Maybe there's more here than meets the eye. I got to go. Thanks for the coffee and the information. I will be obliged, if you fellers'd stop by and pay a visit on the widow McDonnell. I'm sure you know all the right Christian words to comfort her."

"Right, Cole, and do come back. Anytime."

CHAPTER

6

THREE MILES SOUTH OF THE OLD STOUT PLACE RYERSON spotted in the dust of South Range Pass Road the outbound track of a horse he figured was carrying Wayne Slade. Neither of the north-south roads leading to Immigrant Lake was heavily traveled, and the ever-present winds constantly scoured the dusty slate clean. Any visible sign in the roadbed sand and gravel, Ryerson mused, were sure to be recent.

Ryerson had been on and off Jo Shelby a half-dozen times checking hoofprints in the dust before he finally put together the definite track of the horse that must have been carrying Wayne Slade. He found the same print, a bit older, along the road, heading north, suggesting these were Slade's inbound tracks two days before. Ryerson gloated; at last he was slidin' the groove.

Now all he had to do was properly read the sign he had found. The spread of the inbound tracks was different, closer together, telling the aging lawman that the waddy aboard was in no hurry and letting his horse take his ease. He was puzzled by sign of an apparently lame and riderless horse traveling with Slade.

Ryerson learned something else about his fugitive. The man may have just committed murder, knew pursuit was certain. Yet from the apparent pace he set for his horse, the man was considerate, sparing the animal even in his hasty flight. Another man would be panicky and driving his horse for all it was worth.

This horse's last shoeing had not been particularly well done, Ryerson judged. One rear shoe appeared to be a bit loose already, while on the right front, Ryerson could perceive a shoe nail that had bent while being driven and had been clinched over to leave a distinct telltale depression within the print of the shoe's arch in the dirt.

It was all Ryerson needed; he could follow his man clear into hell.

Now that he had his figurative nose to this visible scent, Ryerson urged Jo Shelby at a faster pace, only now and then slowing or stopping to verify the track he followed.

The road went from dust to hardpan as he neared the ford where Wagon Box Creek angled out of the mountains and trickled across South Range Pass Road. The track disappeared against the solid roadbed, and Ryerson knew frustration. Summer winds and the heat had shriveled the stream to a sluggish ribbon of wet oozing out into the desert.

The weather was dry, but the air did not carry the furnace heat that was sure to come in a month or so.

Ryerson followed the twisting road into the mountains a quarter of a mile past the ford, still seeking Slade's outbound track. The roadway turned dusty again, but still no clear sign emerged.

"Damn it to hell," he said to the horse. "Now, where in the name of all that is good and evil do you suppose that track went to? I wish to hell you could tell me. It's one of your kind that I'm after. . . . Judas Priest, talking to a horse about a horse! Sure sign of creepin' old age."

The inbound track was still there, showing where Slade had ridden into Immigrant Lake over the pass. Impatiently,

Ryerson searched the dirt for the outbound spoor. He climbed off Jo Shelby tiredly and walked ahead, leading the animal, intently and minutely studying the dirt; nothing.

"Damn! Been riding along here myself and probably wiped out any of his track up to here. He must've left the road. That was dumb on his part. Son of a pup for sure don't know these mountains. Sure to get lost up in there. Get lost? Sure. That's, for the Pete's sake, what he wants to do! Got to quit talking to myself. Sure sign of old age creeping up on me." Ryerson grunted, realizing he'd made that same observation twice in as many minutes.

He lurched painfully back into the saddle and urged the horse around to head back to the ford, where he was confident he'd find the sign again. Walking had made the old hip wound ache, and his thigh and calf muscles had knotted up. He felt better when he was mounted.

"Sure as sin he left the road at the ford. That's why I haven't seen his sign up here. And he wouldn't double back into the valley. That'd be pure poison for him. Nope, he figured to ride a ways along the creek and probably head up over the crest somewhere, maybe up a convenient coulee. Or maybe he's figuring to hole up in there somewhere until we get tired looking for him, and then he'll come back down and skedaddle out south over the road. Once across the range, he could go a hundred different directions and I could spend the rest of my life trying to track him."

Ryerson reached the ford and headed upstream. For a moment he had the eerie sensation he was being watched, but quickly dismissed it in the hunt for Slade's sign. The water had worked its way down to bedrock, and there was little dust or sand here to leave a track. He knew he was close on the trail now, but he still fought for some kind of confirming sign. "I'll be slidin' the groove again, hot on his trail any minute," he told himself.

He rode two miles upstream and found nothing. Then there it was, and his lawman-tracker's heart leaped. A tuft of grass fighting to retain its toehold in a crack between small rocks was freshly crushed and bent back as if by a horse's dragging hoof, the crippled blades pointing the way Ryerson had come.

"A man's track'll bend the grass forward," he told Jo Shelby. "One of your kind now, a hoss, lifts his foot and swings it back, breaking the grass the other way."

He studied the trail ahead with a seasoned eye, hoping against hope an ambush wasn't being set up for him. "Well, Mr. Wayne Slade," he whispered, "it's just a matter of time now until we find out just what kind of poker player you really are."

He needed a rest and decided to light his pipe over this bit of victory, feeling the soft breeze toying with his face and figuring he was not only upwind but still a long way from Slade. A few puffs on the old briar would hardly give him away.

He unsnapped his canteen swivel and moistened his mouth with a sip of water. He had a hefty bottle of Walt's better stuff in his saddlebags for an appetizer before his supper, and later to help settle his beans. Just now the water suited him fine. He roiled the sip around inside his mouth, gushing it through his teeth before swallowing. Refreshed, he hooked the canteen back in place and nudged his horse's ribs. "Hope I see more sign soon," he told Jo Shelby.

He studied the bleached-blue sky. About four in the afternoon, he judged. The summer sky would stay bright enough for him to see for several hours. Flowing down from the south range, the mouth of a canyon spilled a tributary stream to add more than its share of water to the trickle going down Wagon Box Creek. He found signs of an old camp here, got down to study settled ashes of a fire, and was soon convinced that Duff McDonnell was still sporting with his old lady the night these embers glowed. He had no way of knowing that these ashes had once been the flaring fire that had warmed Acie Casey and Barney Wisner as they decided to try their luck upstream from this tributary's mouth.

Ryerson found no other sign of Slade in this area, but since he was off his horse, he searched minutely for some recent trace. This particular ravine showed plenty of water for this time of year, while upstream, Wagon Box Creek had dried to near-nothing.

Ryerson pondered this fact. "A man figuring to hole up for a while would sure want to be close to good water. If he's smart he would. The chase this Wayne Slade has been running for me shows he's either pretty savvy or operating on blind luck. From what Hadley said about his card-playing, plain blind luck would have driven him out of that poker game hours before. No, I'm figuring our Mr. Wayne Slade for a clever gent. He must've got rattled to have taken Hadley's gun and shot McDonnell. Somehow it don't seem to add up. But then, not much of this damnable law-keeping ever does."

He heaved himself back into the saddle, shoving his warm briar into a shirt pocket. "No, sir, Mr. Wayne Slade, I'm figuring you for a shrewd waddy who might get rattled in a poker game. I'm also figuring you're not so rattled now. You'll be figuring to hole up, or at least move through country where there's a decent amount of water. Come on, Jo, let's go look for some more sign up this defile." Ryerson chuckled at himself that he was still talking to his horse, and now in military terms. They veered up the canyon, away from the main stream.

The sign wasn't long in appearing. Ryerson hadn't gone a hundred yards before he found a rock overturned as if kicked loose by a horse. Moisture still showed beneath it. Ryerson determined to stay very alert. This was good bushwhacking country.

He found other sign, too, but much older. Camps several miles apart and the disturbance of the hillsides where men had gone to dig out wash gravel for sluice and pan. Prospecting had never interested Ryerson; the work was too hard, the prospect of payoff too dim. He'd never known anyone who hit it big.

Still there were those, like Casey and Wisner, who studied the South Range through seasoned eyes and proclaimed there were riches to be had if a man knew where to look and had the strength of a jackass, the patience of Job, and a stomach for loneliness.

The sky was beginning to grow heavy with dusk when Ryerson arrived at a broad apron of open space and gravel and boulders and dots of scrub growth trying to make a go of it on the barren landscape.

Water pattered over a sheer precipice into a small pool below.

"Judas," he muttered, "a damned box canyon. Slade found a way over it, for certain. A good place for me to call it a day. Start out fresh in the mornin' and find a way over that cussed waterfall yonder. Must be up there forty feet. Bet it's a pretty place when there's real water coming over. Ought to come back sometime and camp here just for the hell of it."

Ryerson found a spot where others had stayed some weeks or months before him. It was in a quiet, soul-gentling grove of aspens and evergreens, and he found an old fire ring, an ample supply of seasoned wood chopped and neatly laid up, and some soft, mossy spots for his bedroll. He tethered his horse and rummaged around. Cached some distance from the camp he found a battered and heavy old wood sluice, its baffles splintery and bleached from the work of washing down potentially gold-bearing gravel.

On the side, the initials B.W. had been carved. Ryerson grinned. "Barney Wisner built this contraption. I'm damned. Looks like his work."

Feeling good about his day's progress and sensing it would be hard for Slade to bushwhack him in this grove, Ryerson fished out his bottle for a long pull; he considered it a bit of a victory drink for the job of tracking he'd done this day. He knew in the morning he could easily strike Slade's trail by finding where he'd scaled the cliff.

Had to be something wide enough up in there to take a horse over.

After unsaddling Jo Shelby, Ryerson shook his canteen. It was nearly empty, and he knew the water, hauled all the way from Immigrant Lake, would be stale. He had seen the wide but shallow pool beneath the waterfall, so he dumped out the contents of the canteen and stumbled over the uneven, boulder-strewn flat to the pool.

Water no longer cascaded over the falls but fell in a steady shower of heavy droplets that tinkled into the pool, turning the air around it cool and moist. The more Ryerson hung around the place, the better he felt about it. The quiet evening and puttering at fixing his meal was what his tormented mind needed right now. Back to business as usual in the morning.

"Get me some fresh water for coffee to go with my beans in a few minutes." He felt secure in being able to have a small fire in the shelter of the trees as he warmed his supper.

Beside the pool, Ryerson's ankle twisted with a sharp and fierce wrench of pain as he half stepped on a round boulder. His hip, already aching from the day's abuse of the old wound, buckled. He lost his footing, the canteen sailed away, and he pitched into the pool, shoving out his arms to break his fall.

A new stab of pain rammed into his pelvis as his hip gave up its support. Ryerson fell sideways, pitching over the submerged rocks, sensing that an enormous amount of time was passing before he hit whatever it was he was going to hit.

His left hand and arm plowed into the rocks at the bottom of the pool and he heard and felt a distinct and gutjarring crack, his arm collapsing under him. His head went under, his mouth open in a startled scream of pain and panic, and he inhaled water. He rose up on his right arm, his body shot through with an old forgotten terror of suffocation or drowning as water cascaded into his lungs.

He came right up, gagging at the water, gasping for breath as he coughed and retched to expel the stuff in his lungs that emerged as a liquid vomit. Then he was conscious of excruciating agony in his left arm.

Its lightninglike spear clawed upward with needle talons in paralyzing spasms into his shoulder and chest and back. The muddied water turned red with blood.

"Aaagghh, God!" he groaned. He doubled over in a crouch of sudden agony at the water's edge, trying to raise the left arm, now spread with fiery pain. Out of the water it came, the lower arm bent at a strange angle below the elbow. The sodden, bloody sleeve of his trail coat was torn and something projected from the tear on a direct line to his dangling hand, the fingers still hooked from being jammed against the pool's rocky bottom.

It was bone, jagged and shattered and pink with watery blood. The same blood seeped through the water-soaked sleeve into the water draining off his fingers.

"Oh, Judas!" he groaned. "I've gone and broke the thing clean off!"

Amid the flashes of pain through his body, from the injured arm, the pulled hip muscles, and the twisted ankle, waves of heat poured over him. Still he knelt, soaked and dripping in the chill water of the pool, struggling to lift the shattered arm with his good right one.

His stomach rebelled with the crisis and pinched with nausea. He sensed he was going into shock.

Pain's rising grip turned every muscle rigid. Ryerson bent his head against the agony, gritting his teeth and clenching his eyes, his facial muscles stiff and trembling as he tried to fight down the pain. The searing fire of it inside him throbbed like repeated stab wounds as he forced his eyes open to study the mangled arm. Beneath it, the murkiness of the water gradually settled where his fall had disturbed the rocks and silt.

Something glowed on the bottom, catching his attention despite his pain. His eyes were filmy with tears and the water that still dripped off his hair and eyebrows. Ryerson looked at something with a dull but rich yellow magnificence with the settling of the mud. Cradling the battered arm between his chest and his bent knees, he groped deep into the pool for the bright, gleaming object with his good right hand. His fingers closed over a massive rock they could scarcely encircle. He lifted the massive yellow rock and lifted it up and held it, propping the broken arm with great pain and difficulty over the good one that held the nugget.

Gold! The nugget was pure gold and as large as his own clenched fist.

"Lord God Almighty!" he gritted aloud through teeth still clenched against the unrelenting pain. "Lord God Almighty!"

CHAPTER
7

A MILE AWAY, SECURE IN A HIDDEN CLEFT IN THE MOUNtain rocks, Wayne Slade warmed himself by a small fire in anticipation of another night without food. He had spent this day and the previous afternoon getting well away from Immigrant Lake and doing his best to elude capture.

He knew if he stuck with the road that eventually the law from Immigrant Lake would overtake him. The drying bed of Wagon Box Creek looked to Slade like a roadway to oblivion, leading off into the wilderness and the mountains; surely he would leave little, if any, trace. At one point, when his horse relieved himself, Wayne had gotten down, picked up the soggy, pungent road apples, and tossed them out of sight under some scrub growth to make sure he left no traces.

So far he had no well-organized plan. His last meal had been the hearty Sunday breakfast ordered by Hadley. He figured that would have to hold him awhile. He knew very little about eating certain leaves and roots in the wilds to gain nourishment. He knew a man could survive a week or more without food, as long as he had a way of staying warm, and he knew that water was an absolute necessity. From Wagon Box Creek, Slade had moved up a ravine that showed an ample amount of water. Eventually he had come upon the broad apron of boulders and gravel below the falls.

Panicked, Slade had surveyed the seemingly impassable cliff facing him. He had ridden into a box canyon and perhaps the only way out was to ride right back down into the jaws of the law that surely would be in hot pursuit.

Slade grappled with a mounting fear. He had to figure a way up the face of this sheer rock wall. Certainly trees along the base shielded a means to get up and over it. He dropped the horse's reins to let him crop and drink from the pool, and went on foot to explore the cliff's base.

He found it sooner than he'd expected to. A hundred yards into the woods that skirted the broad flatland he found an inclined shelf of rock wide enough to lead a horse up. Somewhere up above, he assured himself, would be open country and the means to the top of the range. Then he'd search for a way down the other side. It was, he told himself in guarded whispers, good country to get lost in— lost, at least, from the law.

During his second afternoon as a fugitive, Wayne Slade had picked his way a mile above the waterfall.

Now, as the sun set and a gray twilight filtered into this tree-choked mountainside, Slade found a chink in the rocks with a soft gravelly bed, and wide enough for him to move about freely and build a fire. He took a sip of the clear, cold water in his canteen, recently filled at the deep pool below the tall but drying falls.

Staring into his tiny fire, trying to thoroughly warm himself before night fell and before he'd have to kick the fire dead and roll up in his soogans, he thought about the killing of McDonnell by Hadley and about the harsh reality of Hadley's statement that Slade would swing before Hadley did.

He remembered the stark panic and disbelief that this

was happening. He wondered at the odd and coincidental appearance of his old nemesis, Dolan. Slade had hotfooted it to the livery stable, found it unattended, saddled his horse, and galloped out of Immigrant Lake, forgetting Lane's lame horse, already hearing the shouted questions of men as they raced to the source of the recent gunfire.

Slade knew his only hope was to get as far from Immigrant Lake as possible in the shortest possible time. He had but a few dollars with him now, having left most of his original fifty dollars and his winnings in the sprawl of chips on the Water Hole table after the shooting.

The cooling air of the darkening night brought him back to the reality of here and now.

It would not be totally dark for an hour. Slade's horse was hobbled on some flat ground upstream. The horse would be safe there through the night; there was grass enough. Slade's stomach pinched with need at having gone nearly two days without food.

Perhaps, he thought, sleep would make him forget his hunger.

Slade was brought bolt upright and rigid with fear as the echoing report of a gunshot rolled up the ravine. What now? The first report was followed by a second and a third, and all turned quiet.

His mind raced. Why shooting? The shots were evenly spaced. If someone was after him in all these miles and miles of mountains, why was he shooting? And three shots? Distress? He reached over, trembling, measuring his breath, and tossed a handful of gravel and sand on his tiny fire. The flames died, but tendrils of white smoke rose like a pillar. He tossed on more sand, effectively killing the coals and the smoke.

Silence returned to the mountains around him. Slade continued to listen—for anything: voices, sounds of someone coming, more shots. He knew it would be foolhardy to leave this place; he was well-enough hidden.

His racing mind could conceive of no reason for the

shots. He hadn't seen signs of anyone on his ride into this high country, only many old traces of a little prospecting activity. It wasn't that there couldn't be someone. But who? Who, at least, besides the law that was certain to be after him? Only the most stupid of lawmen on the chase would go shooting game for dinner so close to the man he was chasing. And it was no stupid lawman who had tracked him this far and this well.

Slade stayed in his uneasy crouch in the break in the rocks and waited, ears tuned for any sound. Listening this keenly, he clearly heard the trickle of water in the canyon below him, the rustle of leaves when the breeze moved them, and the occasional trill of a bird at its evening recital.

The roar rolled up to him again, ricocheting off the canyon walls. One, a pause, then a second shot. Another pause and a third shot. The spacing was even and deliberate. A distress signal; no question of it.

Someone needed help and needed it badly. Slade debated. The man down there firing distress signals was without doubt the lawman on his trail. Surely, Slade thought, he's convinced he's up against a murderer. He's sure to be a friend of Hadley's. He knows the chance he's taking calling me in with a distress signal.

"It could be a phony," he said softly. "No, nobody would do that. The code of the distress signal. It's sacred, even among the lowest and most depraved. For sure no lawman would try such a stunt. It's real."

He studied the trees, thinking deeply. "I shouldn't have run in the first place. The truth will out, so they say. Justice will prevail. Huh! Everywhere but in the West. Still, a man could be dying. He's signaled twice. He's bad off, no matter how you look at it. He may be after me, and I don't even know the man. He's in deep trouble."

Slade pondered his quandary a moment longer. Then, deliberately, he reached for his still-tied bedroll and his saddlebags and started down. The horse would be secure until morning.

He reached into his saddlebags for Lane's fancy revolver. Well, here goes, he thought. Six of one, half a dozen of the other. Hobson's choice. He raised the pistol over his head and fired into the treetops three times in response to the distress calls.

Despite his anxieties, the special-order Colt had a unique feel of substance; he was glad he owned it now.

He shoved the gun and its fine custom holster back into the saddlebags draped across his arm and started a headlong plunge down toward the base of the ravine, taking no pains to be quiet as he crashed through the underbrush and over the loose rocks.

It was a half mile and more to the lip of the waterfall where Slade judged the shots had come from. He put aside the philosophical thinking about the outcome of all this and concentrated on keeping his footing in the rough terrain and getting to wherever he was going with all haste.

Resolutely he strode out onto the broad and flat lip of the waterfall rimrock with but a thin, narrow stream seeping over the edge to fall in great silvery droplets. He could hear their soft chatter into the pool somewhere down there in the gathering dark below him.

"Halloooo," he shouted.

"Over here," came a shouted response from a grove of aspen and spruce flanking the flat area below the falls. The voice was tight with pain.

"I'll be right there."

"Slade? Is that you?"

"Yeah?"

"I'm stove up bad. Broke my arm. I'm bleeding. Sprained ankle and a bum hip. I got to have help from somebody."

"I heard your signal."

"I've been tracking you."

In the darkness the man's words came clearly to Slade. A chill rippled his muscles. He had never in his life been put in such a dilemma. "I know that too."

"You can go off and leave me. I'll die here without help. Or you can come over here and put me out of my misery. Or you can help me. If you do, I've still got to take you in."

"I've thought about all that, too. I'll see what I can do. I'll be right there."

Slade all but sprinted to the slanted shelf of rock leading down from the precipice. He strode across the broad apron of boulders and gravel in the gloaming as night began to settle softly into the canyon.

The injured man heard him stumbling through the twilight. "Slade! Over here!"

Slade directed his steps to the grove. In the near-dark of the trees a big man in a trail coat lay bareheaded, his hair disheveled and damp. His clothing, too, was wet. The rugged, beefy, and big face was white with pain and shock. He held his left arm with his right as he lay on a mossy spot, his head propped up on a hummock of grass.

The left sleeve of the coat was bright with blood, and the hand jutted out at a strange angle.

"Thanks for coming, Slade." The voice was weak.

"Talk about thanks later. Let's have a look at that arm." He knelt over the man. "Oh, my! A compound fracture. Broke clear through the skin."

"You ain't tellin' me anything I don't already know. The name's Ryerson." The man forced his words. "I'm the law in Immigrant Lake."

"Save your breath, Mr. Ryerson. We'll worry about that later. How do you feel?"

"Like I been mule-kicked. About ten times."

"Feel like you're going to puke?"

"I already have."

"I'm no doctor, but I've been around. In the war and on the trail. I've seen a few broken bones."

"Can you do anything?"

"I'll try if you put up that hogleg Colt. I'll cause you so much pain you'll want to shoot me to make me quit."

"All right. We both know what your options are."

"Right."

"Nothing in my Navy anyway. Emptied it at the sky to get you down here. Got more cylinders in my duffel, but to hell with that. I've got to trust you. Made up my mind to that before I started shooting."

"Okay. I may have to ruin your coat and shirt. Wish I had some straight lumber for a splint."

"There's an old sluice box yonder. I've got a hatchet in my gear. Hate to wreck that box, though. Belongs to Casey and Wisner."

"Acie Casey?"

"You know him, right?"

"Talked with him once. You got any booze?"

"Saddlebags."

"We'll both need a jolt."

"Wait a minute. Stay away from those saddlebags. I don't need any jolt. Well, yes, I do. To hell with it. I guess if there wasn't some decency in you, you wouldn't have come down here in the first place. Now you'll have to shoot me for sure."

"Are you getting delirious on me, Mr. Ryerson?"

Ryerson's words were heavy with resignation. "You're bound to find out anyway, sometime. In the saddlebags. Same side as my bottle of whiskey. Shoved it in there without thinking."

"In here? What? . . . Love of mercy! Where did you get this?"

"When I fell. Slipped on a rock over by that pool. Going for water. When I was trying to pull myself out, there it was. I'm in too much pain to really know what I found. Good, is it?"

"Good? Mr. Ryerson, you're a wealthy man!"

"Then take it all and buy this pain off me. Can you do anything?"

Slade slid the huge nugget back into the saddlebag as he

fished out Ryerson's whiskey. With it he went back to the injured man.

"I can try to set and splint that arm. Hope infection won't set in. How do you feel?"

"I'm slipping. Groggy as hell. Starting to get hallucinotions."

"You are delirious. You mean hallucinations."

"No, these are little ones. Hallucinotions. But I may not be aware of that much longer."

"Maybe that's just as well. If you pass out, maybe I can get the arm set and splinted while you're away visiting somewhere else. Here, have a few good swigs of this."

Ryerson's right hand trembled as he lifted the bottle to his lips. Slade could see his Adam's apple working the fiery stuff down.

"Waagh, damn!" Ryerson smacked, the huskiness of pain clearing from his voice. "That smooths the roughness some."

"I hope you will sleep or pass out, Mr. Ryerson. Make my job easier. I'll be as gentle as I can, but I'm no doctor."

"Out here we take what we can get. I've been worked over by some who seemed to take pleasure in hearing a man howl. Doctors they weren't, except for the initials after their name. Give me another pull on that bottle, son."

Slade handed it to Ryerson for a long swig.

"That feels better by the minute. The pain's still there, but I'm not minding it so much. Wheeooo! My head's dancing like a butterfly."

"Good. Let it work. Doze off if that feels good. I'm going to go hack out my splints. I've got an extra shirt in my stuff and I'll have to tear it up to bind up the splints."

"No, you won't. I've got one, too. Use mine."

"Okay. Mind if I have a jolt of your whiskey?"

"My pleasure," Ryerson said, his voice sounding weaker.

"Aagghh!" Slade grunted, feeling the alcohol's fire etch a path deep inside him. "That'll make my job easier, too."

"I'm slipping away, son," Ryerson said softly. "I've got

to trust you. I've believed for some hours now that I can. What kind of poker player are you?''

"You're hardly in shape to play, Marshal."

"I'm not talking about playing cards now. What kind of player are you?''

Slade grinned, bewildered by the question. "Well, if you promise not to string me up as soon as we get back to Immigrant Lake, I believe I could do a fair job of cleaning out your poke. I'm a fair to middling player.''

"That was my hunch. You're also not a man who's going to take my nugget while I'm away paying a short visit to the angels. Or again maybe with old Lucifer.''

"Don't worry. Try to sleep. I'll wake you up when the war's over.''

CHAPTER
8

READYING HIMSELF TO DO HIS BEST TO SET RYERSON'S ARM, Slade gave little thought to the massive nugget or to what lay ahead when he helped the marshal ride back to Immigrant Lake. There was no escape now; Ryerson would need help all the way back. A dominating thought, aside from caring for a helpless man, was that perhaps the law would look kindly on him for this gesture of mercy.

Regardless of the outcome, Slade knew he could do nothing less for Ryerson. There was no other way. The marshal would die without Slade's help. No matter how the cards were dealt after this, he would not carry Ryerson's death on his conscience—even if a hangman's rope brought that conscience to an untimely end.

With the lawman's hatchet he worked loose a board that would not hamper the sluice's effectiveness and would still make enough straight pieces, when split and chopped, to neatly splint the broken arm.

Slade trudged back through the night, shivering with the thought of the job ahead of him. He hoped the marshal would stay in a semicoma; any thrashing would surely make the job longer and more difficult.

It was hard to see the man stretched on the ground when Slade got back. He poked in Ryerson's saddlebags for the shirt and momentarily hefted the giant nugget in the dark. It appeared to weigh about as much as a small sledgehammer head. He had no earthly idea of the value, but imagined it must be phenomenal. Grunting over all the perplexities life now presented him, Slade found Ryerson's clean shirt, shook out its folds, and tore it into wide strips. He found and sucked and chewed some jerky and wolfed down a heel of stale bread. He was surprised how quickly his raging appetite was appeased.

He built a big fire, knowing he'd need its light, and took another sip from Ryerson's bottle. In the firelight flooding the clearing, he found the can Ryerson boiled his coffee in, poured in a few cups of water and measured in coffee from the cloth sack he had found in the saddlebags. Coffee would hit the spot when his beastly work was done. He had another pull from the bottle, feeling it flood him with the strength he knew he'd need for the job ahead, even if it was a false courage.

The material of the sleeve of the big trail coat resisted his sharp pocket knife. He carefully sawed a slit up to Ryerson's elbow and peeled it out of the way. He decided against cutting off the sleeve; Ryerson might be able to get it stitched up. The bloodstained shirt sleeve was old and faded and tore easily, exposing the jagged tip of white bloodstained bone jutting out of the arm wound. Slade shuddered again. The rest of the arm was pearl white, except for an area around the wound, which was red and turning purple and puffy from battered veins. The bleeding had stopped.

So far Ryerson was sleeping peacefully, or unconscious. His breathing was irregular, and occasionally Slade pressed his ear against the man's chest to hear his heart. It sounded as though it was racing a bit, but Slade was not sufficiently trained to tell.

Tentatively he lifted Ryerson's left arm, seeing the bones move as he did. The unconscious man did not stir, and

Slade was thankful. Gently he tried to work the bone back inside the wound. It disappeared easily. Ryerson groaned a bit, but did not move. Slade breathed a whispered sigh of relief. So far, so good.

He was certain he would have to shove a boot into Ryerson's armpit, and the other against his upper arm to relocate the bones. To put off the brutal work as long as possible, Slade got up, threw more wood on the fire, and realized he was sweating. The coffee can was bubbling and tossing the grounds around. He used his bandanna to move it out of the range of the flames, but close enough to stay hot until he needed it. And he knew he would.

"Well," he whispered, "back to work."

Slade again felt the break, kneading it with his fingers. Still Ryerson did not move. A conscious man at this point would have writhed and screamed in agony. Slade was eternally grateful. He could feel the break and where the bones still lay off-center, the muscles pulling them away from alignment. The muscles would have to be stretched to permit the setting.

Slade knew he must do the job right. It was a long way back to the doctor in Immigrant Lake. If he did a bum job, the arm might have to be amputated.

He wiped sweat from his eyes and hunkered into position with Ryerson's hand resting on Slade's hip and Slade's knees doubled up, his feet in position. Slowly he eased his knees out straight and reached for the hand and wrist. He heaved mightily against the armpit and shoulder with his feet, feeling the arm stretch, sensing the bones lining up.

Despite his unconsciousness, Ryerson deliriously opened up with a bellow of agony, and his body heaved up from the ground, fell back, and lay still, his chest heaving.

Slade eased his grip on the hand and wrist and let his legs relax. They ached, and he wasn't sure why. With his fingers, he vigorously kneaded and probed the break, feeling that the bones were now in place. He sensed there were no chips floating around close to the break. His small amount of knowledge of medicine told him the break had been clean and that the setting was as good as he could do.

He sighed again, trembling with exertion and a natural concern about his effectiveness. The job had been rough, but easier than he thought.

Ryerson rested quietly. Slade eased up and fed his fire again. It flared up and warmed him. His sweaty clothing had turned clammy, and he realized he was close to having a chill and nearly going into shock himself. His muscles twitched, and his joints were stiff, achy, and weak, as if he was coming down with the grippe.

He tore off another bite of Ryerson's jerky and worked it, like a cud of tobacco, into the back of his mouth to suck on. He took a long victory drink from the flask, and it did wonders; he felt it warm him to his frigid extremities. He poured a steaming, crackling cup of coffee and made ready to dress the wound and bind on the splints.

When Slade finally completed his frontier doctoring on the arm, he covered Ryerson's sleeping body with the blankets from his bedroll as well as his saddle blanket. He wished now he'd brought his gear down from up above. He struggled to pull off Ryerson's boots, damp and heavy with odor inside. He checked the sprained ankle.

It was swollen, but not badly. Not much more than just a turned ankle, he thought.

He set the boots to dry near the fire. He found two good-sized rocks and put them near the fire to warm, and again checked the patient's breathing and heart. Both seemed to have returned to normal.

The big lawman, tough as nails, slept peacefully through it all.

Slade rolled the warmed rocks into what was left of the shirt and set them at Ryerson's feet and tucked the blankets around him. He was content he had done everything that could be done to make Ryerson comfortable.

His cup of hot, strong coffee eased the last of Slade's

hunger pangs. He sat quietly, feeling his tension ease like a watch spring winding down. He had another swig of whiskey, noting that the bottle was still half full. The gentling effects of it would make Ryerson's trip to Immigrant Lake a bit easier.

He perched uncomfortably against a tree and tried to doze. Casey and Wisner had left an abundance of wood chopped and split into nice fire-sized lengths. The two prospectors, he mused, knew how to make a good camp. He was too tense to sleep. He tossed on more wood. The fire threw a dancing glow around the clearing and reflected off the dome of branches and leaves, illuminating the campsite in a soft light.

The night was pleasant; still, the fire felt good.

Across the fire from him, Ryerson slept without moving, the makeshift splint bulking under the blankets Slade had piled around him. In the morning, or whenever Ryerson was strong enough to ride, he'd have to find something to use as a sling.

His sleepy mind roamed. Ryerson was now a wealthy man. He would be the talk of the territory and a celebrity. Eventually men would swarm into this area and denude it trying to convince themselves that Ryerson's luck could be repeated. Perhaps Ryerson would be shrewd enough to keep the location a secret.

Maybe only Casey and Wisner would know. Slade would have to apologize, if he got the chance, for breaking up their sluice, and offer to buy the lumber to fix it. Theirs was the closest place he knew of between the camp and Immigrant Lake. Maybe when Ryerson was ready to move, he could take him there and send one of the prospectors to town for help.

Maybe, he thought, he could try to get away again. It might be weeks before Ryerson would be fit to travel. Maybe, with such a magnificent sum of money, he'd even give up his lawman job.

Slade studied the bulk of the inert man again. Ryerson

had laid the cards right on the table as to his intention if Slade helped him. Slade admired the man's guts. Maybe, Slade thought, maybe he's smart enough to have read the sign by now and knows that I couldn't really have killed McDonnell.

Hell, he thought, his eyelids growing heavy, I'm not in such a bad position at that. Hadley did it, and though I don't know the depth of friendship between Hadley and Ryerson, the evidence against me is circumstantial. It's Hadley's word against mine, and I did come out of hiding to take care of Ryerson. That ought to weigh heavily in my favor.

Hadley's conscience, or something, will trip him up, and the truth will come out.

Warmed by the fire, exhausted by his impossible task, Slade leaned his head against the tree and slept. As full night shrouded the two sleeping men, the tiny trickle of water from the pool below the waterfall gurgled softly as it worked its way down to its union with Wagon Box Creek. There, in the darkness where it joined the larger streambed, all was quiet, too. There was no sound except for the occasional rustling of aspen leaves being toyed with by a night breeze.

The area was all but dead silent, as it had been centuries before when far upstream the giant nugget was washed from its lodging of decaying granite and tumbled into the stream, eventually to plop into the pool below the falls to be found by Ryerson. Nothing moved, not even the man who lay in ambush in the struggling bank growth across the streambed from the mouth of the canyon.

Quinn Hadley, in his own heavy trail coat, wore his blanket like a hooded cape. Even though he knew Ryerson was far upstream chasing Slade, he dared not light a fire or venture farther. The summer night was pleasant enough for him to wait out the arrival of morning, his shoulders shrouded in his bedroll blanket.

Stealth was important now, more important than it had

been earlier in the day when he followed Ryerson. If he failed in this mission, he was a dead man, from either the bullet or the rope. Beside Hadley as he crouched on a log in the blackness of night lay a nearly new lever-action Winchester of large caliber, safe in a buckskin sheath.

After leaving the Water Hole Saloon Sunday afternoon, Hadley had gone back to his office, with his little kitchen and sleeping quarters at the back, and had done a share of thinking before he turned in early for his much-needed rest.

Slade's flight had reinforced Hadley's hastily trumped-up yarn about McDonnell's death. Ryerson apparently was satisfied with Hadley's version, even though there was little love lost between the two. Their relationship around Immigrant Lake was not one that would ever erupt into open argument or warfare. It was simply that neither man particularly cared for the other.

Hadley puzzled over his mysterious ally, this Emory Dolan. What, Hadley mused, did Dolan stand to gain? He was certain Dolan had some mercenary idea in mind. Still, Hadley felt confident.

Hadley had friends in other places. There were those in the territorial capital with whom he'd worked on favorable beef contracts. In the end it was the government that paid, Hadley mused, but, hell, everybody did it—everybody smart enough, that is.

Hadley grew fearful, though, that Ryerson would succeed in dragging Slade in. Hadley knew he himself could be called to the witness stand, and under merciless grilling by a clever defense attorney he might let something slip that would incriminate him and lend substance to Slade's claim of innocence, despite any good Dolan might do him.

Hadley knew he was a good bluffer; since childhood he had been glib enough to lie his way out of a lot of tough situations. But he couldn't afford to take any chances that Ryerson would bring Slade in and send him to trial.

If it ever got down to a court battle, Hadley knew pressure could be brought to bear on certain individuals in the territory's judicial system. But he didn't care to have it come to that. Too chancy. He wasn't that sure of his friends in high places. It was just too damned risky. There were other ways, Hadley thought, to save his skin.

Hadley had killed before the morning his bullet had smashed into Duff McDonnell's chest. He was ashamed that neither of his two previous killings had been in a fair fight. That first time, in an argument, he had been egged on nearly to the point of drawing his revolver, then had backed off and slunk away from the confrontation like a whipped pup, but seething. Later, his rage still bright and bitter, he had bushwhacked his tormentor in the dark and fled.

The act of murder from out of the dark had bothered him for a few years, but the next time a similar confrontation developed, he found it much easier to settle the hash with gunfire from the favorable shield of night and save his skin in the process.

Shaving in his kitchen behind the office, Hadley had stared at himself in the mirror. It would be an altogether simple matter, he assured the haggard face staring back at him. He knew Cole Ryerson's habits well enough. Ryerson would leave his place to head out after Slade about sunup the next morning. He'd pick up a hefty bottle of booze from Walt at the Water Hole and go on to Jenkins's Wagon Wheel for a whopper of a steak and eggs breakfast and ride out slow, looking for sign.

After a long, refreshing nap, Hadley let it be known around town on Sunday that he was going to be gone for two or three days on business, but would be back well before Ryerson needed him for further statements on the shooting. Several had heard Ryerson caution him not to leave town. Hadley suggested to several townsmen that he had been planning the trip for several weeks and would not be put off, even by Ryerson.

He carefully avoided confronting Ryerson again that day.

He knew, too, that most of the time Ryerson was tracking

Slade, the marshal's eyes would be straight ahead—certainly not looking back much—as he searched the trail of the fugitive. Hadley planned to stay far enough behind to be out of sight, but would be following a fresher trail—Ryerson's—than Ryerson himself had in tracking Slade.

Hadley was following Ryerson closer than he realized; he was jolted with alarm as he walked his horse past the lane up to the old Stout place to see Ryerson riding for the adobe cabin. Had Ryerson looked back at that moment he would have seen Hadley's horse clearly on the main road. Hadley quickly assumed a nonchalant air and continued his horse's easy walk along South Range Pass Road in easy view of Ryerson, had he looked back, and the cabin itself. His scheming mind composed a glib alibi.

But he had no need for it. He hid himself and the horse up a small draw off the road, waited three-quarters of an hour, and watched as Ryerson came by with more urgency apparent now, eyes again glued on the road before him, checking for signs of the retreating Wayne Slade.

Hadley's game was almost up a second time when Ryerson doubled back and rode north again toward the ford after losing Slade's track. Hadley had stopped to let his horse water in the trickle of stream and heard approaching hoofbeats of a man riding at a canter. He hastily hid himself again and, with heart pounding, watched Ryerson approach, pause at the ford, and then urge his horse upstream.

Ryerson, Hadley gloated after his panic had passed, had no notion that anyone was following him. Hadley lost him in the maze of twists and turns of the stream. He rode cautiously upstream in case Ryerson returned, again rehearsing a variety of alibis in case he was apprehended. It would be easy; he'd persuade Ryerson he had ridden out to help in the search. Hadley reached the mouth of the canyon with its ample supply of water trickling out. A cluster of fresh manure told the story; Ryerson had followed Slade up the tributary.

Chances were strong, then, Hadley assured himself, that

Ryerson would return the same way, sometime. He hobbled his horse out of sight of the stream's mouth and took his stand, well hidden among brush and young trees struggling for survival in the bank sand, but with a commanding view of the canyon opposite him. He settled in, preparing to wait out whatever time it took.

Either way, he would bushwhack Ryerson. With the lawman dead, the search for Slade would be over, or at least postponed for a time. Ryerson's death would confirm Slade's guilt on both counts. Slade would never venture this way again. If the two appeared, Hadley might be forced to shoot both men. Then, when the bodies were found, it would appear they had died in a shootout. Hadley gloated again; any way he looked at it, he had a pat hand.

Sitting through the night rethinking his plan, Hadley pulled the blanket closer around his shoulders as the chill by the creek bottom turned to a cold that seeped through his covering. His head nodded and at last his chin dropped to his chest and he slept.

CHAPTER
9

HADLEY'S CONCERN MOUNTED AS THE MORNING SKY BROKE with dawn, brightened and progressed toward noon, passed its daily zenith and began to wane. Despite his misgivings and the sweat in his palms around the rifle stock, Hadley was convinced that no matter how long it took, Ryerson had to emerge from the canyon's mouth. With or without Slade.

Hadley knew he had never been good at waiting; he was often accused of being impatient. Too many things now crowded into his mind; second thoughts of "maybe I should have," and thoughts that perhaps Ryerson and Slade would come out of the mountains by another route. He was also plagued by the possibility of missing his shots, botching it, and himself becoming the casualty of this elaborate dry-gulch plot.

Hadley was exhausted with waiting and his second thoughts by the time the sun was at a low angle out of the west. Abruptly he heard them coming. He tensed; the sound was clearly that of two horses. His breath choked in apprehension. He slid the rifle up and quietly pried down the lever. The breech opened to reveal a fat and gleaming .44-40 cartridge. He brought the rifle up as easily and as casually as his tingling nerves would allow and trained his sights on the vicinity of the opening of the canyon. His arm muscles twitched and trembled, a sensation he couldn't control, making it difficult to take his sight.

His heart raced, and sweat not generated by the warm afternoon sun poured over his body. He tried to lay the bead front sight into the buckhorn rear and line them on a canyon boulder the size of a horse. His nerves wouldn't obey, and he wondered if he'd be able to bring off the ambush.

Got to get it done, he thought, his mind racing. Otherwise, I'm the dead man. No other way out. Let's get at it and get it finished. When it's over, there'll be plenty of time for relief and easy breathing.

Ryerson and Slade came out of the canyon slowly, in single file, Ryerson in the lead. Hadley's throat tightened and went bone-dry; he tried to swallow and couldn't. In an instant his elaborate plans spun into confused turbulence. The big marshal was hunched forward in the saddle, his head bobbing as though he had been beaten. His right hand feebly clutched the reins; his left arm, like a giant log in splints, was cradled in a makeshift sling.

Instead of firing immediately as he had planned, Hadley stood rooted to his hiding place and watched, mouth agape, his mind racing. The two riders turned now, heading down Wagon Box Creek, within thirty yards of Hadley's stand. He could not imagine what had happened and how Ryerson's condition affected his well-calculated plans. It had to be done, his bewildered mind shouted. He'd figure the rest of it out after they were dead. The moment he realigned his sight picture on the marshal's receding torso, a surge of new confidence and ease rolled over him. Easy now, right there between the shoulder blades; that's it.

The muzzle blast and the roar of sound agitated the aspen leaves in front of him into a frenzied momentary dance.

Ryerson pitched out of the saddle, his body slamming into the rocky streambed. His horse, startled by the explosive sound that had abruptly shredded the silence of the dozing afternoon, bucked on its hind legs and bolted down the wash.

Slade instantly wheeled his horse around, made a short turn, and galloped at an angle back to the cover of the ravine. Hadley fired twice at the retreating Slade, his snapped, confused shots going high and wide. Slade disappeared behind rocks and trees. For a few moments as the echoes of the report bounced off the canyon walls, Hadley could also hear the sounds of Slade's horse slipping and scraping on the rocks, growing dimmer as the man fled up the narrow gorge.

Jittery again and spooked by what he had done, Hadley hastily rolled up the rifle's soft buckskin sleeve and shoved it into his pocket. He grabbed the rifle and jogged anxiously to his horse. He had hitched it far enough away so it would not nicker when the other horses appeared. He mounted unsteadily and carefully rode out to the broad, sun-drenched, and dry stream bed. About twenty yards away, Ryerson lay face up on the rocks.

Desperate qualms persuaded Hadley not to get too close to his kill. In neither of his previous killings had it been necessary or imperative to see if the man still lived. Now he cringed, feeling little muscles in his arms and legs twitching annoyingly as he shrank from the grisly prospect of having to look the dead marshal in the face. His hands shook as they clutched the reins.

This, too, had to be done. The problem was that Ryerson lay face up, his injured arm still in its sling, the other arm thrown above his head. His straightened legs were spread slightly as if he were sleeping. His eyes were closed, Hadley could see as he timidly approached the corpse. Without dismounting, he took a hasty look at it.

An unmeasured fear dictated that Hadley not get down for a closer look. He thought about delivering a coup de grace, but dismissed the idea. Ryerson was good and dead. He studied his quarry a brief moment, a nagging revulsion squeezing his gut with approaching nausea. A bloody circle on Ryerson's shirt marked where the bullet had exited. It looked final. Hadley could see no rising and falling of the chest to indicate that the big lawman was breathing.

He was certainly dead, Hadley concluded hastily, spurring his horse down the dry streambed, only beginning to sense relief that the gruesome chore was over. He was clear. He was free. His feeling of well-being increased the farther he got from the death scene. He thought some that he should have hidden the body. Still, when and if it was found, Slade would be summarily assumed to be the culprit. If the body was eaten and the bones scattered by wild animals, Slade would still be blamed. So, Hadley thought, why worry?

He couldn't figure what had happened to Ryerson's arm. Probably, he thought, Slade and Ryerson had a shoot-out and Ryerson took a slug in the arm. Then, later, Ryerson probably got the drop on Slade and forced him, under the gun, to tend to the wounded arm and had been taking him in.

Slade's hands probably had been tied, he thought; the action had been so fast, he hadn't noticed.

That was without doubt what happened, he reassured himself, and Slade had escaped a second time. It was a cinch now that Slade would ride clear of the territory. What might work through Slade's mind as to the reason for the ambush or the attacker's identity didn't particularly bother Hadley. Slade was still the outlander and was suspect in Immigrant Lake. Most certainly Slade would get as far from Immigrant Lake as he could in the shortest possible time.

Hadley was suddenly engulfed in a heart-swelling euphoria. He was pleased with himself that he had been so shrewd in working through his problem. In something like this, a man had to plan on a few hitches in his scheme. Ryerson was dead, and Slade, for the second time, was making tracks out of this neck of the woods. Hadley could go back and take up where he left off. He would feign suitable grief over the loss of the town marshal.

Maybe, he thought, I'd ought to ride wide of Immigrant Lake and go up north and camp in the North Range country for a few days to carry off the charade of having been away on a long business trip. This would clear him if Ryerson's body was found. On the way back, he figured to visit some of the ranchers north of town, thus reinforcing his guise.

Hadley mentally checked his belongings in his saddlebags. He had enough food to make it. He was angry with himself that he hadn't thought to stop by the Water Hole and pick up a bottle. The days would be long without a little hair of the dog to make the afternoons and the evenings mellow. He knew from experience that after a killing, a strange, unique, and fearful series of thoughts sometimes came to a man alone. His mental condition would demand a drink. His nerve endings still twitched, though as time passed, he grew more and more at ease with himself.

His prayers suddenly were answered. As he rounded a bend on the approach to South Range Pass Road ford, there stood Ryerson's horse, the reins down, quietly cropping some grass that flourished on the dirt banks of the creek.

Hadley had heard Ryerson quip more than once that he never left town without his snakebite remedy. Hadley looked back up the streambed, still feeling nervous. He reined in and walked his horse to Ryerson's mount and got down to dig out the bottle from the lawman's saddlebags.

The horse appeared oblivious to the man's approach. This was a gentle animal, Hadley knew. Ryerson's horse continued to munch, its teeth making muffled grinding noises, the foam at the edges of its velvet lips tinged with green. Hadley's hands hurriedly groped in the saddlebags for the bottle he knew was there.

There was none. Instead, he felt the shape of a rock buried deep among the sundries of survival Ryerson carried for the trail. Puzzled as to why Ryerson would be toting a heavy rock, Hadley hauled out the extra-heavy stone. Late afternoon sun danced off the mass in his hand.

"Judas Priest!" he gasped.

Instinctively darting another glance upstream to make certain he hadn't been observed, Hadley forgot his search for a bottle. Instead, he turned and sprinted for his horse, the giant nugget tight within the circle of his fingers.

As Slade rode upstream a safe distance from the canyon's mouth, his mind was a jumble of confused thoughts. The suddenness of the ambush had startled him out of his wits. He'd seen Ryerson pitch out of the saddle to land with a thud against the streambed boulders, shot in the back. The instinct for survival had taken over as he wheeled his horse and bolted for the security of the ravine they had just left. He couldn't remember if two or three shots had sailed close to him as he made his escape from the ambush.

He rode upstream another hundred yards before easing his horse to a walk, listening for sounds of pursuit. He doubted there would be any. Anyone low enough to back-shoot from cover did not own the guts to ride after a man who very nicely could double back and ambush the ambusher.

As he slowed the horse, Slade's racing thoughts slowed as well. Things began to fall gradually into logical place. It had to have been Hadley. Only for a moment did he think the outlaw Dolan might have had a hand in it, but quickly dismissed the idea; Hadley had more to gain than Dolan. If Ryerson was dead, Slade was essentially free. But, he considered, Hadley had been there to shut both of them up. If Slade and Hadley ever met again, either in town or on the trail, a sudden shoot-out was inevitable.

What if Ryerson hadn't been killed? What if right now the seriously crippled lawman was shooting it out with his assailant? He stopped to listen but heard no shooting.

Maybe, he thought, the bushwhacker was stalking Ryerson to be sure of finishing the job.

Ryerson would need help.

Slade impulsively wheeled his horse around. Taking an oblique route, he urged the animal up the wooded slopes of the canyon. He quickly found a suitable place to hobble his horse well away from the stream. Then he dug out Lane's beautiful pistol and began the long, arduous hike back to the mouth of the stream where Ryerson lay. The long-barreled Colt might have greater accuracy at this range, he thought.

He'd sneak in to whatever vantage point he could find and survey the ambush site. If Ryerson needed help, he was prepared to do everything he could.

Thoughts of the nugget brought him up short. Ryerson had it in his saddlebags! Slade had seen the horse bolt away in sudden fright at the abrupt gunfire as Ryerson pitched out of the saddle.

Silently he cursed the entire hellish business and the unbelievable set of circumstances. Ryerson—Slade's only real hope to clear his name—was probably dead. Hadley was down there someplace with a bullet in his gun with Slade's name on it, and a king's ransom in one giant nugget of pure gold was bouncing around unattended somewhere in the territory.

Never for a moment did Slade think of the gold as anything but Cole Ryerson's nugget. He shook his head at the incredibility of it all. Not since he had left home to cast his lot with Robert E. Lee had Slade been in such an impossible state of affairs.

The going was rough on foot along the crest overlooking the creek. Slade scrambled over the jagged hillside as fast as he could, still moving cautiously, keeping under cover, and gliding across the tree-studded country as quietly as possible. He even drew his breath with care.

Slade emerged on a low bluff overlooking Wagon Box Creek. Because of the mesh of trees, he could not fully see the confluence of the ravine and the creek. He slid around easily, moving downhill now, trying to make out the area where Ryerson had fallen.

Then, in the lengthening shadows, there he was, a hundred yards from Slade's vantage point. The big lawman was sitting up, the broken arm still in the sling. His knees were drawn up, and his head was partly supported by his chest and knees. It appeared at the distance that Ryerson's Navy revolver dangled from the feeble fingers of his right hand.

Slade was moved to shout out to Ryerson, and just as suddenly he held back. The assassin might still be lurking in the scrub growth yonder, assuming Slade would sneak back, and was using Ryerson as a lure to smoke Slade out and still get the two of them.

"Dammit!" Slade muttered softly. "I've got to get to that man!"

Suddenly his thoughts convinced him that such a ploy was not in the makeup of Quinn Hadley. Slade was persuaded now that he had a fair idea of how Hadley's mind worked. He'd played poker with him for fourteen hours, seen him bluff and then kill, and seen how quickly he had put Slade on the spot. Then Hadley had come gunning for Slade and Ryerson from ambush. Hadley was smart in an evil sort of way; but not that smart.

For the second time in two days, Slade threw caution to the winds.

"Cole!" he shouted. There was no movement in the lawman's agonized pose. "Cole! It's me. Slade!"

Ryerson's head rose slightly as he held it up weakly. "He's gone."

Slade could scarcely hear the words at the distance.

Ryerson's pain-riddled body tipped over, and he fell heavily on his side, his knees doubled up. Slade sprinted down the hill, through the bank underbrush, and across the boulder-strewn streambed to him.

"Oh, my God, Cole!" Slade shouted as he saw the blood-stained shirt.

"I'm . . . okay," Ryerson said feebly. "Been hit . . . worse than this . . . before. I'm . . . okay. Damn fool got me on the left side again. . . . I know for sure who killed McDonnell. Hadley's sure . . . I'm dead. Go get . . . the gold . . . my horse."

"I've got to take care of you. That wound."

"Damn you . . . go get . . . the gold. Downstream. Then . . . come back."

Slade took another look at the doubled-up body, cramped with pain. He turned and sprinted down the flat streambed, wondering if Ryerson would die before he got back. He was stopped by a weak call from Ryerson.

"Slade! Watch out . . . for that egg-suckin' bushwhacker!"

FACE DOWN AT IMMORTAL LAKE

CHAPTER

10

THREE QUARTERS OF AN HOUR LATER SLADE WAS BACK, riding Jo Shelby with as much speed as the boulder-strewn streambed allowed. Ryerson still lay where Slade had found him, but no longer were his legs doubled up. Slade feared the lawman was dead as he slid out of the saddle, dropped the reins, and raced to him.

"Cole! Cole!"

"Stop shouting, man," the weak voice said. Ryerson kept his eyes closed. "I may be shot and got an arm busted clean in two, but there ain't nothing wrong with my ears."

"I want to look at that wound."

"The gold. Did you get the gold?"

Slade sighed over the bad news. "Ah, no, Cole, no. Ah, looks like Hadley beat us to it."

Ryerson's eyes opened, and Slade could see fires blazing in them.

"Why, that son of a bitch! That fourteen-karat cast-iron ring-tailed son of a bitch!"

"Easy, Cole, easy."

"Easy, my foot. I told you I been stove up worse than

this in my time. The bullet went clean through, so all I got to do is get busy and mend up two holes. Don't put me down for one of your pantywaists. I hurt like thunder, but I'll be all right."

"I got to clean those wounds."

"Any of that dog hair left, son, or did Hadley get that, too?"

"Whiskey? No, luckily I had it in my saddlebags. There's not much. Maybe enough to wipe your wounds and a decent slug apiece, and that'll be it. I've got to go in a minute and bring down my horse."

"Sometimes the hooch can be more precious than gold. Like now. I figure Hadley was going through my stuff looking for a bottle. I never suspected him for such a sneak thief and a back-shooter. God, I hate that man just now." Ryerson grunted his words through pain-clenched teeth.

"He's more than a sneak thief. That's pretty big business, making off with that much of another man's gold. And he'd have to know it was yours."

"That rotten son of a bitch and bastard." Ryerson's voice gained strength with his anger.

"I'm going to get our bedrolls and make you comfortable and fix those wounds, and we'll rest here tonight."

Ryerson cooled. "Just as well. Casey and Wisner had a camp yonder. Least I suspect it was them, the way it's tidied. Seen it on the way in yesterday."

"Can you get up and walk over there?"

"You just watch me."

Ryerson's pitiful store of strength was largely consumed in stumbling to the old campsite. Slade felt another surge of admiration for the tough-as-nails lawman when he waved away Slade's move to support him. Still, Ryerson was ready to stretch out on the blanket with his head on his saddle.

When he got back from retrieving his horse, Slade pulled back Ryerson's clothes and cleansed the large, bloody punctures front and back high on Ryerson's left shoulder. No bones had been broken or shattered. Slade was well aware the wounds must be sensitive as hell. Yet Ryerson withstood Slade's clumsy cleanup work and the sting of the alcohol without a murmur.

He used what was left of their extra shirts for bandages and wrapped strips of cloth around Ryerson's shoulder to hold the pads in place. He worked Ryerson's shirt and trail coat back over his shoulders and got the broken arm back in its sling. Because of the massive splints, he was unable to remove either garment without ruining it or causing Ryerson great agony.

"Now let me have a shot from my bottle, son," Ryerson said.

"Save me a little. It's been a rough day on me, too."

"Least you're all in one piece. I don't know about me." Ryerson studied the remains in the bottle, mentally measuring his swig. He took a large one. He rasped his good right sleeve across his lips. "There's yours, Slade. Exactly half by honest measure."

"As honest as you could be," Slade said, raising the bottle. Again he savored the throat-paralyzing fire that seared as it dropped into his stomach and spread a burning vigor through his system; his eyes teared up. It was powerful stuff.

"Waagh!" He smacked his lips. "Now, Mr. Ryerson, you lie back and rest. I'm going to get some coffee going and warm up a can of those beans. In the morning we'll have to see what we can do about things."

"You sure know how to look after a body," Ryerson said in a joking tone despite his pain. "I could sure use somebody like you around the place. I think I'll get 'em to convict you and get you remanded to my custody. What do they call it—a . . . manservant?"

Slade felt enough at ease with the big lawman by now to return the joshing. "How'd you like that other arm broken? Shut your yap and your eyes, and I'll wake you when things are ready."

Ryerson settled back on the blankets, grunting a bit with the pain of moving. He didn't sleep, but lay with his eyes open, staring at the aspen leaves above him and the immense sky beyond.

Slade busied himself getting a fire going, starting a can of coffee, and digging into the things he'd need to get a meal of some sort into them.

"It ain't so bad after all, Wayne."

"Things couldn't be worse, and you lie there saying it ain't so bad. You care to explain all that?"

"Well, I ain't dead, though Lord knows with the banging around I've taken these last couple of days, I'd ought to be. After I found my gold, my mind was never really in shape to realize what it was I had. Never had it long enough to really get attached to it. I think probably more important than that damned gold was that out of all this, even though I'm banged up and shot up for a fare-thee-well, we got your name cleared."

Slade brightened. "Yeah, I suppose there is that happy side to all this."

"And soon's I get knit up halfways proper, I'm going after McDonnell's real killer and the owl-hoot that stole my gold. Son, I'll track him through the spitfires of hell if I have to. And he thinks I'm dead. When me and him come up face to face, he's gonna drop dead purely out of fright. I can't wait to see the look on that son of a bitch's face."

Ryerson chuckled in spite of his injuries and coughed a groan at the pain it caused him.

"You'll never find Hadley, Cole. By the time you can travel, he'll be miles away."

"Oh, no. Tomorrow we're riding to Immigrant Lake. I'm getting Doc Wells to take a look at the fine job you already done, and by next Saturday I'm going after Hadley. Won't take no longer than that to get started. He's got my money, more than enough to see me through the end of my days. He's also got a score to settle with the hangman in town."

"Wish to hell you'd sleep, Cole."

"Night was made for sleeping, and the sun's still high."

"Coffee's almost done."

"I suppose if I can't have hooch to ease these lumps, coffee will have to do. Know who makes the greatest pot of coffee in these parts? And I only had one cup of it. Your friend Casey."

"Thanks a lot. You sure know how to show your gratitude. Remind me to let you make your own coffee from now on. Matter of fact, I was thinking of taking you to their place in the morning and going on to Immigrant Lake myself and bringing out the doctor."

"To Casey and Wisner's? Hadn't thought about that. That way I could sit around and drink Acie's coffee for a couple of days. When's Sunday? I'm figuring to sit down at their table for Acie's chicken dinner one a these Sundays soon. If I go there, I'll be ten miles closer to bringing in Hadley."

"You agree to stopping off with Acie and his pardner?"

"Hell, yes. And while I'm waiting around there, I'm going to build a case against that damned Hadley. The lawyer in me would charge him right off the bat with premeditated murder in the first degree. Then, for lying about you, I'll get him for obstructing justice. Gunning me down and taking shots at you are good for two counts of attempted murder or assault and battery, whichever will hang him higher. Then for stealing my nugget I'll run him in for grand larceny!"

Slade grinned. Ryerson's anger was the best medicine he could get.

"You're saying hanging's too good for him."

"You're damned right!"

After a night rolled up in his soogans, Slade was awake with the first gray of morning. He kicked the fire to life and set the can of water to brew with a heaping handful of coffee from Ryerson's sack which, fortunately, Hadley had overlooked when he rifled through the marshal's things.

Slade sipped the tongue-searing brew from Ryerson's one chipped, dented, and splintered enameled cup while the lawman still slept. Slade sat quietly, his mind easy now, and watched the neighborhood come to life. Birds were first to greet the day; their crystal song awakened him when only a sliver of gray broke the sky to the east.

To Slade the morning song of a bird was perhaps the most beautiful music he could think of, next to that of an angel—whose music he could only guess at, having only hearsay as to its quality.

Slade acknowledged he was a morning-lover, savoring the joy of cracking his eyelids as the feathered symphony tuned up for its daily concerto to life. In a half-sleep, under a snugly tucked bedroll on soft sand warmed by his body, he watched the leaves take shape above and around him. When he awoke out-of-doors he loved to sleepily study the morning star, noting how its twinkle dimmed as day brightened.

In these times he was filled with childhood's nostalgia, remembering waking up as a small boy on the Georgia plantation, hearing the same kind of birdsong announcing the approach of day. He'd hear, too, the comforting sounds of movement of people behind the mansion preparing for the day's work. The darkies would be up and breakfasted, and he could hear his father's soft but authoritative voice assigning them their tasks for the day. An ardent slaveholder, and thus an ardent Secessionist, the elder Slade had owned many slaves. To him, though, their ownership represented an obligation. They may have been chattels bought and paid for, but he recognized them as human beings. The plantation's slaves were well fed and cared for and lived in clean, sturdy quarters some distance from the main house.

They were given Sunday off for their religious services and to spend the rest of the day with their friends and families. Slade's father never permitted a family to be broken up by slave trading and, above all, fostered a family-unit feeling among them. If a man turned up sick enough to stay out of the fields for the day, his wife was also given the day to tend to her ailing husband. All the darkies were taught basic rudiments of hygiene and what to do for themselves if they became sick or injured.

Slade still sat quietly thinking about those early days and

the good memories they had left him. Though everything was gone in the wake of war, he thought, at least that was a positive legacy. Good memories that fostered positive attitudes meant as much as tangible wealth. He sipped his coffee and watched the morning zephyrs spin the aspen leaves like tops. He could become more philosophical now about the war and the chaos in its wake. It was, he mused, all a part of building in him what he had become, and then sometimes tearing down and rebuilding. But he knew his basic foundations were sound.

So far, though any form of success seemed foreign to him, he had never stooped to lying, cheating, stealing, or killing to get ahead of the rotten game he was in. He still had no qualms about killing the outlaw Lane or appropriating the dead man's money, his horse, and his magnificent pistol. Slade still wouldn't have traded places with Hadley for the nugget, or for ten more just like it. Hadley now finally and justifiably had taken up Slade's cross of guilt in Duff McDonnell's death.

The sun had broken over the trees and already was warming the rocks and gravel bars along the trickle of stream that was a summer remnant of Wagon Box Creek. Slade's sharp eyes caught the flicker of movement across the stream, as a large lizard wriggled out slowly to toast itself in the spreading sun.

Slade studied Ryerson, still sleeping under the thick bedroll, admiring the lawman's spunk and liking him as a man. Now that his name was cleared, Slade promised himself to ask Ryerson what had happened to his poker winnings. He assumed Hadley had appropriated that, too. That money, like the gold, was probably gone. Ah, well, Slade thought, there will be other games.

Huh, he grunted, almost aloud. I've won the final pot in Saturday night's game: I'm innocent.

CHAPTER
11

RYERSON HAD HIS HAT SHOVED OVER HIS FACE AS HE LAY on his back under the bedroll Slade had tucked around him the night before. Ryerson apparently had not moved in his sleep. His head under his hat was propped on his saddle the way Slade had left him. His arms were crossed over his chest, the heavily splinted arm bulking under the soogans.

Slade was about to wake Ryerson to begin the ride to Casey and Wisner's place. As if anticipating Slade, Ryerson stirred and slithered out his good right arm and shoved the hat back. He rubbed his face with a hand as large as a haunch of meat.

"How's the world treating you this morning, Cole?"

"A touch of the collywobbles dancin' in my belly, but I ain't about to puke. I been awake an hour talking to this damned pain in my arm and shoulder." Ryerson painfully twisted his head to look at Slade.

"Hurt bad?"

"Son, if you ever had a arm broke clean in two and then been shot at close range with a big forty-four through the same shoulder, you wouldn't be asking idiot questions like 'does it hurt bad.' Yeah, it hurts bad."

"Can you ride today?"

"Can I ride? My legs is sound enough to stand in the stirrups and I'll have to guide Jo Shelby with my right hand. But I can ride. Son, when you dressed that wound Hadley give me, you ought to've seen a bullet scar in about the same place."

Slade recalled seeing purplish, puckered welts the size of the end of his thumb, front and back below Ryerson's latest wound. "I saw them."

"With that wound, young feller, I lifted a man's carcass over his saddle, tied him down, and rode fifty miles through the dead of winter up in Montana. That was a number of years ago, I'll warrant, and anymore I just can't seem to take it like I used to. Of course, when we got in, he was a hell of a lot worse off than me. Had to bury him in a grave dug in the shape of a horseshoe. Never could undouble the man to get him into a box. Had to roll the son of a bitch in a tarpaulin."

"And that man was . . . ?"

"An owl-hoot name of Orval Clampett, the same as give me that wound. So don't go asking if I'm in shape to ride."

"Then let's mount up!"

"Whoa there, hoss. I said that was a number of years ago. Just now I aim to get up, go yonder and take my relief, and come back here and stretch out on my soogans and have my prisoner serve me my breakfast vittles and coffee in bed."

"Prisoner!"

"You're the only one I got, and I told you somebody's got to swing in Immigrant Lake for killing Duff McDonnell. Now, you better start right off treating me with the respect due my high office or I'm likely to forget what I said about Hadley's bushwhacking of me clearing your name. And I'll expect 'yes, sir' and 'no, sir' and 'thank you, sir.' "

"Whaat?" Slade was incredulous.

"On second thought, I'll roust about and fix my own

vittles. Anybody as dumb as you couldn't find cow plop in a barnyard."

Slade allowed himself to acknowledge the joke. "No, I'll fix you some grub, sir, and seeing's how we don't have salt or pepper, I may just add a handful of sand to season it up proper."

"One thing's a cinch," Ryerson said with a grunt as he raised his pain-stiffened body to a sitting position and surveyed the day. "It sure as hell ought to improve anything you're likely to put over the fire!"

An hour later they were on the trail. Contrary to Ryerson's broad statements as to his stamina, the long ride to the ford at South Range Pass Road was sheer agony for him. Each of Jo Shelby's jarring steps shot new pain through his battered body. After they had gone but a mile the man who had started the ride tall and proud in the saddle was hunched over, clutching the saddle horn for support with the same hand that held slack reins and fighting not to tumble out of the saddle.

Slade called a halt and gave Ryerson the canteen of lukewarm coffee that he'd saved from breakfast. He figured the coffee would be better stimulation for the wounded man than plain water.

After sipping the coffee, Ryerson sat on a round rock with his eyes shut against the pain. Slade wandered off, letting Ryerson gather his strength and fight down the pain by himself and not forcing him to expend his pitiful supply of energy by talking.

Gradually Ryerson appeared to accustom himself to travel. On their next leg of riding, they made about a mile and a half before Slade could see that Ryerson's condition again dictated a brief stop. Then they made two miles before the lawman needed relief. Each time they added distance between stops.

The last stretch to the Casey-Wisner place was about five miles. Ryerson endured it not quite so hunched over, maintaining his grip on the reins weakly with his good right hand.

Slade smiled inwardly to see Ryerson, riding ahead of him, shove himself as erect as his pride, battling against the pain, would allow. He squared his shoulders as they left South Range Pass Road and began the meandering hundred yards up to the adobe cabin.

He could almost hear Ryerson telling himself it would be a man and not a pantywaist who'd ride up to Casey and Wisner's. Slade grinned again.

The prospectors had seen the pair coming up the lane and waited in front of their new lopsided door as Slade and Ryerson led their mounts up the last rise and approached the house.

"Mr. Casey," Ryerson called loudly, his voice firm, "I sure could stand a cup of your coffee!"

"What happened to your arm, Cole?" Wisner asked.

"Nothin' less than I busted it clean off."

"Get down, man, get down," Casey said. "You look like you been hauled th'ough a ragged knothole." Casey, sensing Ryerson's weakness, moved to help the marshal down. Ryerson was in motion before Casey got to him.

Ryerson feigned anger. "I can make it myself. Much obliged."

Casey shot a mean glance at Slade, still on horseback. "Well, I see you done what you set out for and got McDonnell's killer."

Ryerson's voice still held an edge of impatience. "No, I didn't. The man who killed Duff McDonnell is still at large."

"Marshal, that man you're riding with is the one you're after. That's Wayne Slade."

"Damned if I don't know that, Acie. Will you quit yappin' and let me get into your place before I fall down? The man who shot McDonnell and put a bullet through me and left me for dead was a yellabelly name of Hadley."

Casey shot a quizzical look at Wisner that puzzled Slade.

Slade levered himself out of the saddle and tied his horse and Ryerson's and headed for the door behind Ryerson and Casey.

Wisner mumbled "C'mon in" to Slade and then looked toward Casey with his brows knotted. Hadley's name had triggered something.

"Well, Cole," Wisner drawled, "it appears we got a lot of palaverin' to do when you're feeling up to it. This whole business is getting strange. Want to lie down?"

"Naw, much obliged just the same. I'm just as happy being off that horse for the moment and sitting on something that doesn't jar the blood and the bejeebers out of me. Slade here has the makings of a fine doctor, the way he's been looking after my ailments. I might stretch out a bit after a while. Slade's fixing to ride in for Doc Wells to look me over and maybe put some plaster of paris on this arm instead of this big chunk of your sluice box."

"Our sluice?"

"Tell you about that later. I'd be obliged if I could stay here till Saturday or thereabouts and get knit up enough to ride some more. Soon's I'm strong enough to mount up, I got to get out and try to run that fourteen-karat back-shooter Hadley to ground."

"That be Quinn Hadley, Cole?" Acie asked, bringing coffee to the table and setting the pot in front of Ryerson and Slade.

"You know him? Seen him?"

"No, but along about middle of the forenoon today his horse showed up here. Was trying to eat oats out of the manger next to our mules. We didn't know whose horse it was, so we took off his bridle and saddle and rubbed him down and grained him a bit. Got him hobbled out back."

"Yeah," Wisner added. "We normally don't pry, Cole, but we looked into the saddlebags to see if we could find out who the animal belonged to. We found some papers belonging to Quinn Hadley."

Ryerson and Slade now stared at each other quizzically.

"Well, amigo," Ryerson said to Slade, "at least the hammerhead son of a pup is afoot, or else I got horse-thievin' to add to his bill of indictment."

Slade wrinkled his eyebrows and with his lips formed the word "gold" at Ryerson, who nodded.

"Clean forgot with this arm and shoulder giving me the agonies of the damned," Ryerson said. He looked at Casey and Wisner hovering over him. "Now, I want you boys to be truthful with me. Did you find anything else in his saddlebags?"

CHAPTER
12

F ROM THE MOMENT HE YANKED IT OUT OF RYERSON'S SADdlebag, Quinn Hadley found it impossible to leave the nugget in his saddlebags for more than a few moments at a time.

The night before, as Slade made the twice-injured Ryerson comfortable and kicked up their fire and began to engage in good-natured bantering, Hadley, the subject of many of their thoughts and much of their talk, was already miles away.

With the giant nugget safe in his saddlebags or clutched in his hand for his wondering, gloating eyes to admire, there was little reason now for Quinn Hadley ever to return to Immigrant Lake. He was convinced Ryerson was dead, but had some misgivings that Slade was aware of the gold Ryerson had apparently found by accident high up in the narrow canyon.

Why, Hadley mused, had Ryerson kept up the stupid and possibly lethal chase after suddenly becoming a wealthy man? Hadley was inclined to measure every man's attitudes by his own; he was certain Slade would be elated to find

Ryerson's body and would go slinking back down Wagon Box Creek looking for Ryerson's horse and the gold—if he knew about it. Hadley gloated again; if he did, Wayne Slade would be in for a big surprise.

Or maybe, Hadley thought, it was Slade's all along. He dug again into his bag and slid out the giant nugget to study and be thrilled by. He let fancy put him in elegant drawing rooms and among the elite of bustling, cultured eastern cities. Wealth now was bringing him close to what he'd always yearned for—being close to people of his own kind, people who shared his discriminating tastes.

Reality brought him back to here and now. Maybe Slade found it and Ryerson took it away from him. Either way, it's too much of a temptation to keep Slade running in the opposite direction for long. He'll come back, and when he finds Ryerson dead, he'll know that will buy him at least a little time to go hunting Ryerson's horse. When he finds it and sees the gold gone, he's sure to come looking for whoever took it.

Hadley shot an anxious glance over his shoulder. He trembled slightly. He nudged the horse to pick up the pace. He could be on my back trail right now, he thought.

In his flight with the gold, Hadley had crossed North Range Pass Road and was already in the adjacent northeast quadrant of the Immigrant Lake Valley neatly cut by the Range Pass Road and the Mountain and Central Railroad. He rode the long edge of the quarter-circle, looping up northeast for the railroad.

Of course, Hadley's thinking continued, Slade's probably got it figured by now it was me who did the shooting. He's shrewd. He'll be on my trail for more reasons than one now with Ryerson out of the way. I got him in a jam and stole the gold. I could afford to take the time to wait him out somewhere along here and get him from cover. That'd solve everything.

He trembled again. Nah, Slade doesn't know this territory. He's got no idea which way I went. Either way, I'm watching my back trail in case he does show up. Ah, I don't know. There's also a strong chance Slade doesn't know anything about the gold and is purely hightailing it out of the territory. Yeah, that's it! He's gone. I'm scot-free. Ryerson was slick. He probably found the gold while he was going up that ravine after Slade. Probably just hid it away in his saddlebags until he got back to town. He was taking Slade in for murder, and he sure wouldn't do much crowing about such a find to a cold-blooded killer. Ha! That's it. That's what happened. I got nothing to worry about. He paused in his thinking.

Still, what beats me is how Ryerson hurt his arm. Seems reasonable that Slade winged him. Anyway, I've got the gold now, no matter if Ryerson is dead and Slade is running away or coming after me. This is a damned big valley, and Slade is a stranger to this neck of the woods. By the time he gets his bearings and my trail, if he ever does, I'll be long gone on an eastbound train.

The MC trains, whether loaded or not, traveled slowly over Jackson Saddle, the eastern gateway to the Immigrant Lake valley. Burdened only with his newfound gold, Hadley figured he could easily leap aboard a freight car and ride to the next station, where he could get a passenger seat ticket.

Dipping again into his saddlebags to fish out the huge nugget, he thought again how he would travel east to the big gold markets of New York. He doubted any price-haggling would be possible. Or even necessary. Perhaps he might even find someone extremely wealthy to buy it for more than its market value for the novelty of having that much natural gold in one chunk.

Hadley again wrestled with his fantasies.

Realistically, though, he told himself, he would have to be extremely careful. One false move in his travels, one accidental disclosure of the gold, and his life wouldn't be worth a sliver off the nugget. Men had been murdered for a mere vial of gold dust. This nugget, he thought, could easily provoke a massacre.

The ride to the rail line would be about thirty miles, skirting along the foothills. He would have to be very careful here, too, he told himself, to avoid anyone seeing him. Word might get back to town. The less known of his movements, the better. Cole Ryerson was dead, so in truth he, Quinn Hadley, was a double murderer. It made little sense to broadcast his presence throughout the valley.

Hadley knew the territory well. He had scouted considerably in the area in which he had purchased the thirty acres next to the McDonnell ranch. He was miles from his holdings, but still, the land was familiar. It was midmorning and he knew of at least two ranches whose boundaries ran up to the foothills he would have to cross. Someone would be sure to be out looking for strays or mending fences or attending to any one of the thousand chores ranchers fell heir to.

There was another trail, a rugged one, he knew, that arced into the foothills and got into a bit of the mountains before looping down and meeting the MC rails at the steepest grade of Jackson Saddle.

Hadley debated riding the often hazardous trail or taking his chances cutting across open range. Nah, I'll go the mountain route. After all, what's the hurry now? I'm fixed for life, or will be when I find a rich buyer, and what a life! He dug out the nugget again and held it while his other hand guided his mount toward the foot of the mountain trail.

"You lovely, lovely great big hunk of gold," he said to the giant lump of precious metal. He kissed it for luck before sliding it again into his saddlebag. "When we part company, you are going to make me the happiest man in the world!"

The foothill trail climbed at a steeper angle, and the horse labored up the heights as the trail dipped and twisted around giant boulders, skirted ravines, or switched back and forth to gain promontories before dipping down and then up again.

Though he needed his eyes to watch for trail hazards, Hadley reached into his bag and dragged out the gold for one more look.

If he had not been fleeing from his murders and the theft of Cole Ryerson's nugget, he might have stopped for a neighborly call and a cup of coffee or a late breakfast with any of the three or four ranchers in the area he passed through.

He had visited them often to talk cattle and horses and ranch life in general in anticipation that many of them would bargain their herds with him in Immigrant Lake.

Quinn Hadley owned the ability to be a charmer when he wanted to be, and was held in certain esteem by many of those outlying ranchers and their families. Riding out from Immigrant Lake, he was certain to have a goody or two in his saddlebags for the little tykes on the ranches he visited. A ranch wife was often treated to some little trinket; the man of the place might be given a free copy of some cattleman's journal or another.

If Hadley had stopped this day, however, he would have learned of the repeated attacks of a giant mountain cat that recently had come down out of the hills to raid nearby cattle herds. Three ranchers had lost a combined total of five steers in fewer than four days.

Only one of the ranchers had seen the giant cat, which was as large as a colt. Early the same morning he had taken a shot at it. The cat had bounded off, apparently unhurt.

The cat, however, had been creased along the back of its neck by the bullet. Furious now with the pain and the inability to get at and treat its wound, the cat crouched on a rock above the mountain trail. Its long buff-colored tail snapped, its head filled only with pain and a burning rage at the man-creature that had inflicted the agony on it with one of the noisy spark-sticks the cat was already too familiar with.

With the sound of an approaching horse, the cat tensed, forgetting its pain for the moment. A scent drifted up on drafts from the valley floor, and the cat's nostrils keened on it, its muscles taut under its sleek tan hide. By instinct it could separate the smell of the horse from another scent that made it hiss softly. It was the same smell of the creature that had inflicted the frustrating and fire-sore wound.

The scent was strong, a vivid memory of pain brought on by encounters with these man-creatures who had this distinctive odor.

The great cat could only think of escape; the creature-smell wafting upward was a reminder of the massive pain searing along its neck and down its back—and of the giant hornet sting on its flank another time. Perhaps with this smell would come even greater pain. Maybe even death.

The man-creature guiding the horse carefully along the trail was well down the hillside from the cat. The trail the horse took was wide, the drop below it steep, while the land rose gradually up to where the cat waited.

The breeze off the valley floor swept up strongly now to the cat, confirming the odor of the man-creature even more distinctly. The cat growled softly deep in its throat with the memory of that scent. Around the cat, giant squared-off rocks that had rained down from the granite cliffs above, dotted this hillside, and leggy shaggy-barked pines fought for survival among them in irregular groups or singly. A soft breeze sighed in the treetops most of the time.

Now the cat's eyes slitted on the man-creature as his horse broke into full view in the vista below the cat's position. The man on horseback dipped his hand into a bag hanging behind the saddle and held something in his hand to study. The cat concentrated on the man and his actions, its emotions running between fear and outrage—and hate. Abruptly the man held the object jubilantly in an outstretched hand.

The cat filled with fear. Was this another form of man-creature torment?

Panicked that it was about to be hit by intense pain again, the cat leaped for cover with a great shrill and piercing snarl and bounded up the hillside away from the danger.

Startled by the howl, the horse reared and bucked, throwing its preoccupied rider, and bolted and galloped away up the trail. The man fell stunned to the ground, rolled and pitched down the steep side of the hill below the trail, his body bumped and bruised.

His hand instinctively clutching the nugget, Quinn Hadley rolled and bounced several times as he tumbled and pitched down the slope. His body stopped abruptly as his head collided with a large boulder with a sickening thud. Blood gushed from a head wound and spread into his hair.

Hadley lay still, his chest heaving as his tortured lungs fought for air. Bloody drool glistened at the side of his mouth; he was unconscious.

By midday the sun's blazing heat was intense. In other areas of Immigrant Lake valley, ranchers and farmers and townsmen sought the cool shelter inside their houses, barns, or stores or lounged under the trees. Cattle and range horses gathered in scant shade or stood stock-still to keep as cool as possible under the sun's merciless aura of intense heat.

Undertaker Malcolm Thompson took a pitcher of cold well water and a tumbler and went out to the cave-cool dugout behind his mortuary. In the refreshing, dank interior, he sipped his water seated on a bench-like pallet that had lately been vacated by the body of Duff McDonnell.

High on the mountainside the giant cat lay on a massive slab-topped and cool rock shaded by an **overhanging tree** with thick and shady interlacing limbs and **green needles,** and panted, its tongue out, its sides heaving, and its eyes closed, dozing. It no longer thought of man-creatures and spark-sticks, although a puckering, drawing pain was still evident along the back of its neck.

In the coolness of the old Stout adobe, Doc Wells of Immigrant Lake fabricated a plaster of paris cast around the battered arm of Marshal Cole Ryerson. The light inside the house was dim, and the air dank and cool. It was pleasant enough for Acie Casey to make coffee for Barney Wisner and Wayne Slade to sip as they watched Doc at his work. Ryerson endured the pain without a murmur.

By midafternoon Hadley's mouth closed and his body began to twitch. The twitch grew to a tremor and then a series of convulsive spasms that brought the man awake. He groaned loudly and stirred. His eyes flickered and opened. For a long moment he stared vacantly at the hot, open sky above him. As the heat steamed and dried the moisture from his eyeballs, he closed his eyes, blinked several times, closed them again, and slept.

His legs quivered and twitched in his sleep, and his arms tried to rise feebly, his left hand all but pinned to the earth by the giant nugget. His body ceased its trembling and lay quiet as Hadley slept; his chest stopped its heaving and rose and fell shallowly.

Bleeding from the gash in his scalp also stopped as the blood thickened into a drying clot of scab. His fingers loosened their viselike grip on the nugget. The huge chunk of precious metal rolled a few inches and came to rest.

Dusk eased into black night and the land cooled. Still Hadley's sleeping body lay unmoving beside the giant squared-off boulder. A nighttime dew softened his clothing, and his body was cold without more covering; the man was not aware of discomfort or of pain.

After an eternity of night, morning dawned slowly. Hardly had the light filled the hillside than the air around the unconscious man turned warm. The azure sky was cloudless; the shimmering sun had the world to itself to roast. Hadley's clothing quickly dried and became warm.

His mouth gaped and was baked dry; flies, gleaming and blue, buzzed close, seeking the blood to dab their tongues into and rub their heads in. Others perched on his widespread lips, some venturing inside the parched pink cavern. The man made no movement to resist.

The late afternoon sun was still high, the heat unabated, when Hadley woke, his skull a swollen caldron of burning pain. He raised his hands to gently stroke back the disheveled hair that fell over his eyes. His fingers recoiled when they brushed the long gash of tender scalp wound. He sat up, his head hanging, one hand supporting his forehead while the other gingerly probed the wound. His misery was acute.

A croaking voice, high-pitched, came from his dry, cracked lips. "I got a bad hurt." The words were a childish, self-pitying whine. He seemed on the edge of tears. "Billy got a bad hurt." He was not aware why he called himself Billy; the name seemed appropriate. He had no memory of any other name. He only knew that he was a little boy who had fallen somehow and had taken a nasty bump on the head. "Billy don't like to fall down."

His dry tongue probed his tender, split lips. He was hungry, but the pain in his head concerned him more; his stomach was sensitive and jittery with nausea. Hadley raised himself up stiffly and painfully and stood swaying on feeble, shaky legs. His eyes were wide and unblinking and carried a vacant look. The pupils were dilated. Again he touched the gash on his head, probing the edges carefully, knowing that any rough touch would shoot a jagged pain through his already throbbing brain. When he touched the wound, sweat and grit from his fingers made it smart all the more.

Hair around it was matted and plastered in a mass of drying clot.

"Billy's head hurt bad. Hot, too. Billy ought to have a hat."

He looked around. His hat was out of sight at the edge of the trail above, where his horse had thrown him.

Ignoring the bright yellow boulder of gold that lay a few inches from his foot, the disorganized creature that had been Quinn Hadley began to stagger and stumble away, following an easy course down the hill, but walking in an irregular circle that widened as he moved away from the rock where he had been injured. Some loops of his aimless orbit of the rock took him uphill.

Hadley stumbled around without direction for several minutes before his battered and dusty boots reached a part of the trail he had led his horse along the day before. Confused, he stood a long time at the edge of the trail and dumbly looked down the hill and studied the broad path in bewilderment. He looked up the trail. He shook his head, trying to whisk away the heavy fog that clutched his consciousness. It would not go away.

In an idiocy brought on by the head injury, he sensed no real awareness of his physical body, only of the pain and turmoil in his head. Shaking his head only made the pain throb more. His neck was stiff as wood, and it ached. Movement only heightened the roar of pain in his ears.

He began walking again. His step grew firmer, his gait still shuffling and clumsy. Without knowing why, he chose the uphill leg of the trail he had found. He had walked but a short distance when he found a hat lying in the dusty grass at the rim of the narrow trail.

"Oh-oooh," he cooed through a trace of drool behind his lips. "Somebody lost a hat." He tried its fit, easing it gingerly over his sore head.

He looked around him again, still uneasy as to why he was here. He recognized nothing. He looked down the hillside and remembered the squared-off boulder where he had fallen and lay so long unconscious.

"That's Billy's rock! Billy know that rock. That's Billy's place!" He pitched down the hillside again, half falling as he stumbled and staggered awkwardly over the uneven ground. The hat fell off and was forgotten.

At the large boulder he sat down and leaned against it lovingly and drew his knees up to his chest and clasped his arms around them, feeling comfort in being able to remember something, even if it was only a rock.

"Bill's rock a nice rock," he said. "Billy loves his rock." The waning sun was behind him, large and bright as a giant orange; as though closer to the earth, its rays long and slanted, its shadows were also long and slanted. A beam of light from over his shoulder rested on a large boulder a few feet from where he snuggled comfortably against his warm rock.

"Ooh! Pretty shiny rock. Billy knows that rock, too." He leaned forward on the downslope and fell to his hands and knees to crawl to the bright nugget, picked it up, and scooted back to the large boulder.

"Billy got two rocks he knows. Got play-pretty rock to look at and feel."

Clutching the shiny, heavy nugget with its surface gleaming and smooth as skin despite its lumps, and leaning against the large boulder. Hadley sat for an hour without moving, without looking at the nugget hanging heavy in his hands, his mind empty.

Night fell softly, and Hadley shivered, burrowing closer to the large, familiar rock that still held some of the day's heat.

To the mind which had become that of a very small child, the rock felt good and warm and secure, and he felt love for his two rocks. He inclined his still-aching head against the large rock and slept.

The nugget fell from his hands to thump into the gravel between his feet.

CHAPTER
13

BILLY, THE SMALL, SIMPLE BOY IN A MAN'S BODY, WAS stretched out asleep in the soft gravel beside the large, squared-off boulder when the sun again warmed the earth. Its brightness woke him, and he rubbed the sleep from his eyes with childlike clenched fists. The massive headache had diminished, but the small moronic child remained inside the head of Quinn Hadley.

If his headache was not so intense, he awoke with a powerful hunger and an even more powerful thirst. He sat up and surveyed the morning, finding nothing beautiful in it as Wayne Slade had; in Hadley there was only an acceptance of daylight.

"Billy wanna d'ink. Billy hungry."

He stood up and stared vacantly up the hillside and then down the slope toward the valley beyond. An intuition he couldn't have explained told him people must be in the valley. There he could find something to eat and drink.

Abruptly he lumbered off in the stumbling, shuffling gait of a small child. A remembrance of unfinished business caused him to stop and look about him bewildered. He walked quickly back and looked at his mothering rock.

"G'bye, big rock. Billy come back" He patted the giant rock tenderly. "Oh-oh, where's the little pretty rock?"

The nugget lay near where he had slept. He picked it up, remembering it was very heavy. "You got to stay with big rock. Billy come back, little rock. Too hard to carry you."

Hadley knelt and labored with his hands and fingers to scoop a deep hole in the fine gravel beside the large rock. He carefully nested the nugget deep in the hole and worked the gravel over it, patted and smoothed the tiny pebbles. With an infinite, infantile patience, Hadley had successfully hidden it from anyone but Billy.

Some hours later and several miles distant, two little boys whose father had failed to come home from town the previous Saturday night played in the sand and gravel dugout their dad had carved under a shade tree behind the barn for their play hours.

The two—Martin McDonnell, nearly five, and his younger brother, Ransom—loved the bowl-shaped playground for the many opportunities at fantasy it offered. One day it would be a great lake on which they could pretend to sail boats. Other times they would build roads in it and up its slopes and imagine that sticks were people and rocks were wagons and carriages.

This day Martin and Ransom were fighting imaginary Indians and were using their dugout as a fort with sticks for rifles. In the distance, across a valley shimmering with heat, they made out the figure of a man stumbling toward them.

"It's a Indian!" Ransom cried, and he crouched inside the dirt rim and poked out his stick and pointed it. "Bam! Bam!"

"No, it's not a Indian, Rans," Martin argued, sliding down beside Ransom to peer over the edge of the bowl. "I think it's a big, growed-up man like Daddy. Maybe it's Daddy!"

Quinn Hadley's rugged trail clothes were wrinkled and grimy after nearly four days away from town. Trail grit intensified the lines of his face, and his salt-and-pepper stubble of beard did nothing to detract from his sinister appearance to the two little boys. Sweat from his five-mile trek in the intense heat traced more lines in his dirt-darkened features.

"It's not Daddy," Martin said. "Hide here while I run and fetch Mommy." Martin decided to act brave and not tell Ransom he was scared. He did, however, leap up with great haste and disappear around the side of the small, stablelike barn toward the low cabin that was the McDonnell home.

The man saw Ransom's head jutting out of the bowl in the earth, and strode to him, then stood over him, looking down. For a long moment they stared at each other, the man towering over Ransom as he hugged the sides of his play hole. This miserable specimen appeared ten feet tall from the little boy's vantage point. The man's condition made him frightening.

"Billy hungry," the man pleaded. "Billy thirsty."

Ransom in his little boy's logic was aware something dreadful had happened to his father. This man was dreadful-looking. "Are you Daddy?" he asked.

"Billy thirsty." The man's pleading tone was more insistent.

The menacing-looking twin barrels of a 12-gauge shotgun poked around the corner of the stable. The man who called himself Billy had his attention drawn to them when unmistakably and deliberately the sound of hammers being cocked broke the silence between the man and the little boy crouching in the hole.

Hadley's head bobbed absently, and his arms dangled as he studied the shotgun barrels without emotion. A shoulder belonging to the person holding the weapon showed at the side of the barn, then more of the gun and finally a woman appeared around the corner, the butt against her shoulder as if she knew well how to use it and meant business.

Hadley was uncowed; he simply stood staring blankly at the woman and the gun muzzles.

The woman was young. She looked almost too young to be mother to the two small boys. Her blond hair, bleached to near whiteness by long hours of work in the valley's unrelenting sun, was tied back with a kerchief. Her work dress was long, the skirt full. The long sleeves were work-worn and faded and shoved up nearly to her elbows. Her breasts, thrust against the material of the dress top, would have been described as most ample by a discerning male.

At this moment Quinn Hadley was hardly a discerning male.

Her face was attractive in its youthfulness, the features and bone structure small and petite, as was her body. Her skin was tan but still unlined and soft-looking. Her eyes were wide and large like Martin's and Ransom's, with dark brown irises, not blue as normally associated with blondes. She was hardly robust, but her pose showed she had learned to pull her share of the weight around this ranch.

A widow less than a week, Mary McDonnell was facing the first stern test of her new and unwanted role as head of the McDonnell household.

"Stand where you are!" she commanded, holding the shotgun steady in a direction which, if fired, would have cut Hadley neatly in two.

Duff McDonnell had taught her well how to aim and fire the giant front-loading Belgian shotgun. She had become as adept as he at bringing down doves on the wing and rabbits bounding over the prairie. Duff had believed that if a woman could handle a scattergun, she would be a near match for any intruder who might show up at the place during one of his frequent absences.

Even in this remote location, people with strange and strong motives were apt to appear when least expected, and Mary McDonnell was an attractive woman, provocative even in a hardworking ranch wife's attire.

Now a little boy clutched the stained apron that was tied

around her waist and fell nearly to the hem of her ankle-length frock.

If Hadley had had any wits, he would have noticed the great barrel muzzles shaking slightly. It was not that Mary McDonnell lacked the nerve to protect herself and her two fatherless sons. The core-shattering realization of Duff's death and the abrupt, violent nature of that death was a raging, burning fire inside her. To now confront this vulgar-looking, menacing man was almost too much. Though she had better judgment, Mary's dizzying emotions told her to throw down the shotgun and run. Escape. Any place would be more comfortable than this. But she could not.

Prompted by an intuition peculiar to his diminished mental state, Hadley did not make any fast moves with the scattergun trained on him.

"Billy hungry. Billy thirsty." He pleaded with soulful eyes rolling on Mary.

"Who are you?" Mary sensed her voice trembling and knew that her lips were tight in apprehension. Over the bead front sight down the rib joining the barrels, she studied the man. There was something vaguely familiar in this man who had obviously been on the trail many days. "Aren't you Mr. Hadley from town? The cattle broker?"

A wave of emotion made Mary's shoulder slump and she dropped the muzzles even more. From Acie Casey, the short, fat, and compassionate stranger who had come by to see her days before, she had learned that Quinn Hadley had been an innocent bystander when Duff was killed by a saddle bum named Wayne Slade.

"Are you all right, Mr. Hadley?" Thoughts spun in her head. The man standing on the thrust-up rim of her boys' play hole was obviously ill or injured. She could see the matted clot of bloody hair around a head wound where blood had trickled over his forehead and dried. She sensed his scalp would carry a bad scar when the wound healed.

"Billy hungry. Billy thirsty."

"Are you thirsty, Mr. Hadley? Please, do come in the

house. You probably don't remember me. Mary McDonnell. Duff's wife . . . widow."

The man did not move. Ransom still lay at Hadley's feet, looking up. Martin hid behind her apron, clutching it, only part of his frightened face peering out at the specter of Hadley.

"Billy need d'ink."

The man continued to stare at her, his eyes looking at her and the shotgun and the small boy beside her, but at the same time seeming to stare through her and past her. Blood in his hair, she thought; he's been badly hurt. He's delirious.

"It's all right, Mr. Hadley. You're with friends. Please come in. Can you see all right?"

Perhaps the injury had blinded him, she thought. She lowered the shotgun hammers carefully against her copper caps and dropped the weapon into the crook of her arm. "I'll give you food and water. I have so much to ask you about what happened to Duff. When you've had something to eat and rested a little." She stepped closer to him and took him by the hand.

He continued to stare at where she had been standing at the corner of the barn. The hand that took Hadley's was cool and soft, its touch reassuring. Hadley allowed himself to be led around the barn and toward the low-slung house with the split-shingle roof. He still walked with the animal-like shuffling gait of a large, bewildered child.

Duff McDonnell had cut the logs high up in the mountains and snaked them home and built their place into a sturdy, comforting home. Mary had worked equally hard to make the place as warm and homey as their limited resources would allow.

Now Duff was gone, dead less than a week. She still had not decided how she would face the days, the weeks, and the months ahead—not to consider the years. It was still too fresh, the wound too painful, still impossible to come to grips with. She knew she was operating in something of a daze. Duff was dead; of that she was certain. She'd gone to claim the body and to prepare it for burial at Malcolm Thompson's establishment in Immigrant Lake. It was a wife's duty to care for her man this way; it took more courage than anything she'd ever done in her life. She did not want to see the body or touch it. The very nature of the task required of her had been repulsive and had served only to sharpen the knife-edge of her grief. She had nearly swooned at the size of the bullet hole in her husband's body.

The memory of those first moments and hours of shock were still too vivid. Each night since, she had wakened and reached out for him in the dark of their bed, found him gone, remembered why, and sobbed out a new and burning loneliness into her pillow.

Her life with Duff had been smashed to small bits, and she could see no way to mend them and bring them back together in any bearable fashion.

"Billy thirsty. Billy hungry." The strange-acting man she led across the yard brought her thoughts back to here and now.

"Yes, Mr. Hadley. Come in. You must be very tired. I'll get you something to eat. You can clean up, too. I do so want to ask you about what happened in town Saturday night."

Hadley followed her meekly through the cabin's rude door.

"Sit down. Let me fix you something."

She led the perplexed-looking Hadley to the table in the center of the cabin's main room. He sat in a chair at the table, folded his hands, and stared blankly at the table top. Mary brought him a dipper of cool water from the pail.

When he saw it, Hadley's arm lashed out like a striking snake to jerk it from her grasp, spilling most of the water to splash over the table. He held the dipper in two hands, the handle pointing up as he noisily slurped the water down in one gulp. He smacked his lips with the refreshment of it, then drew his sleeve coarsely across his dripping mouth and grunted. "More," he demanded. "More. Billy thirsty. Awful thirsty."

Mary started back for the pail on the broad shelf, heard a chair scrape behind her, and turned to see Hadley lunging at her. Startled, she sidestepped his movement. He stumbled to the pail, lifted it with both hands and poured the contents in the general direction of his mouth, the excess water cascading over his neck, soaking his filthy shirt, and splashing on the floor.

Unprepared for such behavior, particularly in light of her recent tragedy, Mary shrank from this menace. When the pail was empty, Hadley let it drop to the floor with a clang and staggered back to the table to sit in the chair again, waiting and dripping. Beads of water glistened in the bristle of his beard.

"Billy not thirsty now. Billy hungry!" His childish voice carried a new note of threat.

"Yes, Mr. Hadley. Yes." She was intimidated by him now. Hadley was between her and the shotgun she had unsuspectingly leaned against the door frame. "I'll fix you something."

She had some fresh-baked bread and a lump of cured ham from which she had carved some slices to warm for her sons' breakfast. Both the boys had stayed outside to play, and she was thankful.

Mary's already frayed nerves had gone taut with this new and strange turn of events. She edged to the sideboard, got out the bread and the ham, and reached for the carving knife. With it hidden in front of her and her back to Hadley, she sneaked a look at him over her shoulder. He sat at the table expectantly, hands folded, staring at the table top.

She would use the knife if she had to.

Hadley made no more menacing moves. If he had startled her with his abrupt rudeness over the water, he now sat at the table like a small boy, docilely waiting for something to eat.

"Billy hungry," he simpered again.

"I know, Mr. Hadley. I'm hurrying." Mary said it calmly. She hacked off some slices of ham, cut several thick chunks of bread, put them on a plate, and hurried it to the table.

"Would you like a cup of . . ."

His hands darted out to scoop in most of the ham and bread in one sweep and drag it toward him, scattering crumbs and shreds of meat. He paused, leaned back as if in surprise, and looked at the food. He studied it a long moment as though something was working in his mind.

"Not nice just to start eating. 'God is great; God is good . . .' Billy forgot."

" 'Let us thank him for the food, amen,' " Mary prompted.

" 'Food, amen,' " Hadley repeated, and he crammed his mouth full of bread and ham, the "amen" muffled through the mass of it.

After he had bolted the food in a few enormous bites, he demanded more. Mary gave him the rest of the cured ham and what was left of the bread, a large half-loaf of the good sourdough she had planned to last her and the boys for several meals.

When Hadley seemed satisfied, he leaned back in the chair, his arms drooping at his side. His head lolled as if he was going to sleep.

"Would you like to rest, Mr. Hadley? You're welcome to take a nap."

He turned instantly awake and alert. "Billy not nap! Billy wants to go out and play. Not nap time!"

Panic jabbed Mary like a hot iron. Something was seriously wrong with this grown man behaving like a child. Her two little sons were out there playing. Hadley had already threatened her and was still acting in a most menacing way.

"No, Mr. Hadley . . . Billy. I want Billy . . . I want Billy to lie down."

Hadley's face softened, and the eyes searching hers pleaded as they had when he begged for food. "Billy be good. Billy good boy. Billy wants to play outside in the hole with his friends."

CHAPTER

14

FIVE OR SIX MILES TO THE WEST, AT THE CASEY-WISNER place, Cole Ryerson had never chopped in such tall cotton.

With three concerned friends tending his every whim, Ryerson's road to recovery was destined to be short and all downhill. Doc Wells had helped by responding promptly after Slade's ride to town. A few townsmen who recognized Slade had surprised him by not trying to stop him, but disappeared down alleys and into buildings as he galloped up Range Street toward Doc Wells's office.

In his buggy, Doc brought a large sack of plaster of paris. Around the broken arm he built a cast that seemed to Ryerson to weigh a ton.

"By damn, Doc, if I ain't going to have to have a block and tackle just to haul this dratted thing around," he groused after the plaster had set up enough to move the arm. It was an effort, particularly with the shoulder wound, which Doc had examined and dressed.

"Old Wisner here is full of good ideas," Ryerson continued. "How about it, Barney? Can you build some kind of hoist to lift this damned rock that Doc has hung on me?"

Wisner grinned and reddened and said nothing.

"One of my better jobs," Doc mused, surveying his work as he sat across from Ryerson sipping Casey's coffee. "Michelangelo would be proud of me."

"Who's he?" Ryerson asked. "Sounds like one a them Eye-talian gandy dancers they had working on the section crew when the Mountain and Central straightened that stretch of track out east last spring. Seems to me that was the name of the guy I nearly run in because he was pestering old Walt over to the Water Hole about not having any veen-oh."

"I couldn't expect you to be sufficiently cultured," Doc groused, forcing a scowl. "The least I can expect of an imbecile like you is to lay low for a time until those wounds heal and the bones knit. Slade did good work on you. Now, don't go doing anything to mess it up. You were a fortunate man, Cole, to have that kind of help.

"Son," Doc said, addressing Slade, "if you're ever of a mind to enter medicine, I'll be proud to have you study under me for a time. You have a natural talent, that's easy to see."

"Thanks, but no, Doc," Slade said, grinning. "I guess I'll always be a drifter at heart. May settle down someday, but one of these days soon I'll be moseyin' along."

"You're staying put right here in Immigrant Lake till I tell you you can go," Ryerson said. "You're still my prisoner. Even if I catch up with Hadley, I'll find something to pin on you and keep you here. Malfeasance, to start off with."

"Doc, do I have permission to break his other arm?"

"Probably the only thing that will keep the old bullhead down. At least with another broken arm, I could keep him off a horse long enough for those bones to knit. Cole, I don't see the need for you to do any traveling until I can take the cast off."

"How soon'll that be?"

"Depends if you behave yourself and listen to Wayne and Barney and Acie here. Four, five weeks, I suppose."

"Four weeks! Cripes, Doc, Hadley'll have my gold melted down to bullion by then and be sitting somewhere on his tokus counting my money! I can't lay around here a month!"

"Go ahead, Wayne," Doc said. "You have my permission. Break one of his legs, too, while you're at it. I still have plenty of plaster for the casts."

"These three are treating me like a mollycoddle, Doc. I allowed as to how I'd at least have you in my corner. You see what that gold-grubbing owl-hoot Barney is building for me?"

Wisner, also at the table for a cup of coffee, again grinned and reddened.

Doc had seen Wisner at work as he drove up. Barney was building a narrow litter for Ryerson by lashing thin logs together, then tying in short legs and carrying handles. Over the frame, he planned to closely interlace strips of supple cowhide. This would provide Ryerson with a bed to sleep in as well as a cot-hammock that could easily be hauled outside. Ryerson could bask in the sun or lounge in the shade under the awning Wisner had fashioned on the north side of the house for the mules.

During the long days after Doc left, Ryerson fought against what he knew was his naturally nasty disposition about sitting around. His three companions were particularly patronizing, and even that got on his nerves, much as he appreciated their concern.

Slade looked after the healing of the wounds and regularly checked the arm wound through a breather hole Doc had formed in the cast. Wisner kept on working with his hands and his mind and was constantly thinking about things to make Ryerson's stay more comfortable. One morning he got busy and tore down the front door and used his crowbar to disassemble the old jambs that stood askew. He chiseled away the mortar to true up the frame and widen the door to make it easier to get Ryerson's litter through. He rebuilt and rehung his plank door in the new squared-up opening.

Ryerson considered himself a ten-thumber when it came to building anything and viewed the work as a masterpiece of the carpenter's art and wasn't reluctant to say so. Wisner only grinned over the acclaim, and blushed.

Casey, a culinary master in his own right, built meals for the injured marshal that would have put strength back in ten men. Ryerson was kept full of Casey's coffee—and Casey outdid himself making the best possible brew he could. Ryerson began to feel comfortable enough with the short, pudgy prospector-cook to pay his coffee the highest compliment he could by beginning to complain about it.

Casey made chicken broth for Ryerson to drink between meals, a thick, appetizing soup that made the lawman nearly sit up and crow and flap his wings.

Ryerson's day began with thick and tender sourdough flapjacks. He chided Casey that he'd like one fried extra large so he'd have it to sit around on during the day. Casey followed that with a good-sized steak and three or four eggs. At noon Ryerson got thick slabs of sourdough bread with preserves, greens from Casey's garden, and cold meats and cheeses from a cool storage pit Casey and Wisner had dug in the center of their floor and covered with a sturdy wooden hatch.

The two prospectors, Ryerson allowed, knew how to engineer things for comfortable living.

His afternoons were highlighted by a bowl or two at intervals of steaming chicken broth. At sundown, Casey laid out the best chicken-fried steak, Ryerson said, "this side of Wichita" or a Texas-red chili that "stuck to the ribs" and brought tears to his eyes and, he said, "would have run the San Antonio chili peddlers plumb out of business!"

"Even beats jailhouse chili, Acie," Ryerson enthused. "Down in Texas a man'll try to get into jail just to sit around and eat chili!"

Ryerson sensed his middle growing thicker and heavier by the day.

The shoulder wound, with Doc's medicine and Slade's care, closed up and began to heal nicely. Ryerson began to try to raise the heavy cast himself, despite the injured muscles in his shoulder.

Ryerson was feeling comfortable enough in the surroundings and sufficiently well to get down to the chief business of his life—complaining—and to take notice of others around him. Slade, he could see, was getting itchy.

"What's gigging you, son?" he asked one morning over his after-breakfast coffee. The two of them were alone in the adobe cabin while Casey and Wisner busied themselves with the chores. "Commenced to notice yesterday you were getting jumpy as a frisky colt in a small pen."

"Aw, it's okay, Cole. The important thing is you getting back on your feet."

"Naw, 'tain't okay. I'd like to deputize you and Barney and send you out after Hadley, but he's a killer and if anything happened to either of you boys, I wouldn't rest easy ever with that on my mind. 'Sides ain't neither of you knows this country that well. Not that I think Hadley's even in these parts anymore."

"I wasn't thinking about that, Cole. Just that I don't get along well being cooped up in the same place a long time."

"Hell, you think it's easy on me layin' around here? Why, every minute all I got to think about is Quinn Hadley slidin' farther and farther out of my reach. Why don't you go off and do something? You don't have to mortify here just because I do."

"There's no place particular to go."

"Ride in and see old Walt and have a drink on me. Doc says for me to lay off awhile, and I'll respect his good wishes. Else I'd have you bring me back a bottle. But you go on ahead. Do you good. But stay out of poker games."

"Nah, I don't feel like that."

"Well, go on and ride out yonder, then."

"Where?"

"Why, out there! Anyplace. Go scare up some lizards and some prairie hens. Go out there someplace and set down and meditate on your sins and get to figuring on your salvation."

"What sins?"

"Well, first off for being such a tick under the hide of a stove-up old man like me!"

"Am I that bad, Cole?"

"Son, any time a man comes down with cabin fever, he's due to infect everybody around him. And that'll get men at one another's throats every time. I've had it often enough in my time to have learned how to live with it, and just now I ain't got much choice. Old Acie and Barney there, I never seen two men double-harness like them two. But you're young with a lot of sap in you. Hey! That's it. Ride on out and pay a friendly call on the widder McDonnell. Acie ran over there to tell her about Duff, but he ain't been back since, looking after me and all. I don't suppose any of those loafers from town would have the Christian decency to ride on out and ask did she need any stove wood split or weeds pulled. Go on over and see her. You two must be about of an age. She's some piece of baggage, I'll warrant, though I don't believe I ever seen her. Duff had a good eye for such things, and told me a few times how special Miz McDonnell was."

"Nah, I don't think so."

"All right, then. Sit down and quit pacing the floor. Bring me some of them papers of Jap Jones you hauled in from my place. I want to get caught up on my reading."

Slade rustled up several papers from the short stack that were randomly yellowed at the edges from being stored so long in Ryerson's disorderly heap. He handed them to Ryerson and went to the stove for a cup of coffee. He wandered to Casey's gleaming window and studied the slope down to South Range Pass Road and the prairie beyond. The

McDonnell place was out there somewhere, about due east, he'd been told.

"Well, I don't know," he said to himself as much as to Ryerson. "Maybe I will give my horse's legs a stretch. Miz McDonnell's probably the only one who still thinks I shot Duff. I guess it would be good to go over and clear my name and pay a neighborly call. Might be able to give her a hand with some of the chores."

"Good doin's, son, good doin's. Then you'll leave me in peace to read my papers."

CHAPTER
15

RIDING DOWN THE LANE FROM THE STOUT PLACE TO SOUTH Range Pass Road, Slade was immediately glad he had shaken free of the cabin. There was little he could do for Ryerson for a few days but leave him be. The afternoon was ideal for a ride.

The weather had moderated since the unusually hot couple of days earlier. A soft breeze brushed at his back and moved the shrublike chaparral gently. The wind seemed to bring cool air down out of Weaver's Notch in the mountains to the west behind him.

On those miserably hot days, there didn't seem to be a breath of a breeze moving. The heat settled over the land like a searing cloud.

Today's sky was a balmy clear blue with not a patch of cloud showing anywhere in the grand vista that was of monstrous proportions and seemed to spread upward and away to infinity in any direction Slade looked.

Lizards scooted through the dust of the lane and over the roadside humps to drop motionless beside a rock and wait, alert and poised to dart as the horse and rider appeared. Now and then Slade's eyes caught the quick scamper of a ground squirrel scurrying for cover after being alarmed by the soft plop of the horse's hooves on the tight-packed roadbed.

Slade held the reins loosely and allowed the horse to pick his own pace, an easy walk that set his head and neck bobbing in rhythm with his gait.

It was early afternoon, and since Slade was in no hurry, he guided the horse easily around sagebrush clumps and gravelly knobs that dotted the land. He had veered some in his route, always maintaining a steady bearing eastward.

At one point, two miles after he'd crossed the main road, he struck a wagon road that bore to the northeast. He followed it, sensing that eventually he would have to drop back south to stay on his easterly track. The horse's easy walk lulled him into a soft feeling of contentment. The mild warmth of the day contributed to his sense of buoyancy.

A narrow lane forked to the southeast; a slab of wood nailed to an upright driven in the ground pointed down the lane. The lettering job had been neat despite a crude brush and black paint. The name had weathered, but was legible: McDonnell.

In another mile he could see the place in the distance, a ranch with a squat log house and a squat barn-stable behind it. It lay in a bowl-shaped swale lower and greener than much of the land around it. The greenness suggested that the water table would be higher here, making well-digging easier and the supply more dependable. Even from a distance, Slade could see a few trees trying to survive around the house and barn.

Beyond, in a blue haze brought on by distance, lay the mountains. He wondered casually if Quinn Hadley might still be lurking up there somewhere.

It was another twenty minutes before Slade could make out enough of the place to see that it looked deserted. Nothing moved in the yard. Some white clothing flapping softly on a line between house and barn was the only evidence of life.

As he neared the ranch, a small boy emerged from behind the barn trudging head down, bent on some errand at the house. The boy looked up, saw Slade coming, stopped, and turned and disappeared again behind the barn.

As with the Casey-Wisner place, a hitch rail had been planted at the front of the house, a few steps from the door, the crossarm seasoned and polished from use. Slade rode to it, got down, and tethered his horse.

I'd better move slowly with her, he told himself. No telling what kind of commotion it might stir if I go blurting out my name right off.

The woman who answered his knock was young and small, tanned and attractive.

"Mrs. McDonnell?"

"Yes?"

"I'd like to talk with you if I may. . . . I knew your husband."

"From town?"

"Well . . . yes."

"Glory be! There's someone here I want to—"

"May I come in, Mrs. McDonnell? I assure you . . . ."

"Yes." Her glance at him seemed to reassure her that he had no evil intent. Slade stepped into the dim light of the home's main room. Like the Casey-Wisner place, it had but one window.

"I don't think I've met you, Mister . . ."

"As I said, I knew your husband." Slade stood politely inside the door, holding his hat. The room was dim and cool; his eyes relaxed pleasantly after squinting against the sun.

"Please sit down. I've hoped someone from Immigrant Lake would come by. I've needed to talk with someone about . . ."

Slade took the chair she offered and sat down uneasily, still clutching his hat. "I'm sorry for your grief, Mrs.

McDonnell. That's really what I want to talk with you about. Won't you sit down?''

"I've prayed someone would come by from Immigrant Lake. It's been so strange. . . .'' She continued to stand across from him. He noticed a shotgun leaning against a cabinet within her easy reach.

"What's strange, Mrs. McDonnell?"

"If you're from Immigrant Lake, you surely know Mr. Hadley.''

"That's part of what I came to talk about. I know him only too well.''

"He's here!''

"Hadley? Here? How can that be?'' Slade stiffened. This wasn't possible. Hadley had to be miles away now with Ryerson's gold. What rational reason was there for Hadley to be there at the McDonnell place?

"He wandered in off the prairie three days ago. I can't get rid of him.''

Slade was sure Hadley wasn't in the house. He glanced at the window. He'd go for the shotgun if Hadley came in.

"I haven't let him sleep in the house. He acts very strange. The first day, I thought he was going to attack me. And with Duff gone but a few days . . . I offered him a horse, thinking he'd leave. He's been sleeping in the barn on the straw near the horse he thinks is his.''

"Mrs. McDonnell, that can't be Quinn Hadley.''

"It is. He's bought cattle from Duff since we've been here.''

"Where is he now?''

"Out behind the barn. He seems to feel less threatened with my sons. With Duff dead scarcely a week and now this . . . I couldn't leave for help or even try. If I tried to go away, I'm sure he'd forbid me.''

"Is he armed?''

"No.''

Slade's mind raced. "No time for me to ride for Marshal Ryerson. Mrs. McDonnell, you've got to trust me. I implore you. I'm going out to my horse for my pistol. Get your shotgun and be ready. I'll be right back." He figured he might at least get the drop on Hadley without gunplay.

"I don't understand."

"You will." Slade stepped quickly out the door, watching closely for any sign of Hadley. He was back shortly hefting two six-guns. Slade tingled with apprehension. Holding her shotgun, Mary McDonnell stood at the door watching him.

"We've got to act fast," Slade said. "I don't have time to explain. This is serious if the man is Hadley. On my honor as a gentleman, I have to ask you to trust me completely. And that may be difficult."

"I don't understand. I don't even know you. I've never seen you in Immigrant Lake."

"That's why I ask for your trust."

She studied him closely; he was glad he had washed and shaved and worn his new shirt, bought in Immigrant Lake to replace the one he'd used to bind up Ryerson's wounds.

"Do you know who killed your husband?"

"Mr. Casey, a man who lives nearby and the men in town said Cole Ryerson is out after a man named Slade. You're not . . . ?" Her words ended in a sharp intake of breath.

"Trust me, Mrs. McDonnell. In the name of God, trust me. Yes, I'm Wayne Slade."

Mary brought up the shotgun and held it a few feet from Slade's midsection. "You had better put those guns of yours on the table. Empty them, too."

"No, Mrs. McDonnell. That's why I pleaded for your trust. I've been with Marshal Cole Ryerson these last few days. He's the one who encouraged me to come by and talk with you."

The look of a frightened but determined small animal flitted in her eyes.

"Cole Ryerson will back me up, Mrs. McDonnell. He is

staying at Mr. Casey's place. Please. I was unjustly accused. Ryerson was seriously wounded by Hadley."

"If you're being truthful, then who killed Duff?"

"That's the reason I need your trust and help. The man who shot your husband and nearly killed Cole Ryerson was Quinn Hadley."

"Dear God, no! My boys!"

"Easy, Mrs. McDonnell. We've got to keep cool. You and I have to take Hadley prisoner . . . get him away from your sons."

"How do I know you're not here to kill him?"

Slade felt an edge of impatience with both her attitude and the urgency of his mission. "I had no way of knowing he was here until you yourself told me. And if I were the killer, wouldn't I be miles from here making my escape with Cole Ryerson on my trail? I'd hardly be making a courteous call at your home to offer my sympathies."

"We've got to get that man away from my sons!"

Slade sensed her questioning behavior had been due in part, at least, to the stress she had been under. When she finally decided to trust him, her reaction was almost spontaneous.

"Exactly. Are you strong enough to help?"

"I . . . think so." She raised her chin bravely and sniffed. "Yes. Yes, I can."

"What are they doing?"

"The boys are playing. In a dug hole behind the barn. He hasn't behaved like a man in all the time he's been here. He's been more like an untrustworthy animal. I think it's from a bad bump on his head. He doesn't even own up to his own name."

"Well, I wouldn't know about that. Now I promise you nothing will happen if we surprise him. But we've got to hurry. You take your shotgun around one end of the barn, and I'll go the other way. Be prepared to fire if he makes any threatening moves. Fire one barrel in the air, perhaps. How big are your boys? I think I saw one of them."

"Martin's five and Ransom's four."

"That's pretty small. Hadley's tall. If either of us has to shoot, it must be high to avoid hurting the boys. Either way, they'll probably be frightened and stay down."

"I don't think Mr. Hadley will give us any trouble. He's not sane. That's what's made me so upset. But he really is very meek."

"I hope so. Now, once more, Mrs. McDonnell. Do you trust me?"

"Just now I don't have much choice. Yes."

"Good. Once we take Hadley to Cole Ryerson, he'll bear out my story. Are you ready?"

"I . . . yes."

"Good. You'll be strong. Nothing serious is going to happen."

They walked to the back of the house and toward the barn. From behind it, Slade could hear the muffled chatter of little boys and the low droning voice of a man.

He gripped his guns in piqued apprehension and with them silently motioned Mary to go around the opposite end of the barn. He raised his eyes to the sky beseeching God not to make him have to shoot Quinn Hadley.

CHAPTER
16

RYERSON WAS LAYING OUTSIDE THE CABIN TAKING HIS EASE on his stretcher after dinner when his ears perked to the sound of riders approaching up the lane.

It was a fine western evening, the air calm and moderate as twilight brought the merger of day and night. Since there had been no clouds during the day, the sky had no high color to it. Day simply faded gracefully into the gray of approaching night. It would be a perfect night to meditate on the heavens, he thought. Slade, no doubt, was returning, and the thought struck Ryerson that the two of them might sit that night in the soft dark and talk as they kept their eyes peeled for shooting stars.

Irregular hoofbeats persuaded him that two riders were coming up the lane. He wondered momentarily if Slade was bringing Mary McDonnell back with him. He rose up to catch a glimpse of the approaching riders, then sat bolt upright in amazement and swung his legs over the edge of his cot.

The miserable mess on the horse being led was Quinn Hadley, no doubt of it. Hadley looked as though he had been trampled in a stampede. A hundred questions clogged Ryerson's excited mind. Hadley's clothing was dirty and wrinkled, his hair a messed-up mat swirling around his head. His dirt-stained hands were securely tied, and he clutched the saddle horn to maintain his balance. Slade cantered beside and slightly ahead of Hadley's horse, leading it with the reins.

Hadley's face was bearded and filthy, the skin above the stubble dirty and creased. He looked as though he hadn't washed or shaved in a week. His head hung like that of a whipped dog, and it bobbed loosely on his neck with the jolt of the horse's gait. The man didn't appear to have even the presence of mind to sit a horse properly. Ryerson was bewildered.

Ryerson bounced eagerly from the cot, feeling a twinge of pain in his shoulder as the cast settled into the sling, but paying it no mind. He strode out to meet them, seeing a broad grin slicing Slade's face.

"Now, where in the name of all that is good and evil did you find that dry-gulcher?" Then he shouted, "Hey, Acie! Barney! Come on out here and see what the cat dragged in!" Ryerson was elated. He had doubted he would ever see Hadley again.

"He's been over at the McDonnells'," Slade said. "He's loco, Cole."

"Hell, I have been aware of his diminished capacity since he took a shot at me."

Casey materialized in the doorway as Wisner appeared from around back, wiping his hands on his trousers.

"Look here, fellas, looky what young Slade found in his traps! We are saved a lot of unnecessary trackin'. We got us a Quinn Hadley with the hobbles on. Glory be!"

"Where's your gold?" Barney asked.

Ryerson's heart leaped. "Yeah, Wayne, how about it? Where's the nugget? He have it on him?"

Slade moved to get down, still holding the reins to Hadley's horse.

"Nope. This is all I got. He got himself rapped in the head some way and doesn't even know his own name."

Ryerson's face furrowed. "Then get him down off that horse. I mean to have a word or two with our Mr. Hadley."

"Take him inside," Acie said. "Getting dark out here. I'll go in and light the lamps."

"Time to get down, Billy," Slade said.

"Billy?" Ryerson was incredulous.

"Well, that's the name he thinks he goes by."

At the sound of the name, the man slouching in the saddle came alert. His expression said he'd heard the name before, but he didn't acknowledge it.

"Don't like hands tied. Got to pee."

"Do it in your pants, you bushwhacking son of a bitch," Ryerson said. "Damn, if I had two good hands, I'd yank him right out of that saddle. Get him down and inside."

"Come on, Billy," Slade said patiently, ready to help Hadley dismount.

Hadley slid out of the saddle and stirrups clumsily and stood by the horse looking around him in a kind of dazed bewilderment. He began fiddling with his fly buttons with his restricted hands.

"Watch out!" Ryerson yelled. "He's about to piss all over us like a toad. Turn him around and hold a six-gun on him, Wayne. He looks just loose enough in the head to haul off and do it in the house. Lord!"

After Hadley had relieved himself noisily in the dark near the stoop, Wisner and Slade guided him through the door. He stood just inside, blinking at the light of the lamp on the table.

"What'll we do with him?" Wisner asked.

"Damned if I know," Ryerson said. "He don't act like he's got a grain of sense. Not that I figured he had any to begin with. Sit him down on the floor over in the corner where I can keep an eye on him. And get me my Navy. If he makes a crosswise move, I want to be the one to open his head on the other side and find out what's in it. Or not in it. This damned shoulder is giving me the fantods again, and I'd like nothing better just now than to find an excuse to get even.''

"If I was you, Cole, I'd take it just a bit slow," Acie said. "From what you say, this is the only man that knows what happened to your nugget.''

"Aw, hell, Acie, you know I wouldn't shoot the empty-headed pup. The law'll take its course. But, say, don't you think I wouldn't like to take the barrel of this Navy and rap some sense into him.''

"You say he don't know his own name, Wayne?" Barney asked.

"That's it. Acting mighty strange for a killer and a bushwhacker and a thief. That's how I took him so easy. He was over to the McDonnells', standing around watching Duff's two little boys playing kid games. But don't fool yourself. He's still dangerous.''

"Huh!" Barney grunted. "That do beat all.''

"Tell us about it, son," Ryerson said. The marshal stiffened as he saw Hadley's hands come up; he sat on the floor in a corner behind the table where Ryerson could watch him.

Hadley continued to stare at the floor but brought his hands up and poked a finger deep into a nostril.

"Well, would you look at that," Ryerson said. "Ain't got no more sense than to sit there picking his nose right in front of everybody!''

"Well," Slade began, "I had one hell of a time convincing Mary McDonnell of the truth . . .''

"She's a pretty one, ain't she, son?" Ryerson said.

"Yeah. Well, Mary and I went after him. He was behind the barn, like I said, playing with her boys. Mary has a big double shotgun, and it was no trick to get the drop on him. He didn't put up any fight, Cole. Didn't even act like he recognized me. No fight at all. Just sat there on the edge of this hole they were playing in, looking into the muzzle of my six-gun. He didn't make any fuss until I tried to take some dallies around his hands, and then he started fish-tailing like a bronc. I cuffed him one, and that gentled him some. I piled a loop around his arms and got him down and hog-tied him, and then I could go to work getting his hands hobbled like you see him there.''

"How did Mary behave?"

"Oh, Cole, she's got sand, that one. She'd have come along but for having to look after her boys. I promised some of us would come by tomorrow or the next day.''

Ryerson brightened. "Well, by God, boy, I got to give you credit. You got McDonnell's killer and the one that ambushed me. We'll have some hemp in place of his neck-tie in no time.''

"What about the gold, Cole?" Barney asked.

"He ain't said nothing about it, Wayne?"

"Not a word. All the way here, I couldn't make heads nor tails out of his talk. He just says simpleton things, and says he's Billy. He's gone soft in the head, Cole.''

"Well, somehow he got larruped a good one. See that crease in his skull! Man, I imagine that must've hurt. Barney, get him over here to the table. I want to find out about my gold.''

Hadley was dozing, leaning against the cabin corner, his tied hands between his knees. Slade and Wisner went to him.

"C'mon, Billy," Slade said, urging him up by the armpit. "They want to talk to you."

"Sleepy. Want to sleep."

"You'll be sleepier if you don't straighten up." Ryerson said from the table. "If I have to lay this Navy barrel up 'side your ear, you'll sleep for a week.''

Hadley was guided to a chair.

"He sure don't look none too bright," Acie said.

Slade helped Hadley into a chair and stood behind him, leaning on Casey's cooking counter.

"All right, Hadley," Ryerson said. "Time to quit playing

138

kiddie games. You killed Duff McDonnell, bushwhacked me, and then stole my gold. How about it?"

Aware he was being spoken to, Hadley stared dully at Ryerson.

"Well, damn you. If I didn't have this busted-up wing and this hole you poked in me, I'd get an armlock on your neck and walk you around the lot until some sense started to come out of your mouth!"

"Take it easy, Cole," Barney said. "Can't you see that bump on his head made him simpleminded?"

"All I can see is that the son of a pup put my gold somewhere and is playacting to cover up for it. Hadley, where in the hell did you put my gold?"

Hadley continued to stare blankly at Ryerson; there was no recognition in the eyes.

Slade spoke up. "Why don't you try that name he uses, Cole? Billy."

Hadley swung his gaze on Slade and studied him, open-mouthed.

"All right." Hadley's eyes turned back to Ryerson as he forced a calm tone. "Okay, I'm going to play along with your kiddie game. Now, Bil-lee, where in the everlastin' hell's my gold? My nugget."

"Gold?"

"See the lyin' rascal? Acts like he don't know the word."

"I got an idea, Cole," Slade said. "Barney, you and Acie got any gold stashed around here?"

Casey and Wisner glanced at each other apprehensively. Ryerson got the drift of Slade's logic.

"Come on, fellas. You don't think Slade and me's going to rob you. Just show him some. May help him remember."

"I think it ain't you we don't trust. It's him. He's got a strange record of making off with other people's gold. I'm like you, Cole. I ain't so sure he ain't playactin' myself," Barney said.

"Relax, Barney. He's going to be walking on three feet of fresh air at the end of a rope before long."

"Is it all right, Acie?" Barney asked.

"Uh . . . sure. Okay."

Barney got up, went to the counter and climbed on it and reached into the eaves where the slanted rafters met the adobe walls. He hauled down a buckskin sack the size of a pants pocket.

"We got some small nuggets, Cole," Acie said as Barney climbed down. "Found 'em up in there where you saw the sluice. Could be more up in there. We're going back come spring. But higher up."

"That's where I found mine. Just let me hold one of the bigger ones."

Barney poked in the sack and came up with a misshapen and pocked lump of gold no larger than a .44 bullet. He handed it to Ryerson, who hefted it in his closed fist. Hadley stared at the tabletop.

"Now, Billy," Ryerson said, "you ever seen anything like this?"

He shoved his fist under the soft light of the lamp and opened his palm. The gold gleamed, picking up the lamp glow with a metallic yellow brightness.

Hadley's eyes brightened. "Billy's pretty rock. Billy got pretty rock, too. Billy's pretty rock lots, lots bigger." He raised his bound hands and cupped them to show the size.

"That's it," Ryerson said, handing the nugget to Barney. "That's it! He remembers the damned thing. Now how the hell do we get him to own up to where it is?"

"Probably around where he got hit in the head, Cole," Acie said. "He probably lost it there."

"Or left it there," Slade said. "Acts like he doesn't know gold's value."

"Let me talk to him a minute," Acie said. He slid his chair close to Hadley. "Billy, are you hungry?"

Hadley's eyes widened in recollection. "Billy hungry. Billy need to eat."

"I'll get you some food just as soon as you tell Mr. Ryerson here what you did with the pretty rock."

Hadley's lower lip jutted out in a pout. "Billy hungry. Real hungry."

Ryerson lost his patience. "Tell us where you hid that damned nugget, Hadley, and I'll buy you a whiskey keg of ice cream, for Pete's sake!"

"Take it easy, Cole," Slade said.

"Where's the pretty rock, Billy?" Acie asked again.

"Billy got pretty rock. Billy hungry."

"I think we're getting someplace," Barney said. "He's at least putting the two together."

"Aw, bother," Ryerson said. "Feed the pup and let's get to bed. He ain't going to tell you anything, at least not tonight. This damned shoulder he give me is aching like a sore tooth. I'd just as leave right now forget about that infernal nugget in favor of seeing a mound of dirt with his name on the damned headstone."

Barney thrust in his two cents. "It's none of my say, Cole, but ain't you coming down a bit heavy on this feller? Me and Acie and Wayne there, I know, is the strangers hereabouts, so we ain't in hardly no position to preach. But it's plain that this man has taken a crack on the head that's addled his brains for certain. He purely ain't responsible for his own acts no more."

Ryerson softened. "Yeah, you're right. If he was on top of things, he'd be chasing out of the territory instead of sitting there slavering and babbling like a fresh-hatched baby. Reckon I should thank the Almighty for small favors. He's had the gold. Of that we're sure. Now all it takes is to pry it out of him."

"Right," Slade said, "and now there's plenty of time for that."

"As for mollycoddling him, you fellers ain't been at lawkeeping as long as I have and seen some of the things I've seen. It wasn't one of you hauled young McDonnell dead out of a chair while this man sat right there as close as he is to me now and told me a string of lies. It wasn't any of you that got a bitching-sore shoulder because that man put a forty-four-caliber hole through it. And ain't any of you as found a nugget as big as a sledgehammer that he's stole and hid someplace. And now he's turned so damned dumb he can't tell me. That's why I'm mad. Mad clean through. I can't help it. I'm sorry he's sick in the head, but that don't forgive what he done."

"Think of what Wayne stood to lose on account of Hadley, Cole," Barney said. "You was ready to stretch Wayne's neck on Hadley's say-so."

Ryerson sat silent for a long moment. "Well, as I think on it, I am sorry for Billy here. But this shoulder right now is saying Quinn Hadley is going to pay for his transgressions, Billy or no Billy."

"Can't say as I blame you for that, Cole," Acie said.

"What'll we do with him tonight?" Slade asked.

Ryerson fixed a stare of cold frustration on Slade. He sighed. "I suppose we'll have to post a night guard on him. Let me crawl in my soogans for a time. I'll take the dawn watch. By then maybe this arm'll feel better."

"Yeah," Barney said. "You fellers turn in. I'll watch him till midnight, and then I'll wake you, Wayne."

"Agreed," Wayne said.

CHAPTER
17

And how's Marshall Ryerson coming along?"

"AND HOW'S MARSHALL RYERSON COMING ALONG?"

Mary McDonnell poured a sociable cup of coffee for her unexpected caller, Wayne Slade. His hat hung on the back of the chair, and he sat comfortably, his arms in front of him on the table, watching her move about the cabin's main room, an admiration growing in him.

He felt comfortable there now, the setting and the feel of the place leaning him toward it. Duff McDonnell had set himself up well. It was the kind of a place a man would look forward to coming back to, a place with a now and a place with a future. He thought he wouldn't mind having a home just like this when he finally decided to settle down.

Outside, the afternoon grew warm. The inside of the cabin was dark, still holding the comforting cool of night. That helped Slade's frame of mind, too.

"Mary, if the level of his complaining is any indication, he is back to normal. And then some."

Mary's brows knit. "I never did understand men. If he's getting well, why isn't he in good spirits?"

"Cole Ryerson's at his best when he's finding fault."

143

"You men! If a man's lying around listless and quiet and placid, then something's wrong. He's either angry or coming down with something."

"And if he's crowing loud and long about his aches and pains and what's wrong with the world, he's in fine fettle. No, Mary, you understand men only too well."

Mary glanced out the window with glistening eyes. A tightening emotion and memory of things past clouded her expression. "Duff was like that."

"I'm sorry, Mary. I didn't mean to get on a touchy subject."

"No, I should talk about it. Get it out of the inside of me. Come to grips with it. That's all part of the acceptance. Besides, it wasn't anything you said, Mr. Slade. So many things crowd my thinking about Duff and the things he used to do and say. I have to remember I'm entering a new stage in my life, unexpected and unwanted as it may be."

"At the risk of seeming forward, could I ask you to call me Wayne?"

Mary looked at him, registering neither pleasure nor offense at the suggestion.

"All right . . . Wayne. It was nice of you to be concerned enough to ride out. These days are long since . . . well, Duff's death. The nights are even longer. The boys are such a comfort to me. They are awfully small, but they seem to know my grief and try to make it easier on me."

"They are good little fellows, that's easy to see."

"It's hard not to be constantly reminded of Duff and of thoughts that maybe it's all just a bad dream and he'll be coming home soon."

"I wish it were that way for you, too. I know. I lived with those kinds of thoughts for years after the war."

"You lost someone dear?"

"A bit more, even, than that." Slade paused, reflecting. "I was telling you about Marshal Ryerson."

Mary's expression brightened. "He's complaining."

"Lustily. Doc Wells is having him keep the cast on

longer than he originally figured, and Ryerson holds him personally accountable. The bullet wounds have nearly healed, and I imagine he's gained back most of his strength.''

"That's encouraging news. More coffee?"

"No, thanks. It's funny to see him stumping around town with that bit of a limp of his. He moves as though he's got business that won't keep. You know that bit of a shack he lives in and uses as his office?"

"Heard tell of it."

"Well, he'll be down there a few minutes or an hour. Then he's up to the jail to check on Hadley. From there he'll drop in at the Water Hole for a drink. Doesn't spend too much time there in idle chatter, and then maybe he's over to the Wagon Wheel for a bowl of soup or something else to eat.''

"Got a lot on his mind. Any word on his gold?"

"Nothing. That's one of the things he complains about the loudest. He knows Hadley took it and that Hadley hid it, or knows where it is. Before or after that rap on the head turned him foolish."

"He still thinks he's a boy named Billy?"

"Yes. Sits in that hot and dark little jail day in and day out and only stares at the wall. I've never seen anyone as dull-witted as he's become.''

"Will they hang him?"

"Only a judge and jury can decide that, Mary. I'm supposing they will. That's what happens to out-and-out murderers.''

"But if he's not Quinn Hadley anymore but a boy named Billy, how could they reach a verdict against him?"

Slade sipped the circle of chill coffee from the bottom of the cup. "Believe I might have just a dab more coffee, Mary, if it's still warm."

She got up and brought the pot from the stove.

"You're feeling compassion for the man who murdered your husband in cold blood?"

Mary stopped with the coffeepot in her hands. Her breath came in a sharp intake.

Slade sensed he had again touched a sensitive area. "I'm sorry. I didn't mean to put it that way."

"No. Justice must be done with Hadley and his killing of Duff. But when society takes a person's life in the name of justice, it's about as senseless as the crime he's committed. There ought to be a better way to make him atone. That's all."

"Never thought of it quite that way. Traditionally it's been an eye-for-an-eye kind of thing."

"And I don't understand how the law can deal with Hadley, since he's now so thoroughly a foolish-acting man who thinks he's a little boy."

"I see how you're thinking. I still believe the law must deal with him as Quinn Hadley, no matter who he's become. You know him as Quinn Hadley. I do, too. Ryerson does, and so do the people in Immigrant Lake. He's the same man who committed a serious crime against society, deprived you of your husband and your sons of their father. The Bible, the law, and the people say he must pay."

"Will I have to be there for the trial? I don't really want to be present when they thrash all of it over."

"Ryerson doesn't think so. I knew you'd ask, so I checked before I left. They may want you there. If they do, I'll come for you. I'll stay with you, do what I can to help. Kind of the least I can do under the circumstances."

Mary studied Wayne's eyes. "Thank you, Wayne. You've been very considerate."

"I liked Duff. We could have been friends." Slade knew there was more to it; he could feel himself developing a fondness for this steadfast woman.

Mary acknowledged his statement with a nod.

"Cole says the circuit judge will be in next week. He's wired him about the situation, and they're getting ready for a long time in the courtroom. The defense lawyer and the prosecutor are also circuit riders."

"And Mr. Ryerson's gold is gone?"

"Maybe that's what's making Cole so nervous. He's pledged to see justice done with Hadley. But he knows that when Hadley hangs, all possibility of ever finding the nugget dies too."

"Mr. Hadley doesn't remember anything about it?"

"Nothing. Doc Wells has gone over Hadley with a curry comb. Doc says it's amnesia or some such. Loss of memory. Caused by that rap on the head. We're figuring from the way things looked that Hadley's horse threw him. I told you, didn't I, that Hadley's horse showed up at Casey and Wisner's? If there was a way to find out where it happened, Cole figures the gold's got to be nearby."

"Has he thought of taking Mr. Hadley out there and trying to find that place?"

"Plenty. Got nowhere with that. It's a big valley. And Doc doesn't think it will faze Hadley. He doesn't remember anything from one day to the next. It's doubtful he could lead anyone to the place where he fell off the horse. If that's even what happened."

"So tragic."

"How's that?"

"All of this senseless business from start to finish. Such a simple thing as a card game. Duff is dead. Marshal Ryerson was nearly killed, and his gold is lost. Mr. Hadley has turned stupid and stands to be hanged and will never know why. So much is lost in the process."

She still stood with the coffeepot. Slade shoved his cup toward her. Like someone coming out of a daze, Mary trembled once and then filled his cup.

"I guess all of life is like that, Mary," he said, as she returned the pot to the stove. "As we used to say in the army, take one step forward and slide back two."

"Have you lived in Immigrant Lake long? I don't think Duff ever mentioned you. He seemed to know everyone in the valley."

"To tell the truth, I don't even live here now. Still just

passing through. Rode in from down Texas way the day Duff was . . . the day it happened."

"You live down there?"

"I guess I don't live anywhere permanently anymore."

"You had a home once. You had a good family upbringing. It shows."

"In the South. All gone now. The war saw to that."

"You were in it, of course."

"Most of it. To Gettysburg. Wounded. Spent the rest of the war in a northern prison pen."

"You poor man. It must have been horrible. My uncle and his only son both died at Fredericksburg. They were Iowa men. Nearly broke up that branch of the family."

"A great many families were shattered. On both sides."

"Yours?"

"Totally. A fine plantation home burned to the ground, the land scorched beyond any foreseeable reclaim, taken over by carpetbaggers for outrageous back taxes. Father, I imagine, died of a broken heart. Mother suffered for several years from brain fever before her misery was mercifully ended. Brother dead in the war. Sister lost all her pride."

Mary saw the subject needed changing. Slade seemed about done with it anyway.

"So you, like my parents and me, came west to find a new start."

Slade studied her "And you found it, and lost it."

Mary gazed at the floor. The suggestion of tears glimmered at her eyelids. "I hadn't yet come to grips with it in just that fashion. I suppose you are right."

"Fifteen years I've been trying to find a new start. That's the part that bothers, Mary. Bothers real bad. The end of all that misery, we were told, would bring the fresh start. About the only thing that sustained me through the time in prison was the thought that when it was over, the wind would finally be at my back."

"Maybe it's shifting in your favor, Wayne. It took courage for you to do what you did for Cole Ryerson."

Slade was thoughtful. "That could have been a mistake."

"How can you possibly mean that?"

"I'm not out of the woods, Mary. Hadley killed your husband. You are convinced of my innocence. I'm the only one, really, who knows that for sure. Hadley is in no condition to tell any kind of story to the jury, good or bad. All they have to go on is what Hadley said against me the day it happened. All that is in my favor is that I'm in Ryerson's good graces for going back and helping him when he was hurt. And my sticking around now."

CHAPTER
18

COLE RYERSON'S MARSHAL'S OFFICE AND JAIL FACING ON Range Street had little more dimension than a good-sized three-hole outhouse. Tinier than his shack on the outskirts, the twenty-foot-square adobe shanty was conveniently partitioned down the middle with ceiling-to-floor bars for the south half to serve as a jail.

A glass window over a battered affair that served as a desk looked out on Range Street. A second window, in the cell and barred, faced out the back on a view superior to that of any other *juzgado* in the territory.

From it, a prisoner—not that he cared a damn—could study the sprawling, tranquil Immigrant Lake, its placid, unbroken surface bluer, even, than the very sky.

Ryerson hated the confinement of his side of the place as much as any prisoner fought the claustrophobia of the cell. Still, Ryerson lingered there on scorching and bitter-cold days for the moderate temperatures afforded by the thick adobe walls.

Just now he was leaning back in the battered oak swivel chair, his spur rowels propped up on the desk top. Ryerson absentmindedly rocked back and forth in his chair, rolling the rowels across the distressed desk top, digging new gouges in the agonized wood. When he came around to having to do any paperwork on the desk, he cursed the deeply scarred surface that he himself was responsible for.

His jail cell was more a holding tank for prisoners, with its two battered wood bunks with flattened straw mattresses supported by crude slats. He kept promising himself that one of these days he'd get some fresh straw for the dingy blue and white striped ticking-sack mattresses.

Just now the cell was occupied by Hadley and Doc Wells—he'd locked Doc in just in case—while Doc examined the injured man's head. Ryerson shut out of his mind the low drone of voices as Doc questioned Hadley about his condition.

Doc had cleaned the gaping, healing gash on Hadley's head, cut away some of the hair, and bandaged and wound snow-white gauze around the prisoner's head.

Unbeknownst to Ryerson and Doc Wells, as the doctor worked, Hadley could feel the identity of Billy slipping away and the name Quinn Hadley emerging. The misty hallucination of being a small boy slowly cleared like a shimmering mirage taking on the stark, crisp lines of reality.

With it came a sharper focus in Hadley's consciousness that he was in trouble. Deep trouble. As his senses cleared, Hadley was surprised to see Cole Ryerson alive; a great deal, he thought, had gone wrong.

"Wish to hell you'd got him to me sooner, Cole," Doc groused through the bars at the marshal. "By the time I saw him out there at Casey and Wisner's this gash was too far set to be helped by sutures."

"You saw him the day after Slade dragged him in, Doc. Probably he got knocked on the head about the same day he bushwhacked us up by the mountains. Best part of a week had probably gone by. Besides, he don't deserve better," Ryerson said.

151

"He's a human being," Doc growled.

"And a killer and a back-shooter and a robber to boot. He gonna ever come to his senses, Doc?"

Wells finished his treatment, rubbed his hands on his bandanna, put things away in his black doctor's satchel, and snapped the clasps.

Hadley could barely remember now the time of being Billy. Their conversation and something in his mind, however, told him to play dumb, to continue to affect a blank stare and expression.

Doc's voice carried an edge. "Let me out of here and I'll tell ya."

Ryerson pulled the big jail key and its ring off the hook above his desk and jumped up to open the cell door. One of the spur rowels caught in a deep and old gouge in the desk and Ryerson nearly went ass over tin cup.

"Damn that desk," he said as he caught his balance and heaved his body heavily out of the chair. He let Doc out to put down his satchel and park precariously on the desk's side chair. The glue in all its joints had dried, turning the chair into a thing alive. A front rung was snapped clear through and it was worth the risk of a busted tailbone to try to sit in the thing.

"Wish you'd fix this damned chair, Cole," Doc said, forcing himself to perch lightly on the slab seat.

"I will, one of these days. What's the . . . whattaya call it—prognosis? On Hadley." Ryerson studied his prisoner standing dully in the center of his cell, staring at them with a now familiar imbecilic tolerance.

"I can deliver babies, set broken bones, probe for bullets and bandage wounds, do a fair job of suturin', and prescribe pills for near any ailment that could hit this part of the country. But when you get into injuries of this kind, I confess I ain't got a hell of a lot of savvy."

"Spare me the details of your life, Doc. Is that hammerhead Billy ever going to be fit to tell me where he hid my nugget, and to stand trial for the killin' of Duff McDonnell?"

"I wish I knew. It's evident that that crack on the head brought on amnesia, loss of memory. It depends, I guess, on the nature and extent of brain damage. He had a first-class concussion, and those things, like most everything else that'll ail a body, will take their own good time to heal."

"Dammit, Doc, quit skirtin' around the issue. Just tell me is he ever going to be Quinn Hadley again?"

The man in question had come to stand at the barred door separating him from the doctor and the marshal and witnessed the conversation blankly.

"You got anything to drink in this place, Cole? It'd make the studyin' on this situation easier."

Ryerson squinted at Wells impatiently. "Here," he said. He clawed at the bottom drawer pull and yanked out the drawer. A dusty blue bottle with a few swigs left lay sideways in it, the contents sloshing around.

Beside it were two thick mineral- and dust-hazy glasses Ryerson had swiped from Walt over at the Water Hole. Ryerson pulled out the bottle and glasses and scraped his fingers around inside each glass to rid it of accumulated dust, shook out the grit, and divided the remains in the bottle between them.

Doc Wells watched all this wide-eyed in amazement. "Sometime I'd like to sit down and have a talk with you about personal hygiene, Cole."

"I'd a sight druther you'd drink this and tell me about Hadley. I never knew this High Gene you speak of."

Doc Wells regarded the contents of his glass suspiciously, sighed, and took a hefty sip. He coughed against the whiskey's bite before he spoke. "What I know about brain injuries you could put in your eye. All I know is that it's a toss-up. Like I said, depending on the extent of the injury, his memory may be restored, or he could be condemned to be an empty-head the rest of his days."

"Hell, from his actions since Duff's killing, I got him

153

pegged that way all his life. I commence to think he never did have brain one."

"Stay with the discussion, Cole. He may never remember anything of the past. It might be he'll never be able to remember again. He probably right now doesn't even recall what happened yesterday, or maybe even an hour ago."

"Let's try him. Hey, Hadley!"

The prisoner showed some recognition of the name or that the marshal's raised voice meant he was being spoken to. He looked at Ryerson questioningly.

"See there, Doc," Ryerson said, almost happily. "See how he perked up at his real name."

"Doesn't offer me a hell of a lot to be optimistic about," Doc remarked.

"I believe I'll start calling him Hadley instead of Billy for a spell," Ryerson continued. "Might help clear up the cobwebs in that head he calls a brain." He swung his head back at Hadley. "Remember what you had for breakfast this morning, Hadley?"

"Breakfast?" Hadley asked.

"Yeah, that grub I brought you from the Wagon Wheel on a tin plate."

Hadley's eyes shifted away from the two men and he stood a long time as if in thought.

"Well?"

"Breakfast? I ate breakfast."

Ryerson glanced back at Doc Wells. "His voice commences to sound different, too. Ain't so whiny as it was. But there you have it. We don't know salt and pepper from gold dust. My nugget's gone and I might just as well set my mind to that fact here and now."

"I still say it could be temporary, Cole. A matter of time. There'll be a trial, of course?"

"Oh, yeah. I wired the capital for the circuit judge. They're getting a trip here on their agenda. They'll hang him sure, and there goes any chance of our ever locating my gold."

Doc sipped again at his amber whiskey. "This is pretty good stuff. Tastes better than what Walt usually serves."

"Hell, it's had a chance to age. Not green like most of the whiskey over there. Hell, I suppose that flask's been in that drawer six weeks or better. I don't do that much drinkin' here in the office. The decorum of my position and such."

"A lot you know about decorum," Doc said. "My advice is to play the waiting game, Cole. Don't get impatient with Hadley. And don't roughhouse him. That brain matter is tender now, and as long as he stays quiet there's a chance he might heal and come back to himself in time for the trial. Watch him for any signs of recognition."

"I'll do that, Doc. I'll do that. But every damned bone in my body aches to take him by the shoulders and shake some sense into that empty noggin he calls a brain."

"That won't do, Cole. Leave him be. Keep him clean and feed him well. I'm leaving some laudanum with you. If he gets to complaining about his head hurting, give him a little of this, well watered down."

"All right, Doc. I'll do what I can."

"I'll look in on him from time to time. How's your wounds coming?"

"Well, both my arm and my shoulder are itching to beat hell, so I suppose they're healing okay. I can feel a drawing and a pulling in the bone and muscles around the break. Least that's the way it feels. Sometimes it aches for a fare-thee-well deep down."

"That's probably a good sign that you're on the mend and the bones are knitting. Unless you get other aggravated symptoms, we'll just leave it at that. I'll check on you once in a while, too, while I'm looking Hadley over."

"Okay, Doc. That little sip was pitifully tame. What say we drop over and see Walt? I'll buy you one for your good services."

Doc got up, relieved to be up off the perch that was an accident waiting to happen. "One of these days, Cole, you'll be yelling for me to fix somebody's busted tailbone when that damned chair gives up the ghost.''

Ryerson heaved himself heavily out of the swivel chair that wasn't much better off than the side chair.

"Doc," he grumbled. "You sure are getting to be a persnickety son of a bitch in your old age."

The marshal's office door squealed on dry, loose hinges as the pair disappeared out onto the board sidewalk in the late afternoon sun, and a soft silence seeped into Hadley's tiny cell.

The mists had seeped out of his head, and the superficial scalp pain had subsided with Doc Wells's careful cleaning and bandaging. A dull ache persisted deep in the core, but Hadley sensed that it, too, was seeping away like the daylight that oozed out of his musty cubicle, giving way to the creeping gray of dingy twilight.

To escape the gnawing depression and anxiety and to seek freedom from a suffocating vacuum inside him from the confinement, Hadley was drawn to the barred window as a night-borne zephyr beat back the cell's stale air. He watched a long time as Immigrant Lake began to lose shape and definition as the sun said farewell behind the high ridge to the west. Hadley stood a long time alone with his emerging thoughts.

Dark had nearly descended when his mind was pricked alert with the scraping and crunching of gravel outside the wall. Whoever it was stood so close to the window that Hadley was aware of shallow breathing with a hint of a wheeze.

"Mr. Hadley?" a voice whispered and Hadley, determined to stay in a character he now knew he had been for many days, grunted as if only aware of a presence out there.

"Mr. Hadley. If you can understand me, I'm here to help you." The voice still came as a muted whisper.

Again Hadley mumbled an unintelligible acknowledgment.

"Dammit," the soft voice continued, and Hadley could

see the side of the man's head at the window. "If only I could make sense with you! I was there when Slade ran out of the saloon, and Ryerson knows it. I'm the only person who could support your side."

Clarity emerged fully in Hadley's head. For the first time since his injury, he spoke as Quinn Hadley, and then only in a whisper. "I don't know what your game is, but I'll have to trust you. Who are you?"

"Dolan, Mr. Hadley. You may remember me. Emory Dolan."

CHAPTER
19

COLE RYERSON TOOK THE STAND IN QUINN HADLEY'S MURder trial slicked up and dressed like a churchgoer. He'd had his hair cut, was clean-shaven, and wore a new shirt and his only suit of clothes. The giant plaster cast was off his arm, but he continued to favor it, cradling the arm in a sling. He sat forward in the wood armchair that was the witness stand, elbow on the chair arm, both feet on the floor. He supported his left arm with his right hand.

Two circuit-riding lawyers had come in with Judge Marcus Chase from the state capital, since Immigrant Lake had no one who served in such legal capacities. The two lawyers had spent a couple of days in town, nosing around, interviewing principal witnesses and others, and building their cases. Both had talked at length with Slade and Ryerson. Ryerson grumbled to Slade about both of them, casting aspersions on their mental capacities, calculating both of them only a cut or so above Hadley. Ryerson took a dim view of professional people, especially those in fancy clothes.

Slade had difficulty at first telling the two lawyers apart.

They had nearly the same build and general appearance; they were slight men with no overly rugged or distinctive features. Both had slicked-down hair and wore store-bought business suits.

Algernon Simms had been selected to represent the state against Quinn Hadley. Gregory Madden would defend Hadley's case.

Ryerson grudgingly saw to it that Hadley was cleaned up, put into clean but plain clothing from his house, and brought from the jail handcuffed. He had been washed perfunctorily, but he was not shaved, nor had his hair been cut; Ryerson was too fearful Hadley would jump around against scissors or a razor and hurt himself. The defendant continued to act like some sort of mental cripple. After the jury was selected and sworn in and long opening statements made, Hadley—or Billy—was the first to be brought to the stand.

In response to questions from both attorneys, Hadley babbled so much childish nonsense that Madden asked that he be excused as a witness in his own defense. Simms concurred. The judge instructed the record to show that the defendant was an apparent incompetent, looked at his watch, and recessed the trial until the next morning.

With the opening gavel rap the next day, Simms called Ryerson. He was sworn in and took his seat.

"Marshal Ryerson, how long have you been a United States marshal in Immigrant Lake?" Simms asked.

Ryerson studied the crowd in the packed Water Hole Saloon, which served as Judge Chase's courtroom, as he tried to count back the years. "Three and a half years, to the best of my recollection."

"Before that what had you done?"

"I was bound to a gunsmith in Saint Louis, sir. And I believe that was about the only illegal thing I ever did knowingly. I jumped my bond and went off to Texas and became an officer of the law."

"Thank you for your candor, Marshal. So, you enforced the law in Texas for several years. Then in 1861 . . . ?"

Madden burst to his feet. "Objection, Your Honor. This court is not convened to minutely investigate the life story of Marshal Cole Ryerson!"

Simms turned to Judge Chase. "I won't be long at it, Your Honor. My intent is merely to establish Marshal Ryerson's credibility as an expert and material witness."

"Objection overruled. Proceed, Counselor Simms."

Madden stared a moment at the judge and then sat down angrily with gestures that might have been interpreted as melodramatic. Simms also paused a moment for effect before addressing Ryerson again. "The question, Marshal. What happened in 1861?"

Ryerson glowered at Madden before straightening himself with pride, his eyes sparkling. "In 1861, sir, Texas elected to ride with the Confederacy, and I went along. Rode with the cavalry brigade of the great General Jo Shelby in General Kirby Smith's Army of Trans-Mississippi!"

"And you emerged with what rank?"

"A major, but hell, beggin' your pardon, sir, that was considered pretty good for a shavetail kid who'd joined up as a private."

"And you were decorated for gallantry?"

"Not much of a hand to brag on it, but, yes, sir, I was so honored with a few medals after some of General Shelby's raids into Missouri from Arkansas, and the battle of Newtonia, Kansas, and battlefield commissions and such."

"You returned a major to private life and went into law enforcement again. Am I correct?"

"Yes, sir. Around and about in Texas for a few years. I learned the ropes under the great Mose Laramore in Abilene, and succeeded him in office. Then for quite a spell I served as a federal marshal under Judge Isaac Winfield at Fort Walker in the territories."

"How long, in total, before and after the war, have you been associated with enforcing the law?"

"I have ridden on the side of the law for thirty-five years."

"Excellent. Now, Marshal Ryerson, let us try to reconstruct—from your viewpoint—the crime under investigation here."

"Yes, sir. Well, sir, up to a point, about all I've got is hearsay, really. I was down at my house at the time when I heard shots that morning. Well, it was closer to noon. I came running and found Duff McDonnell dead in this very room. Right over there. Hadley and Slade and Duff . . ."

"Slade?"

"Yes, sir. Wayne Slade. That gent sitting right over there. They'd been playing poker, the three of them. Hadley told me Slade had cold-conked him, took his gun, and shot McDonnell."

"And you believed him?"

"I did then. Had to, I suppose. It was all I had to go on. All I knew was that a drifter named Slade had been there, there was a shooting, McDonnell was dead, and Slade had hightailed it."

"So you went after Slade?"

"I surely did. Just as fast as I could get my gear together. Started out next morning. Didn't think I'd have trouble running him to earth. Thing was, that skunk Hadley coyoted along behind, fixing to back-shoot me on the trail."

Madden jumped to his feet. "Objection, Your Honor! Not a shred of evidence exists linking Mr. Hadley with any ambush. Pure conjecture!"

The judge was thoughtful. "Objection sustained."

"All right, Mr. Ryerson," Simms said. "We'll get to your injuries by a person or persons unknown in a moment. You were tracking Wayne Slade. What's this about gold?"

Ryerson was about to say something more about Hadley, but held his tongue, knowing it would bring Madden to his feet. "That was when I broke my arm and, to my satisfaction, discovered Wayne Slade's true stripe. I was busted up bad; fell in a pool, and when I did, I turned up this big nugget of gold, pure gold, big as this." Ryerson held up a clenched fist.

"You mentioned about Wayne Slade. Where does he come in?"

"My arm was busted up bad, broken bones sticking out and all. I knew I needed help or I'd probably die. Blood poison or shock, one would get me. I'd already done some thinking that maybe I was chasing the wrong man. Slade was the only one nearby. I knew I was close to catching him. I fired a distress signal. Slade answered it and come to my rescue. He found out right off about the gold. I knew right then, if I hadn't suspected it before, that he couldn't've shot Duff McDonnell."

"How so?"

"Well, Mr. Simms, maybe you haven't lived around folks long as I have. A man in my position has to become a fair judge of people and how they think and behave. If your hunches are wrong, sometimes it can get you killed. Here you have a man on the run, justly or unjustly accused of murder. The lawman after him calls him in with a distress signal. He's decent enough to put his own problems second. He finds the lawman out of his head with pain from a busted wing and enough gold to make ten men content the rest of their days. Would a cold-blooded murderer stick around and splint an injured lawman's arm and nurse him along? You damn betcha he wouldn't! And would that man be sittin' right here in this courtroom when he's had ample chance to go skallyhootin' off? And with my gold, to boot. I know my men, Mr. Simms, and I have faith in Wayne Slade!"

"I'm certain you're a far better judge of men than I, Mr. Ryerson. However, I am inclined to agree with your conclusions. But getting back to the other events of your ordeal. You mentioned being ambushed. Be careful, now."

Ryerson ignored the mild admonition. "I did, but I better not say by whom I figure it was, or that 'learned colleague' of yours'll bust a cinch with another of them objections."

"All right, all right, Mr. Ryerson. About the ambush . . ."

"Well, Slade went to work and set and splinted my arm, fed me the next morning, and we started to come on down out of that box canyon where I got hurt and found the gold. Had the nugget secure in my saddlebags. That person or persons unknown back-shot me about the time we hit Wagon Box Creek. My horse run off, and Slade retreated back up the canyon. When Slade got back to me and went for the horse, the gold was gone out of my saddlebags."

"Your hunch was that the ambusher found your horse. And your gold."

"Everything points that way."

"Didn't Hadley, after his capture and even in his diminished capacity—the way he is right now—acknowledge something to you that led you to tie him both to the ambush and to the theft of your gold?"

Ryerson squinted at Madden, measuring him and how he would react.

"Yeah, but that come later. I can't say that, laying there in the rocks of Wagon Box Creek with a fresh-busted wing and a new forty-four hole burning the hell out of my shoulder, I wasn't in a diminished state myself. But whoever bushwhacked me rode by to make sure I was dead. I played a pretty good game of possum, even though I figured he might be fixing to administer my coop-dee-grace. I couldn't've gone for my Navy Colt if I'd've wanted to. I was that helpless. When he started riding away, I snuck a look at him, and I'm dead sure it was Quinn Hadley!"

Madden surprised Ryerson and was unruffled by the statement; he was calmly making notes on a pad on the poker table that served as his courtroom desk. Madden's calm note-taking seemed ominous to Ryerson.

"And the gold?" Simms asked.

"Well, sir, Slade, as I said, he come back after a spell. Before I let him even start to fix me up again, I sent him packing after my horse. And the gold. He found the horse, but the gold was gone. The bushwhacker just about had to ride past where my horse was stopped. My logic says he went through the saddlebags to see what I had that was worth taking, found the gold, and stole it. Slade rode my horse back and again stayed to fix me up. We made it to the cabin of a couple fellers I know, Casey and Wisner. After a few days, Slade went to pay his respects to the widow McDonnell and found Hadley there acting like a baby, like he is now. Miz McDonnell said he just wandered in off the plains."

"With a severe head injury."

"Oh, yeah. His scalp was popped wide open. He took a nasty knock on the head somewhere, and that's for sure. Doc Wells says that's what made him that way."

"Doc Wells?"

"Our local sawbones."

"You said Hadley acknowledged having the gold."

"Casey and Wisner, they let me borrow a nugget, a small one compared to mine. I showed it to Hadley, or Billy, as he calls himself. He started jumping up and down like he was bee-stung. Said he had a big rock just like that one."

CHAPTER
20

MADDEN SURPRISED THE PACKED COURTROOM BY WAIVING cross-examination of Ryerson. After his storm of objections, everyone thought he was prepared to eat the marshal alive on the stand. Instead, he asked that Wayne Slade be sworn in to testify.

Slade caught Madden studying him like a stalking varmint eyeing a mouse as a choice morsel of food.

Sensing something sinister in the wind, Slade took the oath with his hand sweating on the pebbly surface of the Bible's cover; his right hand in the air trembled. He could feel Ryerson's body heat in the wood armchair.

Madden stayed in his seat at the green-felt-covered poker table, a sheaf of notes spread before him. He studied them a long time for effect as he let the jury and the spectators have a good look at Slade.

Slade only hoped his apprehension would not be telegraphed to the judge, the jury, and the gallery. He was still the outlander, and the feeling was uncomfortable. About the only person there he knew he could count on for support was Ryerson. The courtroom was hushed, anticipating the next move.

When Madden spoke, his words whacked the heavy silence in the room like the ring of a sharp ax against a tree trunk. "For the record, your name is Wayne Slade?"

"Yes."

"What is your occupation, Mr. Slade?"

Slade pondered a moment. "Ah . . . cowhand, I guess."

"A cowhand, you guess. That would mean that you derive your principal livelihood from working with cattle."

"Something like that."

"Something like that. Are you or are you not principally a cowhand?"

"When I find work, that's generally what I do."

"When you work. Isn't it true, Mr. Slade, that for many years your profession could best be described as that of a drifter?"

Slade was cautious, sensing he was being drawn into a trap. "I've moved around a lot in recent years."

"In recent years. Isn't fifteen years more precise, Mr. Slade? Since the late war?"

"The war destroyed my permanent family home."

"So for perhaps nineteen or twenty years, since the start of the hostilities, you've been drifting."

"I was hardly drifting while in a northern prison pen for two years, sir."

A murmur of amusement rippled through the room. Madden visibly stiffened. He was already disliked, and felt it. "I take it, then, you fought on the side of the South."

"I was from Georgia."

"Took up arms against the United States government."

Simms leaped to his feet. "Objection, Your Honor. The issue of the Civil War and its soldiers on both sides was resolved years ago. Wayne Slade's loyalty is not on trial here."

Judge Chase thought a minute, musing on Madden's line of questioning. "Objection sustained. Counselor, kindly confine your questions to the issues at hand."

"Like my 'learned colleague,' " Madden snarled, an obvious slurring reference to Ryerson's testimony, "I am merely attempting to establish Mr. Slade's credibility as a material witness in this case."

Madden paused now, got up, and walked closer to Slade's chair. "From all I can gather, Mr. Slade, you are the only competent witness we have to the death of Duff McDonnell."

"I'm afraid so, sir."

"You're afraid so? How exactly do you mean that?"

"Just that. There were only three of us—McDonnell, Hadley, and me—in the game at that point."

"And Mr. Hadley, here on trial for his very life, has been declared incompetent to testify in his own behalf. We have only your word, the word of an avowed Secessionist . . . Beg pardon, Your Honor; I ask that that reference be stricken from the record."

"The recorder is so instructed," Judge Chase said, not seeming to note Madden's ploy.

"We must take your word as to what happened," Madden said.

"Yes."

"McDonnell was dead. What did you do?"

"Hadley told me he was a powerful man in this town, and he reminded me that I was the outsider and, as you say, a drifter, and that he'd see me swing for McDonnell's murder."

"This was after Hadley shot McDonnell?"

"Yes."

"Hadley shot McDonnell?"

"Yes."

"You are certain?"

"Yes."

"You did not shoot McDonnell?"

"No, sir!"

"Are you aware you are under oath, Mr. Slade?"

"Yes, sir."

"An oath in a territory administered by the government of the United States of America?"

"Yes."

"A government you once in your life declared against by your actions—"

"Objection, Your Honor!" Simms screamed, on his feet and red-faced. "Counsel for the defense continues his attempts to discredit the integrity of a material witness."

"Objection sustained," the judge said, rapping his gavel. "Counselor, kindly leave off the attacks on the witness's background and former loyalties."

"Your Honor, the possibility of perjury in this case is very great, very great indeed. We have but one competent witness to this dastardly act. A simple lie could save this man's skin and put the noose around the neck of a totally innocent man."

Ryerson, who had been sitting next to Hadley, guarding him, now jumped to his feet. "Whoa, back up there, Counselor! If you're suggesting that the man who twice saved my life, Wayne Slade, killed McDonnell and would lie to save his own hide, then maybe you got another big think coming!"

Through Ryerson's outburst, the hammerlike thuds of Judge Chase's gavel resounded in the room.

"Marshal Ryerson! Your intrusion into the orderly proceedings of this court is uncalled for and out of order. Please do not make me order you out of this courtroom."

Ryerson glared at the judge a moment, looked around to see that he'd stepped several paces away from his chair, and turned back and plunked himself heavily into it.

Slade sensed a new comfort; Ryerson was ready to risk a lot to make sure the truth prevailed in the courtroom, despite Madden's insinuations.

"Continue, Mr. Madden," Judge Chase said, his angry expression softening.

Slade, glad for Ryerson's support, and sensing a favorable attitude toward him in the room, was nonetheless nervous about facing Madden's questions again.

"All right, Mr. Slade. Let's get down to the facts of here and now. The death of Duff McDonnell and its aftermath."

"Yes, sir."

"Why, Mr. Slade, did you get your horse and race madly out of town after McDonnell's killing?"

"I explained that. Hadley said he'd see me swing for Duff's murder. I got rattled, I guess."

"You got rattled. You, a southern war hero, got rattled."

Slade grew irritated that Madden continued to repeat parts of his statements as though to cast them in an unfavorable light. Madden's penchant for maligning the South was equally irritating.

"I had never found myself in such an awkward position before."

"Have you killed before?"

Slade paused, sensing he might again be getting into a semantic trap. "Before? Before what? I told you I did not kill Duff McDonnell. Hadley did."

"I'd like your answer to the question, Mr. Slade. Have you ever killed a man?"

"Well, I . . . uh . . ."

"The question. Have you ever killed a man?"

Slade sensed tension rising in the room at his delay. Madden was surely trying to trap him. "In wartime. Yes, I believe I did."

"You believe you did."

Out of the corner of his eye, Slade saw Simms gripping the table, ready to pounce to his feet in objection.

"Yes, of course I did. The duty of a soldier in wartime, sir."

"We do not ask an explanation or an apology, Mr. Slade. Just an affirmative statement."

"Yes, I have killed men."

"How many men?"

Simms was up. "Objection, Your Honor! The defense is still trying to impugn the character of the witness."

"Objection overruled. Witness is instructed to answer the question."

A murmur of resentment pealed through the courtroom crowd.

"I don't know."

"You don't know! Was it that many? Was it five? Is that reasonable?"

"I suppose more than that. It was war. A soldier does what he—"

"Please, Mr. Slade. No justifications of your conduct. How many men do you believe you killed?"

"Too many, for God's sake!" Impatience seared inside Slade like a rising fever. "Thirty. Fifty. A hundred. I don't know."

"Very well, Mr. Slade. We may return to the subject of your killings. But for the moment, let me ask you. And be very truthful. You did not shoot and kill Duff McDonnell?"

Slade forced himself back to a calm. "No. I did not."

"But you ran after the killing?"

"Yes."

"And you went up into the hills."

"Yes."

"And when Marshal Ryerson was seriously injured and fired a distress signal, you heard it?"

"Yes."

"Who did you think fired those shots?"

"Someone in distress, of course. In that kind of country I couldn't imagine it being anyone but the man or men who were coming to find me and bring me back to stand trial for Duff's murder."

"You honestly thought that?"

"I honestly thought that."

"Did you not think that the lawman was in serious distress and that if you went back and aided him that you would curry his favor and thus possibly save your own neck?"

"There was that element in my thinking."

"Oh, there was an element of that in your thinking. You had ridden day and night to elude the law and possible conviction for the murder of Duff McDonnell. But when you saw the chance to curry the favor of the injured lawman to possibly save your skin, you seized it."

"I went back to help him, yes."

"Commendable gallantry, I must say, Mr. Slade, from a former enemy of the United States government."

Simms vaulted toward the judge's bench. "Objection! Counsel has been warned against bringing up that portion of the witness's past!"

"Objection sustained," Judge Chase said, a hint of righteous anger now in his voice. "Counsel is advised again to be more judicious in his choice of words."

"My apologies, Your Honor." Madden grinned; a smirk of small victory. He was proud of his performance. He felt he was chewing Slade's veracity to bits in the purest legal tradition.

"Now, Mr. Slade, let's get back to your version of the so-called ambush. You and Marshal Ryerson came down the ravine or canyon toward Wagon Box Creek. What exactly happened?"

"To the best of my recollection, we had come out of the canyon and had just started down the main part of the streambed when a shot rang out. Ryerson pitched out of the saddle and fell. My immediate thought was that he was dead."

"You thought he was dead."

"Yes."

"Did you check?"

"No, sir. Not at the moment. Whoever was shooting fired more shots. I turned my horse and rode back up the canyon to safety. He fired at me."

"Thinking the marshal was dead, you ran again."

Slade's voice came out insistent. "The man was shooting at me. It would have been folly to stay there in such an exposed situation."

"But you came back."

"When I heard no more shooting, yes."

"To make certain the marshal was dead." Madden's questions came off more like statements; the tone of them seemed damning to Slade.

"No, sir, in hopes he was alive."

"In hopes he was alive. I see. Mr. Slade, consider this question carefully. Did you not ride back to confirm your suspicion that Marshal Ryerson was dead, and thus be able to ride leisurely out of the territory?"

"No, sir. I did not ride back. I tethered my horse a safe distance up the canyon and walked back."

"You walked back?" Madden was openly dismayed at a bit of evidence he wasn't prepared for.

"Yes, in the protection of rocks and trees. I had no way of knowing that the bushwhacker was not still there, hoping to lure me into the open to face the same fate he had intended for Marshal Ryerson."

"And you found Marshal Ryerson again wounded but alive."

"Yes, sir. In very serious condition."

Madden gathered himself for a salvo. "I suggest, Mr. Slade, that you walked back to make certain the marshal was dead and then planned to seek out his horse and this alleged bonanza of wealth in gold—if such ever existed— and flee. An honest answer, now. Was this or was this not your intention?"

"It was not!"

"Bushwah!"

Simms leaped to his full height, ramrod-stiff. "Your Honor, please! Counsel has no right to express opinions of the veracity of a witness's testimony. Certainly not in such an unethical and crude fashion!"

"Objection sustained. You are out of order, Mr. Madden."

"Sorry, Your Honor." Again a gloating smirk flitted across Madden's face. "Well, Mr. Slade, there seem to be certain things about your actions and your testimony that I am prevented from bringing out in this court of law." Madden's tone underlined "law" as though mocking the word. "This in the face of an accused who is incapable of speaking out in his own defense. But we have well established certain elements in your thinking. Finding the marshal alive, you could then put your original plan into action, that of easing his misery, saving his life, and further currying his favorable sentiment in your behalf."

"That's not exactly right."

"But as you yourself stated earlier, there was an element of that in your thinking."

"Well, yes, I suppose there was."

"Hmm. Who did you think was Marshal Ryerson's attacker?"

"I had no way of knowing."

"Really? Marshal Ryerson had no doubt it was the defendant, Mr. Hadley."

"I don't think that had really occurred to me until he brought it up."

"So, about the only evidence we have that the man waiting in ambush was Quinn Hadley was that the marshal, nearly delirious, or at best semiconscious with pain and shock, thought that the man riding away from him was Hadley. You yourself never saw Hadley at the ambush site?"

"No, sir. Ryerson's logic seemed to make sense, particularly in light of what I knew of the truth of Duff McDonnell's murder."

"I suggest, Mr. Slade, that your kind and generous gesture of helping the marshal when he broke his arm inclined him toward a belief in your story of Hadley trying to blame you for McDonnell's murder. And I further suggest that the ambush simply made Hadley more suspect and helped the marshal confirm in his mind the version you told him of McDonnell's killing.''

"I question that completely."

"Your opinion, Mr. Slade, is not being sought. I'm not quite finished. I asked you earlier to hazard a guess as to how many men you had killed as a soldier . . . and otherwise."

Slade sensed an ominous inflection in Madden's use of the word "otherwise," as though the lawyer had yet to play some sort of hole card.

"I'd like you to hazard another guess," Madden continued, "since you and Marshal Ryerson seem to have become such fast friends. Do you have any idea how many enemies a man like Marshal Ryerson must have?"

"Why don't you ask him?"

"I'm asking you, his friend."

"Some, I'm certain."

"One?"

"How would I know?"

"Two?"

"I suppose any number of men dislike him for times when, by enforcing the law, he's made their lives difficult."

"Any number, eh? How many of those would you say might despise him enough to want to gun him down if given the chance?"

"You would have to ask him."

"I'm asking you, his friend."

"I suppose there could be some."

"And yet when shots are fired from ambush, the two of you are absolutely certain those shots could have come from the gun of only one man, Quinn Hadley."

"Under the circumstances, there seemed to be logic in the assumption."

"Logic be damned! Total supposition. No more logic than that. And a man's life hangs in the balance!"

Slade thought Simms would jump to his feet in objection. He did not. He sat slumped in his chair as if resigned to Madden's continual badgering of Slade on the stand.

CHAPTER
21

DEFENSE ATTORNEY GREGORY MADDEN WALKED AWAY from Slade acting very dissatisfied and disgruntled with the answers he had received. Slade saw Madden's actions as part of his act for the jury, which much of his examination of Slade seemed to have been.

Madden sat down at the green poker table and busied himself with his notes. He looked at Slade a long time as though merely pausing in his examination of the witness. He sighed deeply to register his dissatisfaction with the testimony and said, "No more questions, Your Honor."

"Counselor Simms," Judge Chase said.

Simms stood up. "Only a few questions, Your Honor," Simms said as he walked toward Slade on the witness stand. His manner was calm, as though he was trying to contrast his approach to the fiery barrage of questioning leveled by his legal opponent.

"Mr. Slade, you seem to have fairly well covered the entire incident as you saw it. There is, however, one matter not touched upon so far in your testimony."

Simms paused for effect and Slade watched him, knowing

Simms was on his side, and hoping his questioning would treat him a bit gentler than Madden's had.

"The matter of the gold missing from Marshal Ryerson's saddlebags. The assumption to this point is that the ambusher was Quinn Hadley, a possibility my colleague seems to want to dismiss. After Marshal Ryerson was shot and you returned to him, what exactly happened?"

"I wanted to attend to his injuries immediately, but he insisted I go in the direction his horse had run and try to find the animal."

"And you did?"

"The marshal can be a very stubborn man."

"What did you find?"

"It was more than a mile, I suppose. I found the horse grazing. I immediately checked the saddlebags. The gold was missing."

"Then you returned to Marshal Ryerson at the ambush site."

"As fast as Ryerson's horse could move over the rough streambed."

"And you gave the marshal the bad news and tended his new wounds."

"Yes."

"Then he told you the ambusher was Hadley?"

"No, he told me before, when he ordered me to go for the horse."

"I see. Now let's switch to some time later. As I get it, at one point, you rode to the home of the widow McDonnell to pay your respects."

"Yes, several days after I got the marshal to his friends' home. I wanted to try to clear my name with her. The marshal was by now convinced of my innocence, and the two prospectors who were caring for him, Casey and Wisner, were also understanding. The only important person left to clarify things with was Mrs. McDonnell."

"And it was at her home that you found Mr. Hadley."

"He was suffering from a serious head wound, was filthy

dirty, and acting very much like a child. Not much different from the way he appears in this courtroom."

"He offered no resistance to your capture?"

"Well, he did some, but not in the way of a person in charge of his senses."

"At the prospectors' cabin, did you four try to get Hadley to reveal what he had done with the gold?"

"Casey and Wisner lent us a small nugget, which we showed to Hadley. He got excited, called it a 'pretty rock,' and said his rock was, as best I can remember, 'lots, lots bigger.' We figured then that he had some recollection of Ryerson's nugget."

"Couldn't he have just been babbling, as he had done since his capture?"

"I don't believe so. No, sir. He calmed down some after he saw the gold. I'm sure there was recollection."

"Thank you, Mr. Slade. No more questions, Your Honor."

Judge Chase dismissed Slade from the stand. As Slade headed for his chair beside Simms, the judge's voice rang out behind him.

"Counselors, does this conclude the testimony, or do you have further witnesses to testify?"

Simms spoke up. "The prosecution has none, Your Honor."

From where Slade sat, he could see Madden waiting tensely, allowing what seemed to be a melodramatic pause.

"Mr. Madden?" the judge inquired.

Madden's long pause continued to hang heavy in the courtroom. Finally he stood up. "Your Honor, the defense calls Emory Dolan!"

Slade's head pivoted, seeking Ryerson's eyes. The marshal's mouth was agape. As he looked at Slade, his lips formed astonished unspoken words: "I clean forgot that son of a bitch."

Algernon Simms looked at both of them questioningly.

Slade turned again to apprehensively watch as the sinister, dark-visaged robber made his way through the packed room. Dolan took his oath from the bailiff, acting as pious as a saint, and walked confidently to the chair lately vacated by Wayne Slade.

Madden was the picture of cool, calm assurance as he walked closer to Dolan. "Your name is Emory Dolan?"

"Yes sir."

"You're a resident of Immigrant Lake?"

"No, sir. Until the, uh, events of several weeks ago, I was merely passing through on the way to attending to business interests farther north."

Simms passed a note to Slade. "Who's this?" Slade took Simms's pencil to write. "It's a long story."

"Had you met Quinn Hadley, the defendant, before the death of Mr. McDonnell?"

"Never in my life."

"Had you met Mr. Slade—the gentleman seated over there—prior to Mr. McDonnell's murder?"

"Yes sir, I surely did. Not by name. But a couple of nights before I saw him shoot—"

Simms was on his feet. "Objection, Your Honor! Mr. Slade's involvement with Mr. McDonnell's death is, to this point, purely hearsay!"

"Overruled. Continue, Mr. Madden."

Simms eased back into his chair, clearly dissatisfied and mystified over the surprise turn of events.

"You were telling the court, Mr. Dolan, about what happened two nights before Mr. McDonnell's death."

"Yeah. That night, out in the mountains, out south of here, Slade shot and killed my partner in cold blood."

Simms again shot out of his chair. "Your Honor, in light of this surprise defense witness, I ask the court to adjourn until tomorrow so that I may myself investigate the witness's allegations."

"Request denied, Mr. Simms. We'll allow the witness to testify for the defense before adjourning. You'll have ample time to prepare your cross-examination. Proceed, Mr. Madden.''

"Your Honor," Simms blurted, "I protest—"

Chase banged the gavel. "We *will* proceed, Mr. Madden.''

Slade went limp, his mind muddled with the shock of Dolan's craven lies.

Madden turned back to Dolan. "Please continue."

Dolan looked at Madden and back at the judge, then at the spectators packing the room. "That night, must've been a Friday," he said. "My business partner, Hank Lane, and me came upon this Slade at his camp on the trail. We chatted awhile, and I could see this Slade was a strange customer. I figured it was smart not to hang around there too long. As we was leaving, this Slade pulled a gun and demanded our money. I yelled at Hank to get the hell out of there, and just that fast, this Slade drilled poor Hank.''

A ripple of astonished murmurs filled the room. The judge rapped his gavel, and Madden again allowed a long pause to dramatize the significance of his witness.

"You know this for a fact, Mr. Dolan?"

"I saw Hank drop."

"And . . ."

"This Slade took Hank's horse and his belongings."

"You're sure?"

"Slade came to town with two horses. The livery man down the street will tell you that. Hank's horse is still there in the livery yard.''

Aghast, Slade turned his wide eyes toward Ryerson, who scowled. Under his strained circumstances, Slade had avoided mention of his dispute with Lane and Dolan.

Again, Ryerson's mouth formed silent words. "Who's lyin'? Him or you?"

Slade looked Ryerson straight in the eye and jerked his thumb at Dolan.

Ryerson accepted the gesture and relaxed in his chair.

"This court and the authorities, I'm sure, Mr. Dolan, will

want to investigate this aspect of the events thoroughly," Madden said. "But back to the deliberations under way here today . . ."

"Yes, sir?"

"The late Sunday forenoon when Mr. McDonnell was killed, you were where?"

"I was huntin' the law here in Immigrant Lake to report the killing of my partner."

"Mr. Ryerson, you mean?"

"I was told that was the gentleman's name. I found his jail locked and didn't know where his house was. I'd been told he might sometimes be found passing the time of day in the Water Hole Saloon."

"This was . . . when? What time?"

"Shy of noon or a few minutes past. Hard to remember."

"You witnessed the murder of Mr. Duff McDonnell?"

"I did. And it was just the way I later heard Mr. Hadley tell Marshal Ryerson."

"And that was . . . ?"

"Slade was standing behind Mr. Hadley. He knocked him over, jerked Mr. Hadley's gun from his holster, and shot Mr. McDonnell!"

"Hmmm. Where were you?"

"In the doorway, just starting into the saloon. The fight and the shooting stopped me, and I stood there, watching."

"Then what happened?"

"Slade threw Mr. Hadley's gun on the poker table and ran for the door. He nearly knocked me over."

"Did you try to stop him?"

Dolan gave Madden a piercing look. "He'd killed my partner two nights before, and I'd just seen him kill another man. I wasn't about to become his third killing in as many days."

Madden tossed a gloating smirk in the direction of the jury. "No more questions, Your Honor."

"Counselor Simms?" the judge inquired.

"Prosecution waives cross-examination until I have con-

ferred with Mr. Slade and otherwise looked into this surprise turn of events. I request a recess or an adjournment."

Judge Chase pulled a large silver turnip watch out of his
vest pocket. "Court will adjourn until nine o'clock tomorrow morning."

Simms turned to Slade and spoke quietly. "Meet me in
Marshal Ryerson's office in half an hour. I want him there,
too."

From across the room, Slade heard the voice of Walt,
the bartender, echo like a deep-seated belch.

"Bar's open!"

The morning light in Judge Chase's makeshift courtroom
reminded Slade of the final agonizing hours of the ill-fated
poker game. Though the saloon was now packed, the silence was almost as heavy as it had been on the morning
of the game. The rap of Chase's gavel resounded hollowly
through the same kind of heavy silence.

"Mr. Simms," Chase called in a stentorian voice. "Cross-
examine?"

Simms rose. "Your Honor, we have heard the testimony
of the witness, Emory Dolan. The prosecution feels that
little would be gained in cross-examination. With the
court's permission, I'd like to recall Wayne Slade."

"Granted. Mr. Slade?"

When Slade had resumed the witness chair, Simms
moved quickly to the matter at hand. "Mr. Slade, your
testimony is already on record as to the events surrounding
Mr. McDonnell's death. Yesterday's witness, Mr. Dolan,
told another version, and it will be up to the jury to deter-
mine if perjury has taken place and which of you is the
perpetrator."

Slade nodded.

"Mr. Dolan has testified that, two days before Mr.
McDonnell's killing, you murdered his partner, a Mr. Hank
Lane, in cold blood. This testimony, if true, could have
enormous impact on the verdict in this case."

Again Slade nodded, realizing a response was not called for.

"Mr. Slade, did you or did you not shoot and kill one Hank Lane?"

Slade fired his answer without delay. "I did!"

Murmurs of astonished shock rippled through the room.

"Tell us briefly your version of those events."

"I was camped that Friday night in the hills about twenty miles south of Immigrant Lake. Lane and Dolan visited my camp under friendly pretenses. Both quickly pulled their guns and disarmed me. They said Lane's horse was lame, and they planned to trade for mine. I had no choice. While they had me under the gun, Dolan rummaged in my saddle-bags and took two hundred dollars I had planned to invest in some opportunity, possibly cattle, in Immigrant Lake. I had a small derringer pistol they hadn't found in my clothing, and as they mounted to leave, taking my money and my horse, I fired. I intended to stop Dolan from escaping with my money. Instead, I shot Lane in the head, killing him instantly."

"Dolan fled?"

"Yes. Immediately. I was left with Lane's body, which I buried as best I could the next morning. I was also left with Lane's lame horse and my own, as well as Mr. Lane's belongings, which I kept as . . ."

"Liquidated damages?"

"That's one way to put it. I was out two hundred dollars."

"You did not, as Mr. Dolan testified, draw down on them, intent on robbery?"

"I did not, no, sir."

"A crucial point, then, Mr. Slade, seems to be the lame horse, which Mr. Dolan and Mr. Lane intended to thrust upon you against your wishes, a point not brought out in Mr. Dolan's testimony. You are certain this was the way the confrontation began?"

"Yes, sir, and in addition, they intended to rob me, not the other way around."

"Very well. No more questions, Your Honor."

Judge Chase looked at Madden. "Any questions, Counselor Madden?"

Madden's look told Slade he was prepared to shoot this testimony full of holes in his summation to the jury. "None, Your Honor," he mumbled.

"You may step down, Mr. Slade," the judge intoned, looking again at his watch. "Now, are there any more witnesses to be called today?"

Simms still stood close to the judge's table. "Only one, Judge, and it won't take long."

"Proceed."

"The prosecution calls Mr. Alexander Handy."

Slade had met Alex Handy, proprietor of Immigrant Lake's livery stable, before he, Ryerson, and Simms paid him a visit the previous afternoon. Handy, a small, wizened man who might have been a jockey in his youth, was sworn in and perched on the witness chair, sitting forward expectantly. It was clear that the spare, wrinkled little man looked forward to being involved in a major event in Immigrant Lake.

"Your name is Alexander Handy?"

"Yes, sir. Usually go by Alex."

"And your line of work, Alex?"

"I run the livery stable here in Immigrant Lake."

"You're familiar with Mr. Wayne Slade?"

"Yes, sir. That Saturday evening before young Duff McDonnell was shot, Slade rode in and left two horses in my care and boarding."

"Do you recall the condition of the horse Mr. Slade rode?"

"Strong animal. Well cared for, though he'd been ridden and used a lot. Sound wind. The army would've qualified him as a cavalry mount, he's that stout an animal."

"And the horse Mr. Slade brought with him?"

"Rough used. Poor care and feed. Hadn't been corned and grained enough. Been months since it'd been curried or cleaned. Coming on to being spavined in the legs. Anybody could see that with one eye closed and the other blinkin'. Probably half the age of Slade's horse, but not near as good. Last few weeks, though, I've got him back to near his proper condition." Alex Handy's pride in his accomplishment with Lane's horse was evident.

"Anything else about the horse's condition when Mr. Slade brought him in?"

"Well, like Wayne Slade told you, he was lame!"

CHAPTER
22

The FOLLOWING MORNING, WITH THE BUSTLE OF THE COURT-room filling, Slade looked the two traveling attorneys over. He wasn't pleased with what he saw.

Madden, scheduled to make the first summary statement to the jury, looked refreshed and well rested. For this portion of his assignment, Madden had saved a brand-new suit of clothes, one of considerably better quality and fit than the outfit he'd worn during the previous days in court.

The brown suit was neatly pressed, apparently by someone in Immigrant Lake. He had taken advantage of the early recess the day before to have his hair cut. His starched shirt was also neat, and he wore a new brown tie, a large bow, tucked under the wings of the pristine white shirt collar. His brown boots had been buffed to a high gloss.

In all, Madden, the attorney who appeared so far to have the upper hand in the trial, had turned up this morning as the picture of readiness, confidence, and assurance.

By contrast, Algernon Simms still wore the wrinkled suit of his previous days. He had apparently been up most of the night studying his case notes. His red, pouched eyes and bearing showed it. His shirt was wilted, and his tie drooped enough to suggest dishevelment and disorganization. If Madden was the image of confidence, Simms appeared nervous, his eyes probing the courtroom, studying the jury, the judge, and the spectators. A lack of total confidence seemed evident.

To now, Slade thought, Madden had not been especially popular with the spectators; the town had accepted Ryerson's word that Hadley had committed the murder and ambushed Ryerson. The man who represented Hadley was not in the town's best graces. But clever men, especially learned and skilled orators, had seductive ways of swaying public opinion—particularly, Slade thought, with such strategies and tactics as were now obvious in Gregory Madden's appearance.

The bright spot, though, was in Alex Handy's testimony that, by indirection, had repudiated Emory Dolan.

Judge Chase called on Madden for his summary statement to the jury.

Well, here it goes, Slade thought. The luck of the draw.

Madden would not be constrained by any further objections from Simms. Slade figured he could expect all the sordid and personal accusations and cheap innuendos to be dragged out.

As he had done while examining Slade, Madden began his statement from his seat at the green poker table. More playing to the galleries, Slade thought. In that position Madden faced the twelve townsmen who constituted the jury. They sat somberly, their expressions blank, reflecting nothing but anticipation of Madden's remarks.

"Gentlemen of the jury," Madden began, "at the conclusion of the summary remarks by myself and the state's counsel for the prosecution, you will be asked to render a verdict as to the guilt or innocence of the man here accused of the murder of Duff McDonnell, Mr. Quinn Hadley.

"To aid you in those deliberations on his fate, I believe it essential to review what has been brought forth in evidence against Mr. Hadley and, to balance the scales of justice, what has either not been brought out against him or with the points in his favor.

"Were I less of a gentleman of honor, I would fall upon the mercy of this court and its jury because of the hopelessly impossible condition of my client. An accident of some fiendish nature has rendered him a total incompetent. He has been altogether incapable of speaking out in his own defense, of telling the court the truth about this charge so ruthlessly leveled against him.

"But I will not do so. Mr. Hadley would not want that. Since he is unable to speak out in his own defense, I shall speak for Quinn Hadley, pointing out to you the aspects of this heinous and malicious charge that threatens, if he is found guilty, to rob him of his very life."

Madden realized he was still seated, paused, pushed back his chair, and strolled into the open area in front of the seated jury.

"Because, gentlemen, as I stand here before you, I have come to judge Mr. Hadley by what I have learned of his conduct before his grievous injury. He was a man of simple honor; upright, fair, and decent in his dealings with one and all of his neighbors here in Immigrant Lake.

"In his business transactions, his reputation is unsullied, of the highest possible order. There is not a man among you who can stand up and, on his oath, say that Mr. Quinn Hadley was not always honorable and generous in a multitude of dealings with his friends and neighbors in this valley during his several years here as a cattle broker.

"There are children on these ranches who will increase to adulthood remembering him as a kind and thoughtful man, with a gentle, understanding way, who brought them little playthings and candies on his frequent visits to their homes.

"There are ranch wives and mothers who remember him the same way for his thoughtful consideration of them. The men of their families carry images of him in exactly the same way.

"Oh, friends, do not believe for a moment that Mr. Quinn Hadley is without friends and supporters, a multitude of them, in this valley of decent, God-fearing people. Even as this trial has been proceeding, his name has been on the lips of countless children as they knelt for their nighttime prayers."

Slade looked at Ryerson, who felt Slade watching him and looked up from studying his fingernails. At the same moment their eyebrows arched in near disbelief.

"But what of the facts? Gentlemen of the jury, you have sat there several days and been witness to the futile attempts to establish any solid or substantial evidence against Mr. Hadley. At this juncture, there exists not a single shred of evidence against him.

"We have a story, a fiction, a fabrication out of whole cloth, that our Mr. Hadley, with malice aforethought, pulled a gun after an all-night card session and shot down without so much as a bat of his eye a young rancher with whom he had transacted considerable business—Mr. Duff McDonnell.

"We are asked to accept this story, built up in the mind of one man, the third party to that card game, Wayne Slade. We are asked to accept the word of a man who acknowledged that in fifteen and more years he has been unsuccessful in every venture to which he has turned his hand. A man who, by his own admission, under oath, confessed that a mere day and a half before Duff McDonnell's murder, he had killed in cold blood!

"The West, my friends, is full of such drifters and malcontents. They are the reason that wives cringe in their beds on nights when the press of work keeps their husbands away from hearth and home. They are the reason stockkeeping has become such a risky venture; after all, how can a man spend his time, his energies, and his money to keep a herd when at the end of it all, a third, possibly a half, of his herd may be rustled away from him?

"The West also has its cities of sin—fortunately Immigrant Lake is not one of them—where the perpetrators of these heinous crimes congregate, where this scum, mostly the dregs of eastern society, go to revel in their debauchery. We know only too well the names of these Sodoms and Gomorrahs of our proud western lands.

"This man, one of that dastardly band, Wayne Slade, has the effrontery to tell us our Mr. Quinn Hadley coolly gunned down Mr. Duff McDonnell. This is the man who saw fit to flee the scene of his crime. I beg you in your deliberations to consider this: perhaps the wrong man is here on trial for his life.

"Then we have this comic chase in the desert. A marshal doing his duty as properly as he could, I am sure, but who long ago should have relinquished the role to a younger, more vigorous and dedicated man. A marshal never known to venture far from town without packing an ample supply of what he refers to as his 'snakebite remedy' in his saddlebags.

"Believe me, gentlemen, I do not find it appropriate to jest about another man's misery, but a doubt has crossed my mind as to the sobriety of Marshal Ryerson when he slipped and fell in the mountains to so seriously cripple himself."

Slade saw Ryerson stiffen as a snicker or two rippled through the room.

"The two had never met before. Yet, when Ryerson groveled in pain and fired a distress signal, Wayne Slade, to his eternal credit, came back to the marshal's aid. But remember Slade's words. He said there was an element in his thinking of the chance that in so doing he would gain the favor of the injured marshal. And at that moment, to Mr. Wayne Slade, his neck was more valuable than all the gold in the world.

"With the favor thus established, Slade helped the injured man back for competent medical help. At some point the marshal was fired upon from ambush and again grievously wounded. And remember the term used in this trial——'by a person or persons unknown.' Slade never so much as caught a glimpse of the attacker. Marshal Ryerson, who by his own admission was nearly delirious with pain, is certain that the man who rode past him was Quinn Hadley. Mr. Ryerson's eyes were closed when the man was near him because, as he says, he was doing a pretty good job of playing possum. When it was safe for the marshal to look, he caught a glimpse of the back of the attacker riding away, probably at some distance by this time and observed through a haze of intense agony. We are asked to believe that Marshal Ryerson, under these conditions, positively identified Quinn Hadley.

"Then we have this preposterous tale of gold, again something of which only Ryerson and his cohort, Slade, were aware . . ."

Slade had watched Ryerson growing more and more tense. He hoped Cole would not explode and lend substance to Madden's fabric of half-truths.

"We are told that the crucial factor is a nugget of gold the size of a man's fist. What do they think we are, gentlemen? Total idiots? A nugget that size simply does not exist, has never existed, and could exist only if all of the gold in the hills around Immigrant Lake were found and melted down. This is ranch country, not gold country.

"Mr. Hadley, with absolutely no evidence that he was anywhere within miles, is again alleged to have committed another sordid crime. He is said to have found the marshal's horse, rifled the saddlebags like a common thief or footpad, and ridden off with this fabled chunk of gold.

"Fable I fear it is, gentlemen. Why did Mr. Hadley not have the nugget with him when he arrived at the McDonnell ranch if, indeed, it ever existed? The only evidence—the only possible scrap of evidence—linking Mr. Hadley to any of these serious charges leveled against him, was that in his diminished mental capacity from a serious head injury, he showed excitement at seeing a small nugget of pure gold. Which of you, even in full command of his senses, would not become excited by a nugget of gold?

"That to me, gentlemen, and I hope to you, is not sufficient evidence on which to condemn a man to the gallows.

"I say instead that this was all trumped up by two men who have spent their lives rootless and many of their years living by the sword and the gun. Isn't it clear, gentlemen, the tie that binds these two? Birds of a feather. It is not difficult for me to see how easy it is for men to lie in these conditions. Marshal Cole Ryerson, war hero; Wayne Slade, hero and victim of the same war. Both veterans of . . . Confederate butternut gray!

"These two, our only so-called unimpeachable witnesses, are both confessed killers, in wartime and on either side of the law, the pair of them once sworn enemies of the government and the flag that now protects them!

"Gentlemen, as surely as I stand here before you, a verdict against Quinn Hadley will send an innocent man to his death and will be both an insult and an affront to that grand American flag and to the Constitution it protects.

"I rest my case."

The closing sentences had been delivered almost rapid-fire. Slade quickly looked across at Ryerson, who sat with murder in his eyes, but calm in his posture in the chair. Slade respected the aging marshal for taking the galling words with as much calm as he did.

CHAPTER
23

From that point Simms would, Slade felt, be walking uphill. He wondered what sort of argument could match the eloquence and persuasiveness of Madden's polished and articulate summary. How would the law stand in such instances? Having heard Madden's statement, the jury could not possibly find Hadley guilty. How badly did the government need a neck to stretch for this crime? Was it possible that the weight of the trial could still shift to his shoulders?

The late morning had turned the air inside the Water Hole hot and humid. Madden, seated at the green table, still seemed crisp and fresh. In considerable contrast, Simms appeared to droop like a wilted flower. His beaten posture only made his wrinkled suit sag more.

Simms got up, holding a sheaf of notes. When he stood, he drew himself erect, and some of the wrinkles seemed to fall out of the suit. He approached the seated jurors confidently, and Slade sensed encouragement. Maybe there was hope yet.

"Gentlemen of the jury," Simms began, "the American

Civil War has been a closed issue for fifteen years. We have bound up our nation's wounds and welcomed our once-dissenting brothers back into the fold.

"My learned opponent has insisted on using the issue of personal grievances in a war long since gone to glory to help build his case. His tactic can only be viewed as a means of artificially inflaming you against two men, one of them doing his duty as a federally appointed keeper of the peace, and the other acting as reasonably as any one of us might act, given similar circumstances.

"Gentlemen, I know not where any of you stood twenty and fifteen years ago on the issues that fostered and perpetuated the American Civil War, nor do I care. Whether or not you had Union or Secessionist leanings matters not in the here and now. The late war must not be used as a vehicle to prejudice this court against doing its bounden duty, that of finding the defendant, Quinn Hadley, guilty of murder in the first degree.

"Admittedly the case against Quinn Hadley is thin, shallow, and for the most part circumstantial. It is at the same time deep, definite, and substantial; the elements are few and quite lacking in complexity.

"There is no other possible culprit. Either Hadley or Slade shot and killed McDonnell. If there is even a shadow of doubt in your mind that Quinn Hadley did not murder Duff McDonnell—in cold blood—you still cannot and must not, in any good conscience, allow your minds to be prejudiced by the actions of Wayne Slade.

"I submit that Wayne Slade did not commit, and could not have committed this crime of murder and that his actions since the shooting, however suspect my learned opponent may have made them appear, are only those that might reasonably be expected of any man in a similar dilemma.

"Given the circumstances of this crime, would any reasonable man, knowing he was the stranger, totally without influence or friends, in what he perceived to be a hostile town, have stayed and pleaded his innocence in the face of the obvious repute of Quinn Hadley—a reputation so eloquently pictured by my colleague, Mr. Madden, in his closing remarks. I think no man among you would have stayed. And I wonder how many of us, given Slade's situation, would have returned to render aid to the injured Marshal Ryerson.

"Survival, gentlemen, is the first instinct of man. Wayne Slade was a very frightened man, and frightened men often act in ways others might think irresponsible or irrational.

"Wayne Slade did not know this town or its people. He did not know the scope of Quinn Hadley's influence. Let us here acknowledge that Wayne Slade's flight was that of a frightened man and not necessarily an act that confirmed even the slightest guilt in the murder of Duff McDonnell.

"Let us for a moment consider the events that have had bearing on the testimony in this case—the injuries to Marshal Ryerson, Slade's care of the lawman, the ambush, and the mysterious disappearance of a fabulous sum of money in the form of Marshal Ryerson's nugget.

"Let us suppose that Hadley did indeed murder Duff McDonnell. Despite Emory Dolan's questionable testimony to the contrary, the only man who knew the truth, Wayne Slade, was still at large. It is not inconceivable, then, that Hadley might have become apprehensive that Ryerson, on running Slade to earth, would be persuaded as to the truth of Slade's side of the story.

"Then might not that man, who had already killed, have gone on the prowl himself, tracking the marshal? Mightn't he then have lain in wait, plotting to ambush and kill both men and thus forever cover the tracks of his own guilt?

"A key factor in support of this assumption, even though counsel for the defense attempted to prove that any number of men might have liked to see Marshal Ryerson dead, a key factor is that Slade, while trying to escape the ambush, was also fired upon! Doesn't this suggest that the ambusher wanted to see Slade eliminated as well? To whom does the finger point? None other than Quinn Hadley!

"The defense also discredits the finding of the gold nugget as a fabrication on the part of Marshal Ryerson and Mr. Slade to reinforce the case against Quinn Hadley. In the first place, it is asinine to imagine two grown, mature men dreaming up a giant nugget as part of the fabric of a lie. The gold nugget *has* to be fact! Secondly, the mere fact that Wayne Slade responded to Ryerson's distress signal would hardly have diverted the marshal from the pursuance of his duty, that of bringing the murderer of Duff McDonnell to justice. In no way are Wayne Slade and Marshal Cole Ryerson conspiring to shift any burden of guilt away from Slade, their only previous connection being that both served in the same army more than twenty years ago.

"In the marshal's case, entering into such a conspiracy would be diametrically contrary to his oath as an officer of the law and of the court and against everything he has ever stood for. It would be out of character for Wayne Slade also to so shallowly conspire. I remind you of the courage it must have taken to go to Ryerson's aid.

"No, gentlemen, the facts are clear, if uncorroborated. Quinn Hadley killed McDonnell, persuaded Slade by threat to flee for his life, became anxious, and followed the marshal and set his trap. When he had shot the marshal from cover, he rode past to convince himself the lawman was dead, then went downstream from the ambush site, taking the same direction as Ryerson's horse.

"Finding the horse, he rifled the saddlebags, found the gold, which he stole, and again went on the run. At some point he suffered the head injury that left him in his present diminished capacity. He then hid or lost the gold and, by the sheerest accident, made his way to the McDonnell ranch to be ultimately discovered by Slade.

"These are the facts—or at least the only plausible reconstruction of them—upon which you must base your judgment. The actions of Wayne Slade were only those of a frightened stranger. The actions which we must assume, by inference, were those of Quinn Hadley—those were obviously the actions of a desperate man, fully aware in his own mind at the time of his guilt in the killing of Duff McDonnell.

"I shan't dwell at length upon the Emory Dolan testimony. I only suggest that you weigh his statements against the opposing version given by Mr. Slade and the evidence offered under oath by Marshal Ryerson and Alexander Handy, which supports Mr. Slade's testimony as to the events.

"Do that, gentlemen, and the only possible verdict you can reach in this case is that Quinn Hadley is guilty of the first-degree murder of Duff McDonnell!"

The Duff McDonnell murder jury had retired to the back room of Seth Carter's general store to deliberate. Judge Chase and the two attorneys also retired—to their respective rooms at the boardinghouse. The Water Hole, for a time, resumed its role as the local saloon.

Outside, a hot summer sun roasted itself in the sky and baked Immigrant Lake. People sought shelter from the heat, and the streets were all but deserted.

After the crowds had cleared out, Ryerson gruffly lifted Hadley out of his chair by his upper arm. "Come on, Billy, I'm taking you back to jail until those empty-heads agree to hang you."

Slade, standing nearby, realized that Hadley had been sitting in the chair in which McDonnell had died. The bullet had nicked the back of the chair as it passed through McDonnell's body; the crease in the wood still looked fresh.

"You!" Ryerson ordered, staring straight at Slade. "You stay right here. I've got some things to talk to you about!"

Slade was taken aback by Ryerson's gruff manner. "I'm not planning to go anywhere," he said, a defensive tone emerging. Filled with his own concerns about the trial's outcome, he wondered at Ryerson's brusque attitude. "I'm figuring to have a drink and hang around. Don't worry."

"Get a bottle for us and a glass for me. Find us a table where we can talk."

Ryerson lifted Hadley so one shoulder went up and his toes barely touched the floor. Obediently he let himself be led out of the saloon and down to Ryerson's small jail. Ryerson was back in ten minutes to find that Slade had done as he asked. Wordlessly, he plunked down in a chair, poured a full glass of whiskey, lifted it to his mouth, placed the rim against his lower teeth, and tossed the contents down his throat.

He quickly poured another, lifted it, sipped a good measure, and put the glass down.

"Just what in the hell was that all about, Cole?"

"What was what all about?"

"You ordering me around like I was about ready to be hauled off to a cell with Hadley."

"Part for show," Ryerson said, his face softening with a smile. "Part because I was just damned mad, and have been mad clear through this whole trial. I swear I would like to run out and find some cow plop to stuff in Madden's head in place of brains. It's empty now, and that's for certain."

"He was only doing his job, Cole. You ought to know that. You've been involved in enough trials before and seen how attorneys behave."

"Yeah, but shifting the rock off Hadley's shoulders onto you, for the Pete's sake. And all that talk about us both being on the side of the South pulling us together to work against Hadley. I'd like to get Hadley cured damned quick and send him out along the road to back-shoot that Madden when he rides out of town like Hadley tried to do to us."

"You wouldn't do that, or want that, Cole. Besides, Madden's taking the train."

"Naw, I'm just talking out of a good mad. How do you think the verdict will go?"

"Some depends, I suppose, on the jurors themselves. How many friends of Hadley there are, and how many ex-rebels on the jury. And whether or not they believe Dolan. That's what's got me worried."

"They'd never believe that cheap grifter Dolan in a hundred years. But yeah, you're right. Madden was taking a chance with that Civil War line of attack, wasn't he? How'd he know how many old Secesh were sitting there listening? All that could work in our favor, come to think of it. But I'll tell you this, even before the killing, Hadley wasn't the sweetheart that two-bit shyster made him out. Sure he went out and cozied up to the ranchers and their families. That was just so that, when it come to totin'-up time after the roundup and Hadley was buying their stock, they wouldn't give him much fight when he flat out gave 'em a rock-bottom price for their beeves—a price that'd hardly earn 'em a cent profit and was sure to give Hadley a good edge on his. That's all. He was worthless even before that knock in the head, Wayne."

"If we could just pin Hadley to the gold. Or if we could have before the trial. It's a damned scary thing, Cole. If they find Hadley not guilty, that'll also serve as proof of Dolan's story about me shooting Hank Lane. You don't suppose they could put the finger on me, do you?"

"Naw, never. At least I don't think so. Hell, Wayne, I don't know the law that well. Nah, but . . . they still won't have anybody to swing for McDonnell's murder if Hadley gets off."

"Don't say it that way, Cole."

"Just facing facts. It ain't going to happen, that's all. Don't worry. I ain't going to let no harm come to you, Reb. Us butternut boys stick together, didn't old Madden just say so?"

Ryerson looked up from his third drink. The jury was drifting back into the Water Hole, none of them looking particularly happy.

"Oh-oh," Slade said.

Ryerson got up. "I guess it's up to me and my authority to go roust out the judge and his two little playmates and haul old Hadley back here. What is it they say? The moment of truth?''

Slade downed his drink. "You sure are a bundle of sweetness and light, you know that, Cole?''

The jury members had found their seats when Judge Chase and the attorneys came in. The judge took his place and rapped his gavel, calling court back into session.

"Gentlemen of the jury,'' he said, "have you reached a verdict?''

Hiram Carter, Seth's brother, the elected jury foreman, stood up. He cleared his throat self-consciously. "We have and we haven't, Your Honor.''

"Whatever does that mean?''

"Well, sir, may I make a statement on behalf of the jury?''

"You may.''

"Well, sir, Your Honor, I have been asked by the fellow members of this here jury to say this, and I speak for all of them. We have sat here all this time and listened to a lot of high-price jawin'· at taxpayers' expense. An awful lot of it was like a sermon that started too soon and ended too late. Out of it, we figure, based on what's been brought out in this here court, that Quinn Hadley is guilty as sin of murdering Duff McDonnell.''

Ryerson jumped up with a "Yaaay!''

Chase rapped his gavel loudly several times and glared at Ryerson. "One more outburst of that sort, Marshal, and I shall have to order you out of this courtroom. And I shall talk with your superiors at the territorial capital. You have disturbed the good order of this court entirely too often.''

Ryerson sat down sheepishly.

"Continue, Mr. Carter.''

"What I was saying, Judge, is that right there we got a problem.''

"You are aware, are you not, that a verdict of guilty of murder, in this case in the first degree, by law, makes a sentence of death by hanging mandatory.''

"Of course we are, Your Honor. We got Quinn Hadley found guilty as can be of murder in the first degree. We agreed that feller Slade never done it. But that jasper over there who couldn't say a word in his own defense, is not Quinn Hadley. That man is some kind of man-size little boy who for the past six weeks has called himself Billy. We figured Quinn Hadley's already dead. Least the man we knew around here as Quinn Hadley is. That may look like him over yonder, but it ain't him."

"Are you recommending leniency?"

"I suppose it amounts to that, Judge, Your Honor. We agree that, based on what's been brought out in court, Wayne Slade didn't do it. No third party done it neither. The only one that could've killed Duff McDonnell was Quinn Hadley. But we're of a mind that Quinn Hadley is dead. Or at least he never was here to stand trial. And, Your Honor, you can't hang a dead man, nor a man that ain't available for hangin'. And Quinn Hadley fits one or both of them situations."

"But you find the defendant guilty?"

"In absentia, you might say. We find Quinn Hadley guilty. But not that feller yonder. Quinn Hadley has left for parts unknown to mortal man."

"Brother Carter," Judge Chase said, "the law is very specific. A verdict of guilty of murder in the first degree carries with it a mandatory sentence of hanging by the neck until dead."

"You can go ahead and hang that man yonder, Judge, but you will go against the wishes and the sentiments of this here jury, if that means anythin' to you. We recommend a verdict of guilty against Quinn Hadley, but we also recommend that that miserable critter be let to live out his life. He's turned foolish, so by our figuring, he's paid the price. Quinn Hadley's already dead."

"You ask this court to set a convicted murderer free?" Judge Chase was incredulous.

"No, sir, but would there be anything in the books

against recommending a life sentence in prison? That way if Hadley ever comes to his senses, then the court could rightly hang the man that done the murder of Duff McDonnell. That, in a nutshell, is this jury's opinion."

Judge Chase pondered a moment. "Will the counselors approach the bench?"

Simms and Madden got up together and huddled over Chase's table with him, muttering things Slade and Ryerson couldn't hear. They all nodded when the muttering ended, and the two attorneys paced back to their chairs.

"Gentleman," Judge Chase said, "I accept your verdict of guilty against Quinn Hadley and again stress that the law mandates that the condemned man must die for his crime. Because of the highly irregular nature of the jury's consensus, I must withhold sentence until I can confer with the judge advocate at the territorial capital—and possibly with Washington as well. Counselors Madden and Simms will return to the capital with me on the next train.

"Until then I am adjourning this trail, but I am keeping the same jury impaneled until our return. I remand the prisoner to the custody of the local federal marshal, Mr. Cole Ryerson."

Slade glanced at Ryerson; he'd never seen such a scowl.

"Considering the round trip," Chase continued, "and the time needed to confer on this matter, I set three weeks from today, more or less, as the date to reconvene this court. Adjourned." Judge Chase rapped his gavel, the sound sending ominous shivers through Wayne Slade; he wasn't out of the woods yet.

CHAPTER
24

"THEY'RE GOING TO LET THAT SON OF A PUP OFF SCOT-FREE sure as hell," Ryerson said. "Then they'll turn softhearted, figuring he's a prisoner in his own mind, and leave him right here in Immigrant Lake. Mark my word on it, Slade."

The two were having a drink in the Water Hole the day after Judge Chase and his entourage caught the eastbound MC train for the territorial capital. Ryerson stared at his drink, his jaw clamped in displeasure.

"Then, one of these days, that damned empty place in his head is going to fill up and he'll be Quinn Hadley again and there ain't a damned thing I'm going to be able to do about it. He'll spend the rest of his life thumbing his nose at me. My shoulder'll get sorer every time it gets cold or is fixing up to rain, and I'll get mad and goad him into a gunfight sometime, and then it'll be my neck that'll stretch in this cussed Duff McDonnell murder."

"That's not the way Carter and the jury want it."

Ryerson's eyes flashed. He felt absolutely no pity or mercy for Hadley—or Billy.

"Words, son, nothing but words. As long as Hadley's

alive, he stands to get off. And as long as he stays muddle-headed, he'll stay alive. I don't trust them lawyer guys. And Hiram Carter and his damned gang of veniremen. Maybe I should say vermin. Why didn't they just go ahead and hang 'im? It's up in the air now, and I don't mean Hadley."

Slade smiled. Ryerson's language, when he was angry, was colorful. "They did what they considered decent, Cole. I can't say as I'm happy about the way it worked out, but I sure see their point."

"Be damned! Maybe you do, but I don't. Them pussy-foot learned counselors'll go back to the capital and huddle with a bunch of them other jugheads, and they'll come back and let Hadley off for good, sure as I got an aching shoulder. Wish there was something I could do to nail him for sure."

"There is one other thing, Cole." Slade sat forward in his chair, alert with a new idea, or at least a new slant on an old talking point.

"What now, for the Pete's sake?"

"What's the penalty for attempted murder?"

"My experience is that it's about the same. Crime's about the same, anyway, except that the man aiming to do the deed botched it."

"Hanging?"

"Been known to happen. They probably would."

"If the court is merciful to Hadley in the McDonnell killing, wouldn't it add weight if we had evidence of attempted murder?"

"Well, they probably for sure wouldn't let him off scot-free to drift around town here, anyway. They never did discuss them other counts, attempted murder and gold-thievin'. Probably would put him away. Down to the state prison. Might even be enough evidence to hang the slobberin' pup after all. Why?"

"Don't you see, Cole? Hadley attempted murder on you. And me."

"Yeah, and that there slick attorney, Madden, tried to pass it off on some other John Doe. At least Madden made a strong case that way, and there wasn't a hell of a lot Simms tried to do."

"What if we could nail Hadley to the ambush with clear evidence?"

"Like what, Wayne?"

"You're as simpleminded as Hadley. How about your gold?"

"Well, Wayne, we been over this before, time and again till I'm sick of it. That gold is where it started and I guess where the fates or God or nature agreed it ought to stay. My mind's well made up on that score. Losers, weepers. Hadley lost it and it's doubtful it will ever turn up. Least not in time to do me any good. Or you. Not while we're alive, anyhow. That's a big territory out there, and I hate to think what's coming."

"Like what?"

"Like some of them New York penny-dreadful writers'll get hold of the legend of Cole Ryerson's nugget. Next thing you know the country'll be chock-full of them eastern dudes tearin' up the land lookin' for it. It's happened before."

"There's got to be some way to find it."

"Not this day. I got business to attend to. They're lettin' Hadley stay at his house, and I got to keep tabs on his welfare. Got to get across there and look in on my 'patient.' I'll pick you up in a couple of hours at your room and we'll go have supper over to the Wagon Wheel. Sound good?"

"Best offer I've had all day."

Ryerson pulled himself heavily out of his chair.

"Maybe tonight we can think about ways to get Hadley to tell us or show us where he hid it."

"I'll think on that," Ryerson said.

Dawn was only beginning to cut the twilight gray of Slade's room in Immigrant Lake's Antlers Hotel when he was rudely awakened by the thumping on his door of a fist as large as the legendary nugget and Ryerson's booming voice calling to him through the wood panels.

Disheveled and staggering his way out of a sound sleep, Slade opened the door and Ryerson muscled in, his red face clenched in fury.

"The son of a bitch is gone! Left him alone at his house last evening, and now the bastard's flown the coop. I knew he was playactin' all along. I told you so, Wayne!"

Ryerson's bootheels beat an angry staccato on the wood floor as he paced angrily, unable to calm down or curb his outrage.

"Now give me a minute to get all this sorted out, Cole," Slade said, his brain still numb with sleep. "Who's gone?"

"Why that lamebrain Hadley, of course!"

"Gone? What do you mean, gone?"

"What'd I just tell you? Hightailed it to dig up the nugget and make tracks out of the territory, that's what. And there ain't sign of hide nor hair of that owl-hoot Dolan in town, neither. For my money, them two been in cahoots since the day Duff was killed. We're mounting a party right this minute to go on the trackdown trail again."

"It's hardly light out."

"And time's a-wastin'. That pair of back-shooters probably left by the dark of night after we went to bed, so we got a sight of riding to catch up on. They'll move slow in the dark, so that's in our favor."

"All right," Slade mumbled. "I'll get ready."

Ryerson was impatient with Slade's sleepiness.

"Now! Pack your war bag and get movin' on out to Casey and Wisner's. Get you a cup of coffee over at the Wagon Wheel and get 'em to put you up a bunch of biscuits to chaw, and then get to ridin'. I'll do the outfittin', get some groceries and the booze and the bullets. 'Bout the time Acie and Barney get their gear rounded up, look for Jo Shelby and me to be headin' up the lane."

Blinking his eyes and shaking his head to rid it of the

vestiges of sleep, Slade pulled on his pants and shirt and sat on the rumpled bed to struggle into his boots.

Ryerson's heels thumped a hasty tattoo toward the door. He grabbed the knob, swung the door open, and looked back at Slade. His tight expression of moments before had softened to a broad grin.

"We got 'em now, boy! We got 'em now," he said. "Before another sun, we'll have my gold back and have Hadley and Dolan dead to rights." The door slammed behind him.

On the way to Wagon Box Creek, Ryerson set as fast a pace for the four riders as Casey and Wisner's slow-moving Missouri mules would tolerate.

As they rode, Ryerson tried to work out a plan of action for them in running Hadley and Dolan to earth, assuming the two were together. Hadley, he said, had wandered into the McDonnell ranch on the east side of the South Range Pass Road.

As he pushed his ragtag posse, Ryerson growled aloud as to how he calculated that the fugitives would be on one of the trails in the hills above the valley's southeast quadrant.

"Hadley likely didn't hit his head on a rock out on the prairie trail," he concluded as they jogged south from Immigrant Lake. "Other hand, there's plenty of rocks on the upper trail, the one that loops into the hills. I'm bettin' we'll track their spoor up thataway."

Ryerson's excitement and zest for the challenge punctuated the rapid-fire cadence of his words.

As they rode, Slade studied the distant hills, their destination, where Hadley and Dolan might this very minute be themselves hunting the nugget. The mist of distance tinted the mountains ahead with a soft purple despite the broadening morning. Their harsh lines were gentled by the gauzelike texture of haze, with only prominent features softly defined. A few puffs of clouds clung to the highest peaks like royal crowns.

Away from the yellow aura of a sun growing intense over their left shoulders, the sky carried the fresh-washed blue of prairie mornings.

Slade sensed an eagerness and anticipation crowding his frame. Catching Hadley and Dolan now was a game of cat and mouse; getting them with the goods would confirm his and Ryerson's stories and clear his name in Immigrant Lake—and with Mary McDonnell—once and for all.

And Ryerson would have his gold back.

They were soon off the main road and, leaving the creek ford, moved over a dusty trail to the east, a path wide and well traveled by men on horseback and by cattle. Ryerson urged them over this rising and then falling track through the land, the mules picking their way cautiously. Ryerson was impatient but endured the pokiness of Casey and Wisner's mounts with an uncharacteristic tolerance.

A mile or more of travel brought them to a fork in the trail, one path veering on a downhill tack toward the plains, the other meandering uphill into thick stands of pine, spruce, and cedar, the hillside also dotted with gray granite outcrops and massive boulders that had tumbled down from above.

"Hadn't we oughta split up here and check both trails, Cole?" Barney's deep voice intoned over the stem of his cob pipe.

Ryerson beamed a squinted scowl on the lean, grizzled prospector. "Your eye ain't so sharp for trail sign as you claim it is for pay dirt, Barney," he said as they paused to let the horses breathe at the forks.

"In this dust?" Barney asked. "Ain't nothin' to find. All looks the same."

"Well, it's here, Barney, take my word. Two horses with men on 'em passed over this trail not more'n two hours ahead of us. I didn't even have to get down off Jo Shelby to tell it. We're slidin' the groove!"

Acie piped up admiringly. "I reckon if you found that gold, you got a sharp eye, Cole." The pudgy miner swiped a sleeve across his sweaty forehead. "I don't know how many mornings I went to that very spot for my coffee water."

"You didn't fall and break your arm neither, Acie," Ryerson said, grinning. "Unless some of you boys wants to get down and water the bushes, we'd best be pushin' on."

Casey answered by slapping his knees against the mule's flanks and starting up the trail. Ryerson urged Jo Shelby past him to resume the lead. Slade moved out behind Casey on the single-file path with Barney Wisner's mule riding drag.

Ryerson's eyes nervously probed the trail and the land ahead, keeping Jo Shelby at a slow walk. From here, he'd told them, anything could happen, even an ambush.

Slade guessed they were only about a mile from the trail cutoff when Ryerson abruptly hauled Jo Shelby to a halt, and that fast his Colt Navy was out.

At the same moment, Slade also heard a weak, plaintive call from downslope. "Help!" The voice was barely audible. "Help me!"

"Cole!" Casey called. "Look. Downhill. By that big rock. It's a man!"

Slade's eyes took in the inert form dwarfed by the huge boulder and at the same instant the name escaped his lips in a shout. "Hadley!"

"Hit the dirt and prepare to take cover!" Ryerson called. "The bastards could be settin' a trap."

The four slid out of their saddles, guns drawn, hugging close to their animals for cover against possible gunfire. Slade looked past Casey at Ryerson. The marshal's head swiveled and his eyes darted to take in the surroundings above and below their position.

"He looks hurt, Cole," Slade called cautiously.

"Sounds it too," came Barney's hushed voice from behind Slade.

"Well, we'll head down there," Ryerson commanded.

"Be ready to dive for a rock if the shootin' starts. I don't put nothing past that pair."

As they moved cautiously downslope toward where Hadley lay, they spread out to avoid making a big target. As if on cue, with Ryerson and Casey in the lead, Slade and Wisner walked sideways or backward, guns poised, watching their back trail for anything suspicious.

As he moved downhill, Slade spied something stuck under a scrub clump of chaparral. It looked like the remains of a hat, brittle and badly decayed by weeks of exposure to the elements. Ignoring its possible significance, he quickly turned his eyes back to the hillsides above and beside him, squinting apprehensively.

Hadley's body was stiffened and cramped with pain. He twitched against his agony and groveled beside the huge chunk of granite large as a small outhouse.

From the looks of his wound, a bullet had entered the tip of his upper arm, passed through the shoulder and exited an inch or so ahead of his neck. The gravel around him was blood-soaked, showing that Hadley had lost a great deal of blood. Ryerson broke the silence as the four, easier now that no attack had come, converged around the wounded man, persuaded that Hadley's confederate, Dolan, was long gone.

"Well, I see you found your voice, Billy," Ryerson said sarcastically.

"Help me, Cole," Hadley beseeched, groaning, his pain-racked eyes searching those of the four clustered over him for a glimmer of mercy and aid.

"You ain't bad hurt, Hadley," Ryerson growled, his voice void of compassion. "You left me a hell of a lot worse off. With what'll be left of that arm, you may not ever play the piano, but you'll live. What happened here?"

"Dolan," Hadley whispered through his pain. "Shot me and rode off."

"With my gold, I expect."

Hadley groaned again. "I was going to divvy up with him, and he shot me down like a dog."

Ryerson scowled at Slade. "So much for honor among thieves."

Slade spotted a deep bowl-shaped hole close to where Hadley lay. A fresh mound of tawny decomposed granite beside it resembled the tailings from a gopher tunnel. "There's where he'd buried your gold, Cole," Slade said.

"Yeah, I expect so."

"What now, Cole?" Barney asked.

"You two had best stay here and look after Hadley. It's the Christian thing to do, even for the likes of him. I'd send one of you to town for Doc Wells, but Dolan might circle back. No, best you stay and take care of him. Keep a weather eye peeled for that other dry-gulcher. Slade and I'll push on to see if we can cut Dolan's trail."

"We'll fix his wounds and get a hot meal into him, Cole," Acie said.

"Seems to me you're always looking out for the sick, the lame, and the halt, Acie," Ryerson said. "You're a goddam angel of mercy, and God bless you for it. Come on, Wayne!"

CHAPTER
25

THEY RODE THE UPHILL TRAIL FOR AN HOUR BEFORE RYERSON, some distance ahead of Slade, held up his hand in military fashion for a halt. The big marshal pivoted in his saddle, his face a mask of anxiety.

"Hell! I've lost him, Wayne. He's left the trail. Back there a ways. I kept thinking I'd cut his sign again. He'll be moving slow through these trees and rocks. Probably had a hunch we'd have picked up his scent by now and the bastard's trying to play foxy."

"What do we do? Go uphill or down from here?"

"Dogged if I know. I don't relish splittin' up, but it's a big country and Dolan's just a little speck in it." Ryerson paused in thought, measuring his options. "Hooey! I can't nursemaid you forever. It's you I guess I been thinking about, worryin' over. Makin' you take my chances. But you've taken on men in your time, too, and landed on your feet. You faced Dolan before. You'll do. You ride along the low ground, zigzag, and hunt for sign. I'll ride the upland. Every man for himself."

"If we don't find anything, suppose we ought to start back to Barney and Acie before dark?"

"I expect. Trail'll be colder than Hogan's goat come morning, but what the hell. Work hard in what daylight's left to us and see what kind of hand we been dealt."

"Watch your topknot, Cole," Slade said, reining his horse downhill, away from the trail.

"*Vaya con Dios,* pard," Ryerson responded, looking uphill for a likely route through the rocks and, seeing an opening to work toward, wended Jo Shelby's way to the craggy, jumbled slope dotted with boulders. Around them, shagbarked, leggy firs and pines grew sturdy and tall before lifting their blue-green-clad limbs in supplication to the heavens. All the while, the ever-present wind brought a soft soul-gentling soughing where their tops touched the bleached-blue sky.

With that peaceful whisper in the pine tops and despite his thoughts for what the next minutes and hours might bring, Slade felt warm inside; it was the first time Ryerson had called him "pard."

The steeps, leading down to the flatlands prairie of Immigrant Lake valley, were tough for the horse to negotiate. Slade helped the animal pick his way, guiding him with the reins toward easy terrain, looping downward as Ryerson had suggested, before riding back at an uphill angle, always keeping his eyes probing ahead for something that would give him a clue to Dolan's whereabouts.

His eyes continued to rove the land around him, hunting for a sign but not really aware what he was searching for.

He rode twenty minutes after leaving Ryerson, conscious that the trail above him must be grading down toward the flats and not far from where it met and probably crossed the grade of the Mountain and Central Railroad as it began its climb up to Jackson Saddle and the east.

Slade came alert to a change, a tenseness, in his horse's shoulder muscles. The animal's ears, relaxed and slightly laid to the side, perked up and canted forward to feel for a sound that Slade had not yet heard. Something out there, he told himself, feeling his heart race and his breathing become shallow. His skin pricked with tingling sensations. Best move on easy, he thought. He'd have to keep the horse quiet, too.

Slade heaved himself out of the saddle and walked beside the horse, leading him by the headstall, alert to stifle a whinny with his hand if the horse sensed another up ahead, which he probably had.

Trees grew stunted here, and the huge boulders were fewer and smaller as the land graded downward toward the flat expanse of prairie.

Slade started into what appeared to be a clearing, an open grassy expanse nearly flat but sloping slightly downward. One glance across the clearing and Slade's breath was stopped in his throat, his senses coming keenly alert.

A hundred yards away at the far edge of a sunlit, treeless meadow, Emory Dolan crouched beside his horse, hunkered down for a rest and having a smoke, staring out over the expanse of flat prairie below him.

Slade cupped his hand over his horse's nose and mouth to avoid a telltale whicker and peeked around his covering tree. There was no mistaking the man.

Nerves tingling with the impending confrontation, Slade dropped his horse's reins and stepped out from behind the tree. Dolan probably couldn't even see him in peripheral vision. Slade eased his six-gun in its holster, loosening it from where it had settled during his day in the saddle.

He felt the smooth, rich-feeling sheen of the yellowed ivory grips of Lane's long-barreled Colt. He had figured its seven-and-a-half-inch barrel was preferable to his shorter-barreled six-gun if long-range accuracy was at stake. Studying Dolan, he knew he'd made a wise choice.

His distance from Dolan was poor pistol range for both men; Dolan's rifle was evident in the horse's under-stirrup boot. Slade stepped farther into the open, feeling his palms and his armpits turn clammy.

Slade straightened his back and sucked in his gut against

a panicked, gripping sensation. It was now or never. "Dolan!" he yelled.

That fast, Dolan spit away his smoke and was on his feet, facing Slade, arms and hands flexed and cocked for gunplay. "Well, by God," he called across the distance. "We meet again, Slade. You sure got here in a hurry. You're alone. Where's that doughbelly rebel pardner of yours that keeps savin' your ass? Or did you skip out on him to get the gold for yourself?"

"For me to know and for you to find out. Drop the gun and walk over here."

"Like hell! So you can steal my gold and ride off? Come on, Slade! You got another think coming."

"Have it your way," Slade yelled, starting a slow, ominous amble across the sun-baked meadow toward Dolan's position. "You're going back to tell the truth about Hank Lane."

"Uh-uh. Ain't you or nobody else going to stop me now from hopping an eastbound freight in the morning."

Slade continued his stride toward Dolan, still out of effective six-gun range, even for the long-barreled Colt. "We'll see about that," he yelled.

Dolan stepped out from beside his horse, his body tense, his hands and arms flexed and ready. "Keep coming, Slade," he called. "Ain't nobody—not you, not nobody—beating me out of my gold!"

Slade was halfway across the open meadow now. A mere thirty yards separated him from his adversary, the distance closing fast. Sheer nerve took over; he would not back away from this one, regardless the outcome.

Slade gritted his teeth, determined not to falter, keeping his eyes and his senses tuned to every move of Dolan's body, ready for the flick of fate.

"We'll have to see about that, Dolan. For the last time, get your hands on your head."

"Not on your life!"

Dolan's right hand abruptly dropped for his six-gun, and

in the flicker of movement Slade unleashed his own, knowing the range was dicey. Dolan's gun barked first, but the bullet whined harmlessly past Slade. His own gun came up, the hammer sliding easily to the business notch under his trained thumb. The smooth trigger sprang with the hollow cough of erupting explosion, and he realized the gun had gone off prematurely.

Dolan's left leg buckled as a circle of red was printed on the faded jeans at his hip. Dolan dropped his gun with the burst of agony and incapacity in his leg; he clutched the wounded left thigh, falling to his knees. Slade raced toward him, further spooking Dolan's horse, which reared with a terrorized cry and sprinted a few feet.

Slade was beside Dolan in an instant as the hard case careened over to lie doubled up on his side, clutching the wound as if holding it would make the incredible pain go away. Slade's bullet had pierced the meat of Dolan's upper leg and exited the same way out the back.

It probably missed artery and bone but did the job. He wouldn't have to haul in Emory Dolan the way Ryerson said he'd handled that Orval Clampett he'd spoken of, over his saddle and buried in a U-shape. A wave of euphoria rolled over Slade; Dolan surely had the gold on his horse. It was over.

"You rotten son of a bitch," Dolan growled through pain-gritted teeth. "I'll get you for this."

"At your service," Slade said. "I'll keep you advised of my whereabouts."

Jo Shelby with Cole Ryerson aboard, right hand at right shoulder height clutching a cocked Navy Colt at the ready, crashed with thundering hoofbeats and crackling brush out of the rocks and trees uphill of them. Ryerson guided his big horse with his once-injured left hand.

Ryerson braked Jo Shelby to a skidding halt scant feet from Slade as he stood over the groveling Dolan, his handsome Colt at port arms.

"Damn!" Ryerson cursed. "I wanted to get the lowlife

myself. There just ain't no joy left in the law-keepin' business anymore."

Ryerson heaved himself out of the saddle and walked over to glower at the inert, wincing Dolan.

Slade moved to slide his six-gun back into the holster.

"Still say that's a handsome piece of ordnance you took off Dolan's partner," Ryerson said. "And from the looks of old Dolan there, it puts 'em on the money every time."

A sudden swell of relief obviously washed over Ryerson, just as it had Slade, as he probed in his vest for his makin's and proceeded to roll a smoke. "They can't kid me," he said. "It wasn't God ner the Declaration of Independence that made all men equal, it was Colonel Sam'l Colt!"

Ryerson glared down at Dolan. "Damned good gun work, too, son. You put him out of action, but left enough for the learned counselors of this world to prosecute and hang."

Dolan moaned, eyes squinted up at Ryerson as if he were a tormentor. "They ain't going to hang me, are they?" Terror was evident in his voice.

Ryerson scowled down at the wounded man. "Just don't you be too sure about that, Emory. You got a lot of counts against you comin' up. Accessory after the fact of murder bein' one of 'em."

His mind on weaponry, Slade picked up Dolan's dropped gun and flipped down the loading gate and ejected the good cartridges and the single spent one into the grass.

"You leavin' them ca'tridges there on the ground?" Ryerson asked. "Such a waste!"

"If you look in Dolan's saddlebags, Mr. Ryerson, you'll probably find an early Christmas present that will make you forget worrying about waste for the rest of your life."

"Yeah, by God, clean forgot! Get his bandanna off him for a tourniquet, Wayne," Ryerson said, heading for Dolan's horse. "We don't want all the life to ooze out of the bastard before we get him up before that fine-haired old fossil, Judge Chase."

Dolan's horse, skittish over the explosions and harsh actions of moments before, reared away from him.

Ryerson's voice was soothing. "Ease up there, son. You're all right." He patted the horse on the neck, holding the reins and dipping a hand into the saddlebag. "Yup, here she is!" His hand came out with the big nugget. "Forgot how big this thing really is! Judas, what a whopper! We're fixed for life, son."

Slade had knotted Dolan's big neckerchief above the bullet wound and was tightening it with a stick. "I appreciate the thought, but that's your nugget, Cole."

"You and Acie and Wisner rightfully deserve a share, all you've done, and part of it'll help little Miz McDonnell and Duff's boys along life's rocky trail, too."

"Well, that's decent of you, Cole," Slade said, getting up and brushing the dust and blood from his hands.

Dolan lay back wordless, eyes clenched against the pain.

"My mind's been on splitting half of it between you all when and if we finally got 'er back," Ryerson said. "There's more than enough to take care of my needs."

"Well, were I to refuse, the others would feel they'd ought to too. So I guess all I can say is I appreciate the generosity."

"I'm thinking you'd ought to ride over to the McDonnell ranch right now and tell Miz Mary. I can get Dolan back to Acie and Barney and Hadley okay. We'll probably transport 'em in the morning to the Stout place and get Doc Wells to come out. As mean customers as they are, Acie'll take particular pleasure in lookin' after 'em, seein's as they're injured."

Slade looked out over the sprawling valley, calculating his route to the McDonnell ranch. "I hadn't given that much thought. I'm sure Mary'd be pleased to know how this all worked out. And certainly your thoughts about the gold and her welfare."

"She's probably got a roast on the stove and a pie baking in a Dutch oven in the hearth coals for her boys, and more than enough left over for you. If you git now, you can be there by suppertime. Sure'll beat whatever whistle berries and side meat Acie and Barney scorch over a campfire.''

"I'll probably stay in her barn tonight and ride on over to Acie and Barney's after breakfast." Slade mounted up and started down the slight grade toward the prairie.

Ryerson hauled Dolan to his shaky feet and gently helped him into the saddle.

"Son?" Ryerson called.

"Yeah?" Slade turned back to look at the marshal.

"Thanks. It would've gone badly for me without you."

Slade waved and turned back toward the prairie. Against the vast distance, over the valley floor, he could make out a dim pillar of smoke, probably rising from the McDonnell chimney. There was a welcoming, a beckoning, in the vista.

He squeezed his knees lightly into the horse's ribs and started off at a trot.